Glamorous Life

THE
Glamorous Life

A NOVEL

*A **Nikki Turner** Original*

One World · Ballantine · New York

Turner

The Glamorous Life is a work of fiction. Names, characters, places, and incidents are the products of the author's imagination or are used fictitiously. Any resemblance to actual events, locales, or persons, living or dead, is entirely coincidental.

A One World Books Trade Paperback Original

Published in the United States by One World Books, an imprint of The Random House Publishing Group, a division of Random House, Inc., New York.

One World is a registered trademark and the One World colophon is a trademark of Random House, Inc.

Library of Congress Cataloging-in-Publication Data
Turner, Nikki.
   The glamorous life : a novel / by Nikki Turner.
     p. cm.
   ISBN 0-345-47683-2 (trade pbk.)
   1. African American women—Fiction. 2. Businesswomen—
Fiction. 3. Rich people—Fiction. 4. Gangsters—Fiction.
5. Revenge—Fiction. I. Title.
PS3620.U7659G57 2005
813'.6—dc22   2004061721

Printed in the United States of America

One World Books website address: www.oneworldbooks.net

9 8

Text design by Laurie Jewell

This book is dedicated to:

The two people who make my life complete
Little Miss Kennisha Turner and Master Timmond Turner

&

To every single die-hard Nikki Turner fan.
How could I not?

I truly appreciate your loyalty and patience as I went through
the motions that the industry bestowed upon me including
changing publishers and getting rid of the typos.

Countless thank-yous for being my inspiration to continue to
keep writing and cheering me on every step of the way.

The best has yet to come!

&

To all the people whose sole purpose and existence is
to live the glamorous life.

Always know everything that glitters ain't gold!

There's an old wise tale that says that you never miss a good thing until it's gone. I have been to so many funerals and witnessed people feeling guilty, they having to carry the heavy burden as they have reflected upon the way they treated someone before they pass on. As I grew and matured, I have learned never to take for granted friendships, and the people dear to my heart, and always try to love as if there is no tomorrow for they could be here today and gone tomorrow.

The following people have all in one way or another, big or small been a part of my life and although they are *gone but they are surely never be forgotten!*

In loving memory of

MARGARET L. SCOTT
GREGORY GIVENS, JR.
SALLIE PIERCE MOORE
TONY MOORE
KEVIN FOUNTAIN
KENDALL "DAWG" WOOLRIDGE
GLEN SWEETING
MELVIN "MO-LINK" SMITH
DOMINIQUE BOSHER
JERREL "STICK-EM" WILIFORD

Glamorous Life

CHAPTER 1

When You Look . . .
You Won't Find

There are two kinds of girls: those who like thugs, and those who lie to themselves and think they don't. As Bambi lay on the king-sized bed in her room, looking at a gold-framed picture of her and Reggie, she thought, *Damn I love this mother-fucka. I never felt more right about nothing in my whole life.*

All of the sacrificing she had done for Reggie had finally paid off. Just a day short of their two-year anniversary it was going to be official: They could start planning the rest of their lives together, like a normal married couple.

Ringgggg, Ringgggg, Ringggg.

The jangling sound of the phone caught Bambi off guard. She located it beneath her oversized terrycloth bathrobe, looked at the caller ID, and saw that it was Reggie on the line. Even his call sent chills up her spine.

"Hello," she said.

"Hey, baby," he purred. "You gon' be looking good for me tonight?"

Even after all of this time, the sound of Reggie's voice still did something to her. Thinking about how good he made her feel sometimes scared Bambi a little and made her feel weak.

"Have I ever disappointed you?" she asked as she looked in the mirror and imagined how gorgeous she was going to look later—although truth be told, she didn't look too bad even without makeup. She was dark skinned with slanted eyes, five feet seven, with long firm legs and a Coke-bottle figure. Her straight shiny coal black hair grew past her shoulders.

"Boo, straight up I don't think you would know how, and that's from the heart," he said. "Anyway, I just wanted to make sure everything was a'ight."

Bambi could sense something else in his voice. "I'm good, baby. I just need to know that you're okay?"

"I'm good, Boo. I just had to get some shit straight. This mark-ass nigga owed me some money, and when I got over there, don't you know this nigga came with some short money?"

"For real?"

"Yup, matter fact, dude was a few thousand short. Me and him got da rumbling and that bitch-ass nigga had the nerve to scratch me on my fucking neck and shit."

"Oh, my God! Baby, are you all right?" Bambi asked. She knew he could fight, but she also knew how cruddy dudes were on the street.

"I'm a'ight, I'm just going to put some peroxide on it. This shit just got me running all behind schedule. I'm going to need you to meet me at that restaurant at the Brander Mill Inn. Don't forget I want you to wear that sweater I had specially made for you, the N.T. Original."

"I know, baby. I'll see you in about an hour and a half then?"

"That's cool, and make sho it's an hour and a half and not

two. I know you and time," Reggie teased before hanging up the phone.

Chicks better understand that tonight is my night, Bambi thought to herself. *This is the night my man gives it all up for me! The streets, the quick money, the dope slaying, the late nights, and the whole nine yards. He's going to stand in a room, in front of all our friends and family, confess his love to me, slip a fat engagement ring on my finger, and look into my eyes and wait for me to say yes to him. And everybody knows I'm not going to say no. See, everybody thought I was crazy in the beginning. Not me. I knew it was love at first sight straight from jump!*

Two years earlier Bambi had been out running errands for her mother on a hot July afternoon. Frustrated with the traffic and a "to-do" list almost a mile long, Bambi hopped off the expressway. After taking a shortcut, Bambi found herself in one of the busiest crack-slaying corners in Virginia's capital city and smack dead in the middle of a dangerous housing project. The closest she had ever gotten to this side of town was when she visited her grandmother, who lived in one of Richmond's oldest historic neighborhoods. When she went to Grandma's house, it was always during daylight hours and she was never allowed to play outside. So before that day she had only seen this side of town from the highway or during News Six television crime reports. Seeing it up close, she found herself mesmerized by all the excitement going on around her.

The area was like a small village within the city. Three-story apartment buildings lined both sides of the streets, some with clothes hanging over the balcony. The once-yellow buildings were now covered with dirt and graffiti. She read the words "Boo is a slut" and "Kiki was here" scrawled in huge letters across one wall.

The hustle and bustle of the area was a sight to see. As she sat at the stop sign, which had black writing all over it, she noticed a braiding shop to the left. Well "shop" may have been a bit of an overstatement. A girl was getting her hair braided in a black and faded gold lacquer chair on somebody's front porch while two other girls sat waiting their turns. One swung two white plastic bags of horse hair in her hands. To the right there was another girl walking down the street in a hoochied-up outfit. The black and gold striped shorts should not have been worn by anyone but Daisy Duke on *The Dukes of Hazzard*. The short black fringes were the only thing that kept the cheeks of her butt from being visible, and an enormous amount of cleavage spilled out of her too-small halter top. The way she strutted in those platform shoes made it clear the outfit wasn't intended for daylight.

A yellow school bus with the words "Meals on Wheels Snack Truck" was parked on the side of the street, and a crowd of children in the neighborhood were huddled around it. One guy stood at the front of the line passing Popsicles to all of the children. A grown man rode around on a child's bike, and a woman on her knees behind a Dumpster gave a blow job to a young boy who didn't look old enough to buy a pack of cigarettes.

Bambi took all this in as she drove. When she pulled up to a red light, a tall, skinny, light-skinned dude with a mouthful of gold teeth walked up to the car and asked, "Yo, shawdy, you looking?" He spoke slowly with a deep down-South drawl.

Bambi looked him over, from head to toe. She knew she should have been afraid; but he was very handsome, and the whole atmosphere kind of excited her.

"Do I look like a mother-fucking junkie?" she asked, knowing good and well that he was a drug dealer, and she wanted him to know that she was hip.

The dude answered, "Nah, shawdy, I wasn't asking if you was looking for no drugs, I was asking was you looking for me?"

Bambi looked him up and down again like he was crazy and said with as much attitude and spunk as she could, "Nooo, I wasn't looking for you either. And I would have thought a dude thinking himself as cool as you think you are could have or would have come at me with a better line than that one."

He nodded his head and smiled. "Well, they say when you ain't looking, you find. And sometimes it ain't the line, it's the nigga's style that attracts."

Bambi tried to hide the little smirk on her face, but she was enjoying his come-on and he knew it.

"Look, baby, I ain't catch yo digits," he said.

"Maybe because I didn't throw 'em," Bambi said.

Just then a Datsun with what sounded like a hole in the muffler rolled up beside them. A toothless, scary-looking lady with the short of a cigarette in her hand hung her head out the window. She had no shame in her game.

"Yo Reddggie," she slurred as slobber ran out of her mouth. "I got seven dollars, can you work wit that?"

"Hold on, I'm coming. Just pull over there and cut that loud-ass car off before you make this block hotter than this shit already is," Reggie responded.

Bambi gave him a look, saying nothing. Reggie could sense her awkwardness, but before he could smooth over what had just taken place, two dudes rode up on a bicycle: one was pedaling and the other was on the handlebars.

"Reggie, man, we struggling badder than I don't know what. Look, we ain't got but twelve dollars in quarters, can you look out real decent for us?" the rider on the handlebars asked.

Reggie just shook his head. "Man, what the fuck I'm gonna do wit forty-eight quarters jingling round in my pockets?" He smacked his lips. Bambi could tell he didn't want to let that money get away from him. "Damn man, I got y'all. Just park and gon' head in da store and get me some dollars for all the gotdamn change."

Just as he said that, a little boy who didn't look old enough to be out of elementary school, apparently working as a spotter up the block, put both of his hands around his mouth and called out, "Yo, Regg, five-oh coming through the cut!"

Reggie looked Bambi in her eyes. "Look, give me yo digits. I'm going to remember it, cuz the police coming and I am dirty as a fat baby's shitty ass."

She called out her number to him as she pulled off.

"A'ight baby, I am going to hit you up in a li'l while," he yelled, and then took off running into someone's house.

As Bambi continued her mother's errands, she couldn't help thinking about Reggie. Most girls who had lived such a sheltered life with an overprotective mother would have been scared off, would have run as far as they could get from the whole scenario of the 'hood—the crack heads, dope fiends, the scary-looking whores out tricking, willing to sell their body, their temple, their prized possession for a rock (they would suck the devil's dick for a quick escape from the pain and misery), not to mention the police running through the cut—but not Bambi. She wasn't the average suburban girl from the Valley. This life excited her and got her blood pumping, her heart beating, and her adrenaline rushing. Her own life had always been so safe. She liked the feeling of desperation that the streets offered, but her mother had done everything in her power to keep her away from that lifestyle. Bambi saw Reggie as a conduit to feed her desire to know and to experience life firsthand.

Bambi was naïve, but she was far from stupid. No matter how much her mother sheltered her and kept her tight under lock and key, Bambi had a thirst for excitement, drama, and living on the edge. She could tell exactly what kind of hustler Reggie was from his gold chain down to his brand-spanking-new Air Jordans. She had read enough and heard enough to know that the real drug lords lived in Colombia or were vacationing on a yacht somewhere or held a powerful position in the government, and no matter how much the police raided the projects, it would never stop the real problem with drugs.

Bambi figured that Reggie was a small-time hustler. He hustled for tennis shoes, hotel money, and rims for his hooptied-out Cadillac. His pockets were bulging because he probably carried every penny he owned around in his pocket in a wad of cash. She was intrigued with the way people tracked him down for his product. Just from that brief meeting, there was one thing of which Bambi was certain: This dude was hungry and determined, and from what little she could see or feel in her gut, he had the potential to go from being a nickel-and-dime hustling shorty to becoming "the Man" one day! By the way he dictated authority over his surroundings she felt that his domain should be larger than just a few measly street blocks.

He was also fine as all outdoors, the kind of man who could make any chick want to get up the nerve to smack her mother. Reggie stood six feet tall. He was light skinned with three gold teeth on the bottom and three on the top of his mouth. He was thin, and his oversized Levi jeans hung off his butt. She could tell by his sideburns that they were not artificial waves under his black do-rag. When she looked down at his shoes, he was definitely in. He wore the new Air Jordans that came out that day.

The phone rang as Bambi returned home. She hurried across the foyer to the hall and picked it up.

"Hey, how you doing? This is Reggie."

Bambi looked around for her mother. Thankfully, she was nowhere to be seen. Bambi tried to sound relaxed: "Oh, hey, Reggie. How you doing?"

"I'm cool, but look you're going to kill me."

"Why?"

"Because I never caught your name."

"It's Bambi, and don't even ask me how my momma came up with it."

Reggie laughed. "How did she come up with it?"

"A deer hit my dad's car when he was on the way to the hospital. So, my mom thought it would be cute to name me Bambi." Of course, that was the only time her sorry excuse for her father had gone out of his way to see her.

Reggie laughed, then cut to the chase. "Look, come and scoop me up so we can go eat."

"I don't have a car right now; the car I was driving was my mother's. Don't you have a car?" Bambi asked.

"I got a Cadi. You might have seen it parked on the corner. Da police is round here deep, and I ain't got no license so I can't go nowhere."

It was funny how in every single 'hood in Richmond, every hustler's first car is a Cadi. Bambi learned later that it makes no difference to the young, up-and-coming drug dealers what year or style. It could be ten years old, and they would invest in rims and a stereo system that cost more than the whole car. Seventy-five percent of the time the first car that they hustle for is a Cadi. They are so proud of that car, taking it to the car wash damn near every day. It was once said that a Cadi made a brother feel like he had status in the drug or pimp world. Some move on to Benzes, BMWs and Lexuses but most never lose their love affairs with the Cadi and always have one around.

"How you got a nice-ass Cadi, suited all up with rims and everything and no license?"

"Baby, that's just 'the Life.' Rich girls like you wouldn't know nothing about it," Reggie said.

"Yeah, whatever," Bambi said with a little chuckle.

"Look, we could talk all night, but how about you give me your address so I can have my driver pick you up."

His driver? Bambi liked the way that sounded. She gave him her address, and within ten minutes he called her back and said, "My cab driver will be there in forty-five minutes. Oh, before I forget, write down this number. This is my pager number."

She jotted down the number and then asked, "What's my code?"

"What do you want it to be? One, oh-oh-one, three ones, what?"

"Naw, baby, two-two-oh!"

"Why two-two-oh?"

"Because I am second to none!"

Reggie chuckled a little. "No doubt, baby. When I see two-two-oh behind any number, I am calling right back!"

Reggie paid the cab driver as he pulled to a stop in the projects and helped Bambi out of the backseat. He handed her the keys to his Cadi, and they took off for Western Sizzler.

As she drove he looked her over. She looked even better than she had that afternoon.

"You pretty as a ma'fucka. I never saw anyone so black and pretty as you are."

"Thank you." She blushed.

"Boo, you could be first cousins with someone from the Motherland. You are as dark as those Ethiopians they show on TV," Reggie said with admiration. Bambi knew she didn't have the "beauty queen" looks of some girls, but she was proud of her midnight complexion, her high cheekbones, and her exotic eyes.

As they ate their meal, Bambi laughed to herself, imagining what her mother would say if she knew that her daughter was being wined and dined at Western Sizzler. For sure it was a few steps down from what she was used to. She didn't hold it against him. She knew it was probably the best that he could do or the best he knew of, anyway.

Reggie was easier to talk to than Bambi might have imagined. He was the kind of guy who would say anything just to get her to smile. He was funny, too. One minute acting all tough, and then the next he was so kind and gentle.

After dinner, he tried to impress her when the check came by peeling off a few bills from his thick wad of twenties, fifties, and hundreds. Bambi acted as if she wasn't looking as he peeled off the money like it was nothing to him, but indeed she was. There was no doubt that she had seen money, but the money that her mother and her mother's rich boyfriends peeled off was different—checks and credit cards. Reggie didn't have to go to nobody's bank or ATM; his stack of money was the best kind—cash, always accessible, right in his pockets.

As they got up from the table, she asked, "Did you leave the waitress a tip?" She had caught him off guard.

"Yeah, I left her a tip a'ight," he said, and burst into laughter. "Look both ways when she crossed the street."

Bambi stopped in her tracks. "Look, you ran her around in circles, worrying her to damn death to get you some ketchup, steak sauce, napkins, a refill, and on and on. So you better leave her a tip."

Reggie was not embarrassed at all. He went into his pocket, pulled out some change, threw it on the table, and walked off. Bambi didn't say anything else. Instead she reached into her mother's Chanel bag (which Tricia had no idea she had borrowed) pulled out a five-dollar bill, placed it on the table and walked away.

Reggie saw her place the money on the table. Far from being mad, he seemed to realize that she wasn't like the other chicks from the 'hood, scheming on his "riches." He was quiet as they got back in his car, and for a moment he just sat there. Before she put the car in reverse to back out of the parking space, he wanted to say something to her.

"Hold on," he said as he looked deep into her eyes. "Look, I know you think I'm some ol' little poo-putt dude, beings that you met me out in the jungle. But, baby, this shit here, nickel and diming, is only temporary for me. I ain't gonna be a corner hustler forever! I just came home from jail, not even two months ago, and had to start over from scratch. My momma gave me a hundred dollars to go get me sneakers. I took that and flipped it, and I ain't never looked back. I got my Cadi, and I'm gonna get me a business soon, real soon."

After he'd said his piece, Bambi couldn't help but be impressed. "I know you will, baby, and I'll have your back every step of the way." She wondered for a minute if she sounded too hard-up after one date, but she didn't care because these were her feelings.

Just like that Bambi found something in Reggie that she'd never seen in any of the boys at her school. He made her feel wanted and gave her something to believe in, and she was as intrigued with him as he was with her. Without a doubt, this was love at first sight in her eyes.

CHAPTER 2

The Come Up

Reggie hadn't lied to her, Bambi thought to herself as she drove across town to the engagement party. Within a year, he was large—not Tony Montana large but surely large in a Nino Brown kind of way, and definitely a major player by the standards of Richmond, and big enough to hold it down with a lot of those I-95 cats in DC, B-more, and Philly, too. Some cats who had spent many years hustling in the street never saw half the bank he saw in only one short year.

The cornerstone of his growing fortune was a lucrative car-detailing business. He ran his business during the day, and in the evenings and in between detailing jobs, he would make his moves, working off his pager selling weight in heroin to a select few.

They were living the glamorous life. Bambi had a closet full of designer clothes purchased at the finest boutiques across the country. Many of the shops were the very same ones where her mother shopped. Reggie was even more flamboyant and showy.

He traded in his thugged-out street gear for pimped-out full-length Gucci furs with hats to match. His twelve-year-old Cadi had been upgraded to a Cadi straight off the showroom floor, and Reggie had outfitted Bambi in her very own black-on-black convertible Allante Cadillac. Just one week before the party, she somehow persuaded Reggie that since she was his doll baby, she needed a Corvette just like the real Barbie dolls. Without hesitation Reggie traded in the Allante and got her a candy apple red Corvette. Not only did they have an array of vehicles, but they had a driveway to keep them in at a brick, three-bedroom starter home they rented in a quiet section of the 7-4-6. Most of all, Reggie seemed to enjoy the getaways—the extravagant trips to Belize or the Bahamas, weekends in Las Vegas and New York City. These were a welcome break from the mayhem, chaos, and confusion that surrounded his high-risk life.

Although they moved to the suburbs of the 7-4-6, they couldn't escape the drama that came with the 'hood. Many times Bambi was awakened in the dead of night by Reggie's pager or his cell phone ringing with somebody who wanted to purchase heroin and had the major paper to make it worthwhile for Reggie to get up from next to Bambi's warm body. Lying awake worried that something could happen to him, she would wait for him to call her to confirm that everything was okay. Just when she'd think that something must have gone wrong, he'd call. Losing sleep was one of the prices she paid for dating a high roller!

Bambi couldn't be absolutely sure Reggie was being faithful to her, but apart from some late unexplained nights and rumpled clothing, she never saw any direct evidence linking some gold digger to his dick, nor did she ever hear any ghetto rumors about her man running around with this or that woman. Until she did, she was going to keep all suspicions between herself and Egypt, who was her best friend since middle school.

But there were other issues closer to home causing her pain. For one, her mother was hot as fish grease when it came to Reggie. She did not like the hold that Reggie had on Bambi. Early in the relationship Bambi had left home to go shack up with Reggie in a hotel, abandoning her college dreams without hesitation. Her mother, of course, was outraged.

"This nigga can't even get an apartment for you. He got you living with him in a hotel. Baby, it's not like he got you living in the Trump Plaza. This monkey got a nerve to have you in the Econo Lodge. Baby, it ain't no dick that good in the world."

Reggie was an easy one to profile for an old pro like Tricia. She peeped him for what he was immediately, exactly the kind of no-class-having, straight-from-the-gutter, thug nigga that she had been trying to protect her daughter from for so many years.

Tricia's feelings on the subject of men like Reggie ran deep as the Dead Sea. Having clawed herself up from nothing to something, Tricia had given her only child the finer things that life had to offer, including private school and enrollment in a charm school. Tricia was sure that her daughter would bring home, if not a politician like her father, maybe an astronaut, a surgeon, a lawyer—a true provider and gentleman. But never in her wildest dreams would she have imagined a thug.

When it came to men, Tricia knew what she was talking about and could lecture like any Ivy League university professor. She was thirty-nine years old, but she was an old-school playerette to the highest degree, if the East Coast had ever seen one. She used her exotic looks and charm to get the best out of life. But she hated to be called a gold digger. Gold digging was beneath her, and she was insulted if anyone ever referred to her as one. According to Tricia, gold digging was something strippers and groupies did. Tricia's beauty—her stock in trade—always hooked the wealthiest men, the certified big fishes. Somehow the richest and most powerful men became powerless when they came under the spell of her bewitching laughter. Although the men treated her like a queen, wining her and dining her with nothing less than the best, the only men she *ever* truly loved were the dead presidents on their currency.

Bambi's father, Bob, was one of the men who had been hypnotized by Tricia's high cheekbones, caramel complexion, and bright eyes. He had fallen victim to her wiles. In the midst of his courtship, he'd neglected to mention the fact that he was married and had been for ten years, with two small children. She found this out when she told him she was pregnant. When he demanded that she have an abortion, Tricia had spit in his face. "You dirty motherfucker, you want me to get rid of my baby? Did you tell your wife to get rid of those two little crumb snatchers she had for you?"

She'd been young, but the experience had hardened her and taught her a very valuable lesson. By this time Bob had revealed too much of his life to Tricia, not to mention he was a politician with an upcoming election and didn't need the scandal. To keep Tricia quiet he made sure she never wanted for a thing. Tricia moved out of her mother's house when she was seven months pregnant, but she didn't move into a low-income government-subsidized apartment or a small one- or two-bedroom apartment, like most of her friends. No, at nineteen years old, she moved from her mother's fifty-year-old house in the middle of the 'hood into her own four-bedroom home. The car, house, and everything in it were all paid for by Bob.

In the years that followed, Tricia had accepted money from

some of Richmond's finest, consisting of rich men and even richer men! Men who should have known better, but simply could not deny her, they let lust blind their vision. Tricia knew that Reggie was definitely an imposter when it came to having money, and he was nothing she wanted her daughter even looking at. Seeing her daughter falling victim to Reggie turned her stomach. She had to do something to snap her daughter out of the spell of a nickel-and-dimer like him.

Soon after Bambi and Reggie moved into a one-room effi-ciency apartment, Tricia decided that if Bambi was going to keep the company of, and shack up with, some uneducated, no-good hoodlum, then she was going to have to do without her mother's support.

"I love you, Bambi," Tricia said, "but I'm not about to stand by and watch you throw your life away on trash. If you want me to reappear in your life, then you do a Houdini and make his ass disappear."

Bambi was hurt when her mother washed her hands of her. If it had not been for Ms. Dot, Reggie's mother, who embraced her like her very own daughter, Bambi might have had a ner-vous breakdown. After Bambi's mother rejected her, Bambi couldn't sleep, and often she cried for no reason at all. But Ms. Dot took care of her, often bringing her soup and brownies, sometimes talking and sitting with her or just watching the sto-ries on television. Finally, Bambi would be able to sleep again, but she continued to hope her mother would change her mind about Reggie.

But the biggest drama-filled episode occurred one morning with a knock on the door at 6 a.m. Bambi awoke to find their house surrounded by Richmond's "finest": the county deputies and city police. They were very familiar with Reggie's reputation, so they showed up with more than enough backup when they came to arrest Reggie on an outstanding warrant: a petty trespassing charge.

"I can't believe you motherfuckers got the damn nerve to run up in here for some bullshit-ass trespassing charge. I'm sure it's a child molester somewhere out there that you needs to be running up on," Reggie screamed as they put him in the police car.

Once free on bond, Reggie told Bambi that he was sure he was going to have to do about thirty days because this was his third trespassing charge.

"Baby, it don't matter how much time you gotta do, I'm going to be right here for you, holding it down like only I can," she told him.

Reggie had underestimated the authority of the judge, who gave him ninety days in the Richmond City Jail. Reggie would call every day, and Bambi would sit by the phone accepting the collect calls; and when the twenty minutes was up, she demanded that he call right back. Every Thursday she visited Reggie, a thick glass separated them.

At first, the whole jailhouse visit had her on pins and needles. The clanking doors, the surly guards, the ugly peeling paint on the walls—all of it turned her stomach. It especially made her sad when she observed the women who brought their kids to see their fathers. One time a little girl was crying, begging her daddy to come and leave with them as visiting time came to an end. The guard showed no emotion as the little girl begged for more time with her father to say good-bye.

Sometimes she waited for an hour and a half just to get in for the twenty-minute visits, which annoyed her. She still was there every visiting day enduring the frustrating wait, from the babies crying at the tops of their lungs, to the musty smells and not to mention the eyeing of the guards looking down on her as if she was nothing because she was visiting her man in jail.

Reggie knew he had two sure things to come home to: First and foremost, he needed his money and his Boo. He told Bambi that he would listen to so many dudes in the jail whine about their girl running around wild, fucking anything and everything moving because they had not prepared them for the possibility of having to do time. Reggie said that 85 percent of the chicks moved on to another dude solely for money. On the streets their men lived for the moment and never planned for the future. They left the females, who were so accustomed to the street lifestyle, no other choice really but to move on to the next hustler. So Reggie made sure his money was together. Besides, he didn't want to start from the bottom with a hundred dollars like he had the last time he came home from doing a bit.

So he took care of some things from the inside. He got Bambi to call his supplier Big D on the three-way and make arrangements to meet him. He instructed Bambi to go into the stash and give Big D the money in exchange for a kilo of crack cocaine. During the prison visits Reggie would walk her through how to weigh it out. He even sent her a chart as to what the scale needed to say to get an ounce, big eight, and so forth. After it was bagged up into ounces, he called three of his homeboys to let them know to call Bambi for the weight. At the price he paid for the kilo, he was able to sell cheaper than almost anyone else in town and make a profit. He only allowed Bambi to deal with the three dudes directly.

Every day she sat in the house at the mahogany wood table, feeling her heart beat as she bagged the coke up, knowing at any minute the police could kick up in there. She thought about how proud Reggie must be of her, the way she was holding it down. In the middle of the night when the dudes wanted to re-up, she just grabbed Reggie's nine millimeter and headed to the gas station to meet them. Although she knew she was doing wrong, as soon as she left out of the house, she prayed and asked God to take care of her anyway.

Even though Bambi didn't like it and Reggie knew it, not once did she complain. Instead she handled her business like a seasoned pro.

One day while on a visit, he looked into her eyes. "Boo, I'm sorry I got you all caught up in this. This is only till I get up out here."

"Baby, you were out in those projects trespassing, hustling, selling drugs for us, for us to survive and have the best that life has to offer. You made sure both of us benefited to the fullest. So it's not even a question for me to hold this down while you're gone. It's my duty to keep your books stacked and take care of whatever needs to be taken care of while I'm out here and you're in there. It's done, and if it ain't, baby, you can lay down and do that time and bet that I got you on this end."

Reggie smiled a big Joker smile.

"Without a doubt, I know I got a soldier right by my side."

But dealing drugs wasn't the only indignity Bambi had to face. All the guards admired Bambi. She always looked her very best when she came through the jailhouse's double doors. One guard at the prison saw her submission and love for Reggie as a weakness and said, "Look, show me some 'PG' and I'll get you a visit every visiting day, instead of once a week."

"What's PG?"

"Personal Growth."

"What? Mothafucka, are you crazy? Have you bumped your head?"

She strolled right into the visitation room and told Reggie

exactly what he'd said. She was even more shocked by his response: "Shit, I'm trying to see you every visiting day, let that ma'fucker pat yo ass or something. Don't you want to see me?"

Bambi did a lot of soul-searching after that. She'd been shocked that Reggie would willingly allow another man to touch her. *Damn, do he really love me? I know he's under a lot of stress, misses me and wants to see me as much as I want to see him. This has got to be hard on him. He saw me every day, and now all of a sudden he can't see me. But I can't let another man touch me. Why would he want another man to touch what's his? I know pimps do it all the time for the money. I guess with Reggie, desperate times call for desperate measures.* Bambi felt horrible, but she thought it through and allowed the guard to look down her shirt to get to see Reggie every visiting day for the next few days.

Although it was only ninety days that they were separated, Bambi had lots of time to think—time for reality to sink in. Bambi loved the lavish lifestyle that they lived, but all good things had to come to an end. She knew that no fairy tale lasts forever. Bambi hoped Reggie would decide to quit while they were ahead, but three months after he was released from jail, he kept right on dealing, never slowed up. Finally, Bambi couldn't hold her tongue any longer and said something. "I can't stand the thought of you going to jail again—and one of these days, some envious hater is going to send five-oh our way."

"So what do you want me to do?"

"I want you to get out of the game."

"Okay," he said with a smile. "I'm out, but I need about another month to be on the grind so I can tie all my loose ends up."

That had been a month ago, and as far as she could tell, Reggie was still slaying more bricks than a little bit one hundred miles and running. So now the clock was ticking. Hopefully after the engagement party there would be no more hustling for Reggie.

As she pulled up to the restaurant and prepared to say good-bye to the crazy life and embrace her destiny, Bambi couldn't help but think how lucky she was.

CHAPTER 3

What's Done in the Dark . . .
Will Come to the Light!

"**H**ey, girl!" Egypt greeted Bambi with a hug as she stepped into the restaurant lobby. She handed her a drink—her favorite, a Passion-fruit Alizé. "You are never gonna believe all the people in that back room, and they are all here for you."

Although she hadn't let on to Reggie, Bambi had known he was throwing her a party, thanks to Egypt, her best friend since sixth grade. Reggie had asked for Egypt's assistance not only in helping to pull the party together but also in selecting the five-carat engagement ring. Too bad he never suspected that Egypt would consult with Bambi about which ring she wanted, and that was exactly the ring that Egypt selected for her friend. But Egypt made Bambi promise to act surprised when she arrived at the party.

As she looked around, Bambi couldn't help but be touched by the effort Reggie had made. The restaurant had been beautifully decorated with what seemed to be thousands of white roses, their smell enveloping her as she looked around. Throughout the lobby and all over the ballroom, there were enlarged pictures of the couple from their many travels, and also from their two-year journey from the 'hood where they'd met to their first apartment and finally to their personal paradise.

It took everything in her not to cry. She knew she couldn't because she hadn't applied waterproof makeup on her face.

"Now, you sure you want to go through with this?" Egypt asked, laughing.

"The party or the wedding?" Bambi asked with a straight face.

"Real funny, real funny."

The party was already going crazy—there must have been about a hundred people in there, along with seafood buffet tables and three open bars. A DJ was playing "The Men All Pause," that golden oldie by Klymaxx, and the guests had been liquoring up nicely at the open bar. At the sight of Bambi, the music stopped, and so did everything else, and Bambi could feel every set of eyes in the room glued on her, their smiles paying respect to the queen.

Bambi couldn't believe all of the people who had blessed her with their appearance. She saw a man who was obviously Reggie's dad. She had never met him before, and she was touched that he'd come all the way up from New Orleans. Of course her favorite cousin, Zonna, was there. But there were her friends and family there, too—folks Reggie didn't even know but somehow had managed to invite, like her Grandma Ellie.

Grandma Ellie was her mother's mother, and when Bambi was growing up, Grandma Ellie was her only ticket to the free world. She'd loved to go over to her grandmother's house. It was there she got to let her hair down and have fun. Grandma Ellie wasn't snobby at all, unlike the rest of her mother's friends or anyone that Tricia had let into the invisible bubble that surrounded Bambi. Grandma Ellie had always been the one to keep things in order when Tricia was out of whack. For the old lady to be anywhere other than church this time of night was a miracle in itself.

Grandma Ellie put her hands on both Bambi's arms. "Let me look at you. You look so perty. I'm so happy for you, baby. He better treat you right." Just then Bambi felt a pair of hands slide over her eyes.

"Is that my prince? Is that you, baby?" She knew it was. She could smell his Issey Miyake cologne, and, boy, did it smell good!

When Reggie removed his hands, she turned around to face him. *Ummp, ummp, ummp!* Lord have mercy, could thugged-out Reggie rock a suit or what? It was a crisp white Armani double-breasted suit, hemmed perfectly to lie well over his shoes, with a white pimp-daddy hat cocked a little to the side over his white do-rag, which covered his neatly braided cornrows. Reggie had his collar pulled up to try to camouflage the scratch on his neck from the squabble earlier, but she noticed it anyway. *Ulll*, she thought. Thinking of the pain that scratch must have caused turned her stomach, but that only lasted a moment because seeing him done up so nice made her wet between the legs. For a second she thought about pulling him to the ladies' room to hop on his dick real quick, but then she remembered that she'd have him for a lifetime.

"May I have this dance?" He extended his hand to her and smiled with his gold teeth glistening.

"Yes, you may," she said with a smile, giving him her hand as they took to the dance floor. Reggie usually just stood against the wall and nodded his head. Tonight was different. He knew Bambi loved to dance, and tonight and from this day forward her wish would be his command.

The DJ began to play Tony! Toni! Tone!'s "Anniversary." Straight old-school all of the way. Could things be any more perfect?

After the song was over, someone tapped her on her shoulder. "May I cut in and have this dance with your handsome man?" Bambi was surprised at the voice. It was her mother, and although she hadn't seen her mother in months, as always she was as clean as the board of health. She had on a soft pink Chanel suit with the shoes, hat, and bag to match. It didn't even matter to Bambi that her uptight mother was tipsy as hell. Bambi knew she had not only had a few drinks but she had probably dropped a Valium or something to have her so laid-back and relaxed.

She hugged her mother and said, "Thank you so much for coming, Mommy! I'm so glad you are here with me."

"I would not have missed this for the world! Now, baby, go to the restroom and fix your makeup because your forehead is glowing, and let me get my dance on with my future son-in-law," Tricia said, speaking with perfect composure the entire time and holding her breath as she looked directly into her daughter's eyes.

Bambi went to the bathroom to check her face. When Bambi was growing up, her mother had made her go to Sunday school and church every week. Since she had gotten with Reggie, she wasn't as religious, but looking in the mirror, she said a silent prayer:

Lord, God up in heaven, I just want to take this time to thank you for showing me all the signs and for giving me a reason not to walk away from this relationship. God, you know all about my problems with this man, how I was holding on to my sanity for dear life while he was in jail. Thank you, Lord, for revealing the big picture to me and, most importantly, for helping me maintain my peace of mind. And had this not worked out, Lord, I knew you had my back as long as I was steadfast. God, I could go on thanking you all night because you do so much for me. But I am going to keep this short and sweet! In Jesus' name, I pray. Amen.

Bambi hurried and washed her hands. When she exited the bathroom door, she couldn't believe her eyes. Some dude was standing right in front of her, blocking her path, wearing the very same sweater she had on: an N. T. Original, cut from the same cloth.

Ain't this some shit? I thought these sweaters were handmade and one of a kind. To top it off, how dare somebody show up at my *party trying to outshine the queen herself. But whatever—it's cool because it's my night and can't nobody, and I mean* nobody, *take my shine away from me. It's a whole bunch of divas up in here tonight but I am "that diva," and everybody here knows it, too.*

It was a whole lot easier to forgive a man than a woman. Now, if some chick would have come stepping into "her" party wearing "her" sweater, words would have never been exchanged. The only thing she would have said was, "Security get this imposter up out of here."

The dude had a nice build on him, caramel complexion, hair neatly braided to the back. His linen pants fell perfectly over his Italian loafers, and he was wearing that sweater well, to the point she just had to compliment him. "I really love that sweater, and you're wearing the hell out of it, too."

The guy just glared at her. "You just ought to, 'cause your man bought it for me."

"What did you say?" She knew her ears must have heard wrong.

"You heard me. Your man bought this for me, and everything else he buys or has bought for you—guess what, Boo?—he buys one for me, too."

"What?" Bambi could barely get the word out.

"That's right. You heard me, Ms. Two," he said, jabbing a finger in her face. "I said 'your man.' That's right, yo man, Boo, is in love with me!" The tone of his voice lifted as he dropped the bombshell in her lap. "Your man be laying pipe all up in me, and I slobs the hell out of his knob on a regular, Boo. When I say regularly, I mean just that. But to clear the smoke in the air, I mean seven days a week, and twice on Sundays."

Bambi couldn't believe what she was hearing. "Who the hell are you?"

"Jack, but you can call me . . . Jackie, beeaaiiitch."

"Now, I know you just didn't say what I thought you said," Bambi said, getting hot.

"Look, let me give it to you in plain ol' English, because you act like I am speaking Spanish. What I'm saying is that your man's a homo-thug!" he said, twisting his neck. She was so close to him she could smell the Big Red gum on his breath, which he had the nerve to use to blow into a bubble in her face.

He continued. "And every time you kiss him, you are sucking my dick or eating my ass." He ended that statement with a snap of the finger as if he was reading her.

Now, that last comment snapped Bambi out of her trance, and she did what was natural for her to do. She drew back without even blinking or thinking twice and popped him one right in the jaw. It never dawned on her that she wasn't fighting an average chick. She was indeed fighting a man, and while her blow might have been hard enough to send a big woman to her knees, it only made Jack, or Jackie, or however the hell he liked to be addressed, stumble a little, but not enough to lose his balance.

Before Jack could retaliate, Egypt appeared. That girl had a sixth sense when it came to Bambi and always had her back.

Egypt didn't hear the exact content of the conversation, but truthfully, she didn't care the least bit. She just knew by the astonishment written all over Bambi's face that whatever it was, it wasn't nothing nice.

Egypt began to pummel him, and Bambi threw a hell of an uppercut; and Jack began to scream, falling to his knees. Bambi tried to stomp him, but Jack pulled her to the floor and somehow grabbed Bambi's long, flowing hair, holding on to it for dear life.

The three of them were rolling around on the floor making a commotion when Reggie and some of the guests heard them and hurried into the hallway.

A couple big fellas pried the girls off Jack. They had beaten him around pretty good. One of them turned to Reggie, laughing. "Damn man, what type of shit you into, Reggie? Hope you know what to do with all of that."

Reggie didn't smile. He pretended not to notice Jack, giving no indication of their relationship. "Security, get this man the fuck up out of here," Reggie said as one of his homeboys got the crowd under control and sent everybody back inside of the restaurant.

"Redddggie, oh no, you didn't say *have this man removed*! You wasn't saying that three hours ago when you was laying pipe all up in me."

"Shut the fuck up!" Reggie demanded, giving Jack an evil look.

"Reggie, please tell me it isn't so," Bambi said, with hurt written all across her face. With all her heart, she wanted to believe that this was all some type of cruel joke.

"Look, I can explain! We'll talk about this later."

"Bitch!" Bambi uttered, as she spit in Reggie's face. "Tell me he's lying."

"Baby, I said we gonna talk about this later. There really ain't no need to make no scene," Reggie pleaded to Bambi. Bambi saw guilt written all over his face. Before he knew it, he felt the smack from her Gucci high heel cluck the side of his face.

"Oh, hell no. We ain't escorting a soul up out of here. We are going to get all this BS in the open because it's just that! Bullshit!" Bambi shouted almost at the top of her lungs.

Reggie was cold busted, and so he did what any coward would do in his shoes. He punched Jack dead in the face.

"You lying ma'fucka," Reggie shouted. But Bambi knew it was just an act.

Jack fell to his knees with tears dropping from his eyes.

"Oh, this is beautiful. Just such a great part of the entertainment, Reggie, but tonight the entertainment is on me!" On that note, Bambi stormed off.

Reggie tried to follow Bambi, but Egypt pushed him out of the way and followed closely behind her.

"Girl," Egypt said, "that was an Oscar-winning performance, and I can tell this definitely isn't the time for a commercial."

Bambi got to the closed door that led into the grand ballroom. As she stopped in her tracks, she turned around to ask Egypt, "Is my face a'ight to go in here in front of all these folks?"

Egypt simply grabbed a napkin from a nearby lobby podium. She spit on the napkin a little and wiped the blood off of Bambi's face and combed through Bambi's hair with her fingers to try to get it back in order as best as she could. That's when Reggie walked up.

"Look, Bambi, we can work this out. I invited you here to ask you to marry me. I love you," Reggie pleaded.

"Love? You brought me here to marry me? You think I want to marry a freaking bitch with a damn dick?"

"Ouch," Egypt said, looking at Reggie with a smirk.

"I'm not wit that gay stuff," Bambi continued. "I mean, let's be real. What could I do for you now? I mean, come on now, jump in any time. How and where do I start to compete with a man? There is no competition, and I am not even going there with you."

Reggie dropped his head in shame as Bambi went to put the icing on the cake. She pushed the doors open and began to search for her prey. Misery loved company, and if she was hurt, a whole bunch of other people were going to leave there feeling her pain. She scanned the room like a surveillance camera. She walked toward her potential target as Reggie trailed behind her begging her not to make a scene. Bambi didn't care about making a scene. Hell, the damage was already done. Her night was ruined; the good life that she had worked so hard for was gone down the drain, thrown out of the window, and flushed down the damn toilet. It was no turning back now.

Bambi was the victim and hadn't done anything wrong but been a fool for love.

"Bambi, please, don't do this. Please don't embarrass yourself," Reggie pleaded with tears in his eyes. He had no idea what she had up her sleeve.

"Oh, it's not for me to be embarrassed, and I don't care if these people know or not, but there is one person I want to know—yo damn momma!"

At that very moment, she walked up to Reggie's mother, Dot. Dot was on the dance floor doing a combination of the old-school dances—the robot and the funky chicken—having a jolly old time with her ex-husband.

"What's wrong, Bambi? Is everything okay?" Reggie's dad asked.

I feel like asking him, Do everything look okay? This is even bet-

ter, a father to feel the pain of his son being gay. There will be someone coming out of this more hurt than me.

"Hellll nah! No! Everything's not okay. I just found out that your son is fucking men now. He's gay, a fucking faggot."

"What?" he said, more confused than angry.

Before she could explain further, Ms. Dot looked at Bambi with deep sincerity, took her into her arms, and pulled her tight to her bosom as only a mother could comfort a child. "I am sorry you had to find out like this," Dot whispered in Bambi's ear.

For the first time that night, Bambi let loose the tears she'd been holding back. But then she realized what Ms. Dot had said and started to get very angry. How could Ms. Dot, a woman just like she was, who had claimed to love her like the daughter she'd never had, withhold such a heart-wrenching secret from her? How long had they expected this charade to go on? Did they not think that such a skeleton would ever fall out of the closet? Hadn't Ms. Dot heard of that saying: "What's done in the dark will always come to the light?"

Bambi pushed away from Ms. Dot and did something she'd wanted to do from the first day she had met her, but would never have dared to do till now. She reached over and snatched off that funky-looking wig that Ms. Dot was certain made her look like Foxy Brown but which actually made her look like Foxy Clown. Bambi wanted to make her feel as humiliated as she herself felt.

As she tossed the wig on the floor and turned to go, she realized it was going to be a long time before her broken heart mended!

Bambi lay in her hotel suite crying, mascara everywhere, still wearing her party outfit, when she heard a knock on the door. She didn't want to answer, but whoever was knocking wasn't going to leave her alone. Finally, Bambi got out of bed and was surprised to see Tricia with a bottle of Dom Perignon in a bucket on ice.

"Do you mind if I join you?" Tricia said. Her voice was a little slurred, but she wasn't too far gone.

"Come on. Just don't tell me 'I told you so.' Because, Ma, I can't take it right now."

Tricia kicked her shoes off and pulled up a chair in front of the bed. "Look, baby, I know this is not what you expected to come out of tonight, but better you know now than ten years from now."

"I know, Mom."

Tricia popped open the bottle and poured champagne for herself and Bambi. "Over the years I've seen you and your grandma look at me sideways because I've only been interested in a man's possessions. Well, in all your years have you ever seen me cry over a man?"

Bambi looked at her mother and then shook her head no.

"Do you know why?"

Bambi was silent as she looked at her mother and waited to hear what she had to say.

"I was never emotionally attached to those men, just to their bank account. I loved what they had, what they could give me. And when the money ran out, there was nothing for me to like about them." She added, "To sum it up, when the money was gone, I was gone."

"You don't have to tell me all of this, Ma."

"I know, baby, but it's important," she said, pouring herself another drink. "I need you to make me a promise. I need you to promise that you're never gonna give a man your heart again."

"The way I feel right now, I could kill every man in sight."

"No sense hurting them physically, baby. You already done enough of that tonight. Next time you hurt them, do it where it hurts . . . in their pockets!"

For the next few weeks, Bambi would play those words over and over in her mind, time and time again!

CHAPTER 4

He Done Messed with the Wrong One

Bambi didn't let any grass grow under her feet. In a matter of days she had found herself a new place and had moved her things out of Reggie's house. The relationship was over—there was no negotiation, compromising, or counseling. Bambi knew she had to move on.

Weeks passed without Bambi leaving her new apartment. She cut off communication with everyone as she wallowed in her misery. Her emotions ran wild, and a cold bitterness set in her veins. Although she avoided her incoming phone calls and never answered her door, there were two people that she couldn't ignore. One was the UPS man. He came about three times a week with the catalog and Home Shopping Club purchases that she ordered while trying to convince herself that one day soon she was going to go out and face the haters.

They may be popping that trash, pointing and giggling behind my back, but you best believe they won't be able to say that I look bad. Because when I do step out of that door, I'm going to be clean as the board of health, and hos can lay flat and bet that.

The other person was Egypt, who, no matter how rude Bambi was to her, came around to give Bambi her unconditional love and support. Every day about five in the afternoon, Egypt stopped by Bambi's apartment. There was no need to knock because she already knew that Bambi wasn't going to answer the door. So Egypt simply put her key into the door and waltzed into Bambi's crib, immediately opening all the blinds and windows. Most of the time, Bambi acted as if she didn't want to be bothered, but deep down she looked forward to those afternoon visits.

On this particular morning Bambi could feel Egypt's presence in the doorway, yet she never turned around to acknowledge her. For the next few minutes, Egypt stood there with her arms folded.

"Go ahead and say what you got to say," Bambi said, feeling Egypt's stare.

"Look, B, you've got to snap out of this funk you're in. I mean, look at this place. You've been in this apartment for five weeks straight. That's thirty-five days, and how many baths have you taken? This house smells, and this bedroom is a pigsty. Girl, this ain't you. It's time you got yo shit together."

"Well, if you don't like how it smells, you don't have to come over here. You can leave the key on the table and carry your ass on," Bambi said defensively as she rolled her eyes.

But Egypt wasn't budging. "Look, Bambi, I'm not trying to dis you. Hell, I am your girl, and all I'm saying is you are losing touch, B. This ain't you. Why you tripping on me? Today is November twenty-first, and you have no clue."

When that date rolled off of Egypt's tongue, Bambi's whole

disposition changed. She jumped up, ran over to Egypt, and hugged her.

"Oh, my God, how could I? I am so sorry. I forgot my best friend in the whole world's birthday. Your twenty-first birthday, at that! I am soooo sorry, and you came over here yesterday, and didn't even say anything to me. If I was you, I wouldn't even be talking to me."

"It's cool, because now you owe me."

"Oh, my God! Egypt, anything. I am telling you, anything! I'll make it up to you. Please forgive me."

"Anything?" Egypt said with a smirk on her face.

"Anything!"

"Well, since last night I couldn't go out and use my ID to get into a club, why don't you take me out tonight?"

Bambi agreed, although she didn't feel like going out in public yet, but there was no turning back. Egypt was her girl, and she had to make it up to her.

"Well, you better get it together, because I am coming back over here to get dressed and make sure that you don't stand me up. And don't try to say you don't have nothing to wear, because all these boxes and packages tell another story," Egypt said, pointing to a stack of boxes in the corner that Bambi had not even opened yet.

"In that case then I guess I better finally get up and wash my funky butt and go get my nails done and call and see if I can get something done to my hair."

Bambi didn't have a lot of time to play with, and she couldn't let her best friend down. Egypt had been her friend through thick and thin, the meaningless drama as well as the good, bad, happy, and sad. It was always Egypt who lent her ear when Bambi needed someone to listen, and it was on her shoulder Bambi cried. At the very least, Bambi felt she had no choice but to summon the strength from deep within and pull herself together, if not for herself, then for her friend. It took everything in Bambi to swallow her pride and get her act together, because she knew she would have to paint a picture for the haters and gossipers and to give them all the impression that she was fine, that life without Reggie was grand and could not have been better.

With the help of her cell phone, Bambi worked wonders within a few hours. In addition to inviting their friends, she arranged to have the VIP area at the Spade Club decorated with balloons and streamers and ordered a scrumptious-looking penis-shaped chocolate cake with white icing to be delivered to the club. When the invitees arrived that night, they were in awe that Bambi had thrown together this blowout in such a short period of time.

Bambi herself was a showstopper. Although she had put on about twenty pounds, the weight didn't look bad. She was dressed to kill, turning heads of both male and female partygoers, as she made her rounds and played the perfect role of hostess. Under her full-length white Russian mink coat, she wore a snow white leather halter dress that hugged every voluptuous curve in her perfect hourglass figure. Her dark chocolate skin and long jet black hair resting on her back, accentuated the whole ensemble and showed her off as the queen of style. She thought about what her mother had once said: "You know you's a fearless bitch when you can pull off wearing white in the wintertime. And I am not talking about cream or off-white color. I am talking about snow white." And if nothing else was certain and no other facts could be documented for the night, let it be known she was wearing white like no other woman could.

Lots of folks stopped by to give their condolences to Bambi as if a loved one had died instead of her being kicked to the curb by her man for another man. She simply smiled at them, not revealing her true emotions. She wanted to break down, but it wasn't an option, not here, not now anyway. The party went well, and Egypt was having a ball. Bambi stayed glued to the VIP area, acting as if she was keeping everything intact, but truth be told, she couldn't bear the thought of being around too many people. She was happy Egypt was mingling with the crowd among the rest of the club, collecting her gifts, mostly monetary, from a lot of the clubgoers instead of trying to comfort her. Before the party, Bambi had tipped the DJ fifty dollars to announce "Happy Birthday to Egypt" and to give her shout-outs on the mic every ten minutes. Egypt was being shown much love by the folks she did know and even some she didn't. It was Egypt's night, and Bambi wanted her to make the most of it.

Egypt would come back to the VIP area every so often to give Bambi an update on who she had seen, who was wearing what, and who was with whom. Bambi knew it was more to check on her and to see how she was holding up.

"Girl, I just met this fiiiinnneee dude named Smooth."

"For real?"

"Yup, girl, he is fine, and he look like he got plenty bank. Girlllll, I can just tell. And he is at me hard!"

"That's right, Boo. Go, E. It's yo birthday!" As Bambi started to sing, she held up a glass, and they toasted.

Someone came up and tapped Egypt on the shoulder, and she was off again. This time she was gone for about an hour. Normally, Bambi would have left the VIP area to search the club for her friend, but she was too busy keeping her own emotions in check. While she looked happy, what she really wanted to do was run off to the bathroom to break down and cry.

"Hey, girl, you all right?" Egypt asked, coming back to Bambi.

"Yup, girl, I'm good. Where you been?"

"Girl, I was in the lobby talking to Smooth. I am really feeling Smooth. He wants to take us out for breakfast. I'll understand this one time if you don't want to go. I am just grateful you came out tonight wit me and did all this for me."

"I'm not really feeling it, but I want you to go."

"You sho?"

"Yup, I really want you to go. You feeling him, and he kept you away from your own party for like an hour. Girl, go and have a good time."

"You sure?"

"Yup, I am. I'm going to get this stuff cleaned up, and I didn't really drink much, so I can make it home fine."

Egypt looked into Bambi's eyes for a sign of disapproval. They both knew she was going off for a one-night stand with this man, someone she had only known a matter of hours. To her surprise she got something that was almost mind-blowing: Bambi's approval. This was very unusual.

They hugged, and then Egypt grabbed her pocketbook and coat and headed out of the VIP area to the lobby to meet up with Smooth.

Judging from Smooth's conversation and his persona, Egypt was slightly impressed, though not surprised, when Smooth hit the alarm on a brand-new, shiny, candy apple red Mercedes Benz coupe that looked like it was fresh off the showroom floor.

She knew if she got in his car, there was no turning back. She had to be able to deal with any repercussions that came with getting into this car—specifically giving it up, the kitty cat, that is, and having a one-night stand. She knew exactly what came with leaving the club at 2 a.m. with a man she just met or any man for that matter: giving up the coochie. She dissected the whole situation as she walked to the car on his arm.

I can't believe I am about to go and have a one-night stand with this ma'fucka I don't even know. What do he think about me? Will he even call me after this is over? Damn, is he gonna tell all his boys that he fucked me on the first night? Well, I am twenty-one years now, a fucking grown-ass woman, and whether he calls me or not I'm cool with it. This is something that I want to do.

He went around to the passenger's side of the car, opened up the door, and being the perfect gentleman, made sure her coat was inside the car before closing the door for her. After he shut the door, he hurried around to the driver's side of the car and got in. Once he was out of the club's parking lot, he asked, "What do you want to listen to? Grab the CD case out of the back and see what I got."

With butterflies in her stomach, Egypt sat nervous as a virgin on her first date. Though she wasn't a virgin, she was brand-new to this whole one-night-stand ordeal. This was something she had never done before.

After selecting *Ghetto D* by Master P, Egypt looked at Smooth, admiring his sexy appeal. Inside the club, he'd seemed a bit conceited, but once she'd actually talked to him, he was cool. Although he was tall and slinky, it was apparent that he had a membership at someone's gym. His body seemed hard and fine. His almond complexion went well with his dark brown short hair, embedded with waves. He had thick eyebrows that met in the middle and could have used a good waxing, but it only enhanced his sexiness. His cream suit with the cream-and-brown gators put the icing on the cake. Not one woman—black or white, young, old, or middle-aged—could deny that he was fine.

Egypt became turned on as she watched Smooth drive. She really wanted to skip breakfast and head straight to his house or the hotel, motel, or wherever he had plans on taking her after breakfast. She knew breakfast was just the way to ease into the sexual encounter.

They went to an all-night seventies-like restaurant in the fan district on the campus of VCU and continued talking long after they had eaten and the bill had come.

"So, how does it feel to be twenty-one?" he asked.

"It feels the same, but I am glad that I am legal now."

"Do you have a man?"

"Nope, do you have a girl?"

"Yes." He grabbed her hand. "You my girl."

She smiled. The night was going better than she had expected.

When the waitress came over and informed them that she would be getting off soon, they knew that was their cue to leave. He reached into his pocket and gave the waitress a tip and looked at Egypt.

"Look, let's go to Byrd Park and talk."

"That's cool with me," she said.

Maybe he really is a gentleman. Maybe after all, I won't have to have a one-night stand with him. Shoot, who knows? He just could be "my man."

He cruised through Byrd Park and finally parked in a secluded area away from everything, but he left the car running with the heat on.

"Take your coat off, and put it in the backseat. I got the heat on, and if that's not enough you can always turn on the heat for your seat."

She did as she was told. He pulled the sleeve off so she could ease her beaver-fur coat off. Then she threw it in the backseat.

He looked into her eyes, leaned over, and gave her a long, passionate kiss. Another kiss followed—even longer and more erotic. It made her whole body tingle. He struggled to unbutton her pants, then put his right hand inside her underwear and began to fondle her while inching her pants down with the other. Then he grabbed her hand and placed it on his rock-hard manhood and looked into her eyes. He pulled her big breasts out of her halter top and began to suck on them as she stroked him. Before she knew it, she was completely out of her halter, and he whispered in her ear, "Help me take your pants off." He stopped for a few seconds as she slid her legs out of her painted-on leather pants. He continued to play with her clit, and within a matter of minutes he was caressing her and rubbing her in all the right ways. He reached on the side of her seat to put the seat back so she could be more comfortable.

I cannot believe I am about to fuck this nigga in his car. Now, is that some straight skeezer-type shit or what? Shoot, I don't care, because whatever that nigga is doing, that shit feel so good!

She opened her legs wider as he unbuckled his pants. She was working him with a killer hand job, wanting him to get off. She reached in the backseat and grabbed some lotion out of her pocketbook. Once she poured it on her hands, she stroked the head, and when she did, she could see by his expression that he was thoroughly enjoying himself. He looked into her eyes as he came all over the leather seats. He could see how blazing hot she was and that she wanted him inside of her right that very second. At that instant, as turned on as she was, she didn't care if it was inside of a car, on the backseat of the car, under or on top of the car. She wanted him right then and there.

With such an intense tingling feeling throughout her whole body, she couldn't resist. Waiting another minute was not an option. "Come on and put it in," she said breathlessly.

As he was trying to catch his breath from his own orgasm, he looked at her with a devilish grin on his face, and out of nowhere he pulled out a big-ass chrome .357.

"Get the fuck out of the car, you trifling bitch!" he shouted as he pushed open the passenger's side door. She had no choice while looking down the barrel of a .357 but to obey. She tripped, falling to the ground on her way out of the car. Without hesitation he put the car in gear and pulled off, screaming out the window at her, "You dumb bitch! Didn't yo momma ever teach you, don't get in the car with fucking strangers?"

As Egypt lay on the ground, she cried hysterically, whimpering, humiliated, and cold with nothing on but her skimpy lace thong that Smooth had put a hole in while he was fingering her. What was she to do? There weren't any phones anywhere in sight, and her cell, money, ID, clothes, shoes and, most importantly her coat were all in Smooth's car.

A day passed, and Bambi had not heard a peep from Egypt, which was very unusual. They usually talked every day—three, four, sometimes five times a day. Bambi had left her a few voice mails but assumed that Egypt was mad because she didn't go have breakfast with her and Smooth. Bambi was getting worried, and if she didn't hear from Egypt today Bambi was going to call her stepdad, Jeff. He was the only family besides Bambi that Egypt had. Her mother had died from cancer when Egypt was sixteen, leaving Jeff and Egypt to take care of each other.

But Jeff called her first, and Bambi didn't even let him finish before she hung up. She rushed to the hospital crying, blaming and convicting herself the whole time.

If I was in my right state of mind, I would have never, *ever in a million years allowed her to go with no stranger. Instead I was all caught up in my damn drama, having a pity party for myself. This is all my fault! What did he do to my friend? What if something happens to her? What if she dies? How would I be able to look at myself in the mirror?*

As soon as she saw her friend laid up in a bed with barely a pulse, Bambi started to cry again. Jeff explained to her that a park ranger had found her the day after her birthday. For nearly ten hours she'd lain in the park almost naked. Her skin was blue and purple. Egypt was suffering from frostbite and severe hypothermia. He explained to her, "She was a Jane Doe until someone who worked in dietary recognized her and called me."

Although Egypt was doped up over the next three days, Bambi sat at her best friend's bedside around the clock. As soon as Egypt came around, the first thing Bambi said to her was, "I'm soooo sorry. I know it's all my fault, and if it's the last thing I do, I promise on everything I love, I swear I am going to get this nigga back. I swear to God. God can take the breath out of my body if I am lying. He done fucked with the wrong bitch this time. The only way I won't is if the sun don't shine and the creek don't rise. I'm going to get this clown back. "

Egypt gripped Bambi's hand tight and just cried.

Once Egypt was released from the hospital, Bambi waited on her hand and foot. That was the essence of their friendship. When one was down, the other never kicked her but instead lifted her up, unconditionally. They had each other's back—no backbiting, no backstabbing, no two-facing, no larceny-hearted BS, none of that. They had a friendship that came only once in a lifetime.

"Come on, you have to put something on your stomach," Bambi said as she tried to feed her friend some soup.

Egypt didn't want to eat or talk. Egypt blamed herself for the whole incident. She felt like it was a warning from God because it could have been much worse. She could have been raped, beat up, had a train run on her by five or six dudes, or even killed. So this was her warning from God. Not an hour of the day went by that Egypt didn't wonder or ask God why this had happened to her and what He was trying to tell her.

"I never went on a one-night stand before or slept around with a whole bunch of niggas. I ain't never been on that kind of trip. I only been with like three dudes in my life, so why would this cruel shit happen to me?" Egypt asked her friend.

"Look, E, it wasn't you! Trust me when I tell you, it wasn't. It's that crazy-ass nigga Smooth. Blame him, not you or God. That whacked-out nigga is the one with issues. Maybe he had a flashback. Has that dude ever been to jail before?"

Although Egypt felt the question was irrelevant, she still answered her friend, "Yes, he did mention that he had went when he was a juvenile."

"Well, that explains it all right there. For him to act like that he probably got juked up the ass or something when he was in the slammer, and now when he's got the upper hand, he feels like he can just be on some Psycho Sam–type shit."

Egypt didn't say a word; she only listened to her friend as she continued. "And sure if my name is what it is, oh, his ass is going to get it. I don't care. It could take me forty years. Trust me, I am going to get his ass."

"What you going to do, fight him?" Egypt said, trying to crack a joke.

"Nope, it ain't no need," Bambi said confidently. "Oh, you can say or think what you want, but baby, this here ain't no joke. I promise you this one is on me."

Egypt heard every word her friend said and knew she meant well, but what were the odds that Bambi would run into Smooth and that Smooth would even talk to Bambi? He knew that Bambi was her best friend, and how many Bambis were there running around Richmond? None besides her. But Egypt never took into consideration that this was Richmond and that with Bambi's knowledge of the streets, the odds were more in Bambi's favor than Egypt could ever have imagined.

CHAPTER 5

The Gig

It was 8:07 a.m., and the phone rang as Bambi sat at the kitchen table, writing checks to cover the minimum payment on her credit card bills—at least on the ones she felt were most important—and deciding which ones would have to wait. The stash money she had been saving when she was with Reggie was almost gone.

"Hello, can I speak to Bambi?" the caller said, like she was an old friend.

"Who's calling?"

"Janey."

"Janey, she's not here." Bambi knew that it was a bill collector.

"Well is her husband in?"

"Nope, and do you know what time it is?"

"If she'd pay her bills, then I wouldn't have to call at 8:00 a.m., but I'll call again tomorrow morning and wake you up again," the bill collector said, and hung up the phone.

Now these people must know that times is hard on this end.

That's why I didn't pay them. If times were sweet, then they'd be paid. These people call at eight o'clock in the morning, talking shit to me and think for one minute I am going to pay them because they are rude? I know for a fact that they get paid by commission off of how much they get me to pay them. Seems to me if they had any common sense they'd try to be a little courteous. As long as they get smart, I'll never pay them—as simple as that.

But some bills *had* to be paid—the electric bill, the rent, the phone bill, and the water bill. Just covering the basics was dwindling her bank account balance. *Damn how they gonna charge me for water? Water should be free, but it ain't a damn thing free in this world, believe that.* The phone rang again, but this time it wasn't a bill collector. It was the answer to her prayers and her worries.

The voice on the other end belonged to Disco, the owner of the club where she'd had Egypt's birthday party. He was so impressed with what Bambi had done with the VIP room in such a short amount of time that night of Egypt's party that he wanted to meet with her and possibly bring her on as an events planner for the club. She agreed to meet with him the following morning.

On the way to the club the next morning she remembered that the night of Egypt's party, some hater had broken off the side-view mirror of her car and she needed to get it repaired before she got a ticket. So she decided to drop the car at the dealership and have the oil changed while it was there, too. The dealership was only a block away from the club, and she could walk to her meeting.

Bambi arrived at the dealership and drove around back to the service department, where she was greeted by Joe, a middle-aged man with salt-and-pepper hair. Joe had checked her in the few times she'd brought in her car before, and every single time he was always nice, giving her pointers and helping her however he could.

"Joe," she said, pointing to her mirror. "I am going to need you to fix my mirror for me."

Joe nodded. "Ms. Bambi, that mirror is going to have to be ordered. It will take about a week or so to get here and it's going to cost a nice piece of change."

"Like how much?" she asked.

"Almost three . . . four hundred bucks, I'm guessing."

"What?"

"Yes, sweetheart, you don't have yourself a Chevette. You got yourself a Corvette."

"Well, right now I got a Chevette budget," she said.

He put his hand to his chin. He then put his finger up, motioning her to wait a minute.

"Ummm, let me check on something else first," he said as he picked up the phone and made a call.

For several minutes he was on the phone, talking as if it was an old friend instead of a business associate. Finally he hung up, smiled, and said, "Look, Ms. Bambi, I found that mirror that you need for your car, but it's at the junkyard."

She frowned as he told her, "Hold your horses and let me finish. My friend owns a junkyard of salvage cars, cars that are wrecked, with the mirror you need. We can go down there when I get off. I can take it off the wrecked 'vette and put it on your car. He'll charge you about ten or fifteen bucks for the mirror."

Smiling, she asked, "And how much you gonna charge me to put it on?"

"Ummm, just buy me a cold beer, that's all."

"It's a deal." Bambi smiled and shook his hand. "I'll make it a six-pack."

Joe promised her the oil change would be done in thirty minutes, and that they could go get the mirror later. She left her car and headed to the club, eager to hear what Disco had to say.

Once behind the closed doors of Disco's office, she walked around the room looking at all the expensively framed photos on the wall of what looked like pimps and players to her, but were actually snapshots of Disco and his friends who also owned clubs. She could tell he had put a lot of effort and time into his Wall of Fame. Disco took the time to explain who each and every one of them was, as if they were his kinfolks. She asked questions as if she were truly interested, but actually she could give a solitary fuck. She was mostly interested in the business at hand. Once he was done giving her the history of what seemed like every major club owner in America, they got down to business. She listened as Disco went on and on for about thirty minutes straight about how impressed he was with her.

"Bambi, I believe party planning is your niche, your gift, your talent, and if you play your cards right, it could be a hell of a hustle for you."

Bambi had never quite looked at it like that before, but she was glad Disco had brought it to her attention. She nodded and smiled as he went on and on. The more he talked and flattered her with all the praise and glory, the more the wheels began to turn in her head.

Then he finally told her, "Look, let me cut to the chase. I want to bring you aboard, put you on my payroll, make you the special events coordinator for the club. I'll pay you a nice salary—one that you can't refuse. You know I heard all about that sad little incident." He shook his head. "*Uump, uump, uummp,* so sad, but ummm . . ." He paused for a minute, then came around and sat on the front of the desk to be closer to her.

Gesturing with his hands to express himself better, he continued. "I know things gonna get a little tight for you right now, if they ain't already. Especially since you don't have a job and all, no income coming in and that old punk up out yo' life, so I know it is a struggle for you emotionally and financially, too. And the type of money that I'll pay, it ain't a doubt in my mind that you still can keep up that extravagant lifestyle that you used to."

Bambi sat there as the words rolled off his tongue. She laughed to herself because Disco was throwing game like a quarterback threw a pass. It was a good thing that she had intercepted the game a few yards ago.

Disco was one of those old heads, in his sixties, who tried to be young. He wore the same clothes the twenty-year-olds wore, but he had a way of putting on a suit that made him look not like a dirty old man, but like a classy, disgtinguished old man. Although he was straight out of the heart of Richmond, Virginia, this old joker could dress like he was one of the real Ohio Players. He'd owned plenty of clubs in his day—strip clubs, jook joints, sugar shacks, after-hours clubs, motorcycle clubs, even a country-western club, but now he owned *the* biggest nightclub that the city of Richmond had ever seen.

Since Disco played his position well, he had the women flocking to him, young and old, but his famous saying was, "I don't want nothing old but a dollar bill, and as soon as the bank open, I'm trading that in, too." Bambi had secretly always had a crush on him, but she would never become one of his harem. He had a sandy red complexion and was bald. He had green cat eyes and a beautiful set of pearly whites. They were probably false, but who cared? He had bought them, so they belonged to him. He may have been pushing sixty-one or sixty-two, but he was in great physical condition and had a body of steel. His muscles were enough to make any thirty-year-old man jealous. He walked with a slight limp, and bragged to everyone that the limp was from carrying around such a big weiner, which was no lie. Every girl who had been with him confirmed that fact and also revealed that his balls were the size of grapefruits.

Women congregated at his doorstep, wanting a piece of "Disco Almighty," knowing that since he owned a club, he had money. And since he was an old head, he jerked off money on young girls. But instead of the women working him, Disco worked them to the fullest, any way he could.

Bambi knew he didn't see her any differently from the other women, but she was sure that she had already peeped his game a long time ago. She knew Disco bullshitted a lot and was a slick-talker of old. There was one thing for sure and two things for certain that she knew weren't a mirage when it came to Disco: He had money and a lot of it, and she knew for a fact if she rolled with Disco, her money would flow like water. It was no secret that Disco was a hustler on a whole other level, and if she made the wrong move, he would damn sure take full advantage and hustle her. And that she wasn't having, so the game he kicked to her, she kicked right back to him.

"I mean, do you understand the opportunity I am giving you? It's a hell of an opportunity, that's fo real, if I must say so myself. I mean, baby, I can go get a renowned party planner from DC, Chicago, LA, New York, or somewhere to come in, and they'll gladly take this job and run with it."

Now you are taking it too far. You are really exaggerating now, Bambi said to herself as she listened to him carry on.

"But I want to offer it to you, because you home-grown. You are from here, and you always used to come to my clubs to show love and spend dough. So, now that I see your skills, I ain't gonna overlook them. I want to give you some work. I mean, we can work out the details. I know the caliber of female you are. You don't want to be working on front street, because, see, the mentality of our people is if they see you out there, it looks like you struggling or gotta work since that faggot left you. So I understand, and I can make you a behind-the-scenes type or however you want to do it. So, what do you say? You want the gig or not?"

Bambi knew she had Disco right where she wanted him: on the front burner, brewing. She looked into his eyes and said, "Look, I am just like you. I work for myself. I call the shots. So, as far as you hiring me, that's not going to work. But"—she put her finger up once she saw his lip on the floor—"you can hire my company, if you'd like."

He frowned, trying not to show that he was caught off guard.

"Your company? What company?" Disco somehow managed to close his mouth from the shock and asked.

"Yes, sweetie, Events R Us." Bambi said it with such finesse that it sounded like the company had been in business for years, but she had just made it up seconds ago.

"Ummm . . . ," Disco said, still in shock.

"Is that a yes, or do you need a day or so to think about it?" Bambi asked him as she stood up.

"No. I mean, yes, I want to hire your company."

"Good. I'll have my secretary call you to set up a time when we can go over the contract," she said, slipping on her full-length sable mink coat. She put her Gucci bag on her shoulder and casually strolled out of his office.

Just like that, out of an hour meeting, Bambi created her business and vowed to herself that it would be a lucrative one.

CHAPTER 6

Car Troubles

Bambi couldn't wait to call Egypt to share her good news. She picked up her car and promised Joe that she'd be back to get him later to go and get the mirror. She kept trying all Egypt's lines but couldn't get in touch with her, so Bambi decided to head to DC to go shopping. There was traffic on the highway, so she took Route 1, a two-lane highway that ran parallel with the interstate. When she was past Ashland, Egypt called her back.

As Bambi was boasting about her happy news, she suddenly noticed that her car was smoking like a forest fire.

"What da hell?" she shouted, which threw Egypt for a loop.

"What's going on, girl?" Egypt asked in a worried tone.

"It's my dang-gone car, and it's smoking like a chimney. I got to bail out before this bitch blows up. I am going to call you back."

"Where you at? I am coming to get you." The phone went dead before Egypt could get an answer.

Bambi pulled into a little bootleg, jackleg mechanic shop where she was greeted by a light-skinned, sloppy grease monkey with his belly hanging over his pants and sweat rolling off his face even though the weather was rather brisk outside. He had come out of the shop when he saw all the smoke pulling into the parking lot. Bambi was furious when she hopped out of her practically brand-new Corvette that she had literally just taken from the shop. But with the grease monkey looking at her eye to eye, her car wasn't the first thought that came to her mind. The first thing that ran across her mind was, *Shit, he takes grease monkey to a whole 'nother level.*

"I need you to look at my car," she said.

"Pop the hood, ma'am."

She did as she was told. While he fumbled around under the hood, she called Joe, who was busy with another customer at his shop. Egypt called her wanting to know what was going on and got there within ten minutes while Mr. Grease Monkey supposedly diagnosed the car. Looking around at all the broke-down, old, halfway-taken-apart cars on the lot, Bambi wasn't comfortable with the idea of leaving her car, but what choice did she have? She gave Grease Monkey her cell phone number to call her if he found anything, and she and Egypt went to get something to eat.

While they were eating, Joe called back and explained to Bambi that the smoke she saw wasn't anything to worry about. Oil had probably spilled on the motor when the oil had been changed. He assured her that it would eventually burn off in a day or so. Although it seemed a little crazy that a professional dealership didn't have a way of avoiding spilling oil on the motor, she believed Joe. Egypt said she had heard that before, too.

Within minutes after Joe's phone call, Grease Monkey

called. "Miss, I got some bad news and some good news. Which one you wanna hear first?"

"Give me the bad news first," Bambi said into the phone, while rolling her eyes at Egypt.

"Your motor is in bad condition."

While Bambi was thinking, *This is some bullshit,* Egypt questioned her with her eyes.

"Your motor is about to go any day now. I can always fix it for you, less than the dealer or any other mechanic shop will, but as pricey as these cars are, you are better off getting you a new car."

"Is that right?" she said nonchalantly.

"Yup, but I do have some good news, too."

"Ahhh, let me hear it," she said.

"Look, I can take the car off yo hands if you want to sell it."

"Is that right?"

"Yup, I mean I fix cars, so I can make you an offer so you can have enough to get a down payment towards a new car."

Bambi listened as the Grease Monkey tried to run game on her. She told him that she would talk to him when she got back to the shop. When she arrived back at the shop, she told him that she had to think about it and would be calling him.

She later met Joe at the junkyard. While he removed the mirror off of the junk Corvette, she went inside to pay for the part. She sat down in the dingy blue chair that had permanent oil stains and filed her fingernails. The man who owned the junkyard was Joe's friend, and he asked Bambi, "May I make a suggestion to you?"

Bambi did not really want to hear his comments, but she was willing to listen to him.

"The parts on your car are not cheap. Now I have that Corvette out there that has been wrecked. Corvettes are not something that come through this junkyard or any junkyard much, so what I am suggesting to you is you should buy the whole Corvette. I will give it to you at a good price. I would let it stay here, and whenever you need a part, it's here for you to get. And if anyone else needs parts off of it, they'll have to call you and pay you for them."

She thought for a minute, and all of a sudden filing her nails didn't seem so important. *Hmm, it's like an investment, huh? I guess like Reggie would say, I can wholesale the car. It's like buying a key of coke and breaking it down to flatfoot it, selling other people parts of it.* She smiled because it sounded like a good idea.

"How much?" she asked.

"Ummmm, give me 900 for it?"

"Oh, hell no, I'll give you six for that smashed-down, beat-up looking car."

"Deal." They shook. She wrote a check and realized she was just about down to the wire, but soon she wouldn't have to worry—as long as Disco kept his word.

He left and went to the back and got the title. "Keep this in a safe place. You never know when you will need it."

CHAPTER 7

Good Help

Bambi headed over to see her cousin, Zonna, who lived with Grandma Ellie. Grandma Ellie lived in Church Hill, one of the oldest neighborhoods in Richmond. Her house was three blocks away from where Patrick Henry gave that famous "Give me liberty or give me death" speech. Grandma Ellie's house was the prettiest house on the block. It stuck out like a sore thumb since the surrounding houses were so run-down. She always changed the color of the two-story house, which kept it looking new although it was old. Now it was pink with white shutters; the professionally landscaped flowers and grass complemented the colors.

Zonna was Bambi's older first cousin by four years. Zonna's father was Tricia's brother. Zonna's mother and father had divorced when she was eleven, and when she'd turned fourteen, her mother had married and shortly after that had claimed that Zonna was getting into an excessive amount of trouble and had shipped her down south to live with Grandma Ellie. Once

Zonna arrived in Virginia, there was never a peep out of Zonna's mother. To this very day Grandma Ellie will tell everybody how Zonna's mother sent her away for a man.

Zonna and Bambi were close. They never hung out together, but they were always there for each other. Zonna was light skinned, with sandy brown hair that she wore in a neatly maintained ponytail. With a petite frame, she stood at only five feet two inches tall. Although she was a grown woman, she could easily fit into a girl's clothing. She wore wire-framed glasses and was a computer wiz.

Grandma Ellie firmly told Zonna when she was fourteen, "You can stay here, as long as you stay in school. The day you leave school, you've got thirty days to get up out here."

Zonna took full advantage of those living arrangements, completing one educational program after another. For some reason she never saw fit to get a job. It wasn't that she didn't want to work. The girl was a computer genius, and surely she could have gotten a job at Microsoft, IBM, or any of those places making a top-dollar salary, but she had decided early on she wasn't taking any orders from any white man.

"You think I am going to build up them folks' company and devote my all to their company and the next thing you know after I put in years of playing fair, they come handing me a pink slip talking 'bout *we are downsizing*?" she said.

The bottom line was that she wanted to work for herself, but was too shy to get clients. She did, however, have a few folks that she met at school; she typed and composed resumes and letters for them to earn some money. The computer was Zonna's best friend. When she wasn't in class, she could always be found at home with her eyes glued to the monitor. She was addicted to it, like crack.

When Bambi decided to start her business, Zonna was the

first person she wanted to recruit. She offered her a position as office manager/vice president of the company. If it had been anyone besides Bambi, Zonna would have declined the job, but since it was her cousin, the closest thing to her sister, she had no choice.

"So, do you have my back or what?" Bambi asked.

"Of course I do."

"I can't really afford to pay you a salary, but as soon as I get paid, then you'll get paid," Bambi told her, knowing that Zonna would agree anyway.

Zonna said, "You ain't never been selfish when it came to money anyway. Besides, I know that you would mess things up without me by your side," Zonna teased. "You're very smart, but at the same time, working together I know we could move mountains." Then the cousins hugged and discussed Bambi's next steps.

"I need you to do a contract for me to get the ball rolling," Bambi added.

The next day Bambi pulled up to Grandma Ellie's house to pick up the contract from Zonna. As she got out of the car, she was greeted by Ruby, who lived next door with her mother. In the state of Virginia, Ruby Lee Meedlepoint was a legend that went back to the mid eighties, and even now her name still rang bells throughout the state.

Back in the mid eighties, Ruby was a pretty, young, carefree factory worker who had everything going for her: a house, a late-model BMW, lots of friends, and a job that paid well where she could get all the overtime she wanted. She dressed sharp as a tack. She had long, flowing black hair and a smooth Hershey complexion. She was big on the social scene, and she had a man, Uno, that she loved. Uno was fine and always had plenty of cash.

They lived high on the hog until the cops showed up at her doorstep, wanting to question her about Uno's drug empire. She wouldn't cooperate. Although they tried to strong-arm and threaten her, she never budged. She knew everything about Uno, and with all that pressure, she could have sung like a bird—especially after she was locked up and indicted on the same charges as Uno. But to their surprise, she stayed true to the game and her man and never breathed a word. The media had a field day labeling them the "Bonnie and Clyde of the eighties."

While she sat in jail, she lost everything, including her job and her house. Friend after friend fell off, and everything that she had worked so hard for went up in smoke. Still, she maintained. She got beat down badly several times by some of her fellow inmates as she awaited trial. To someone on the outside looking in, she had every right to tell on him, especially since he was out on $100,000 bond and living his days on the street to the fullest, never bringing her a dollar. She had the perfect opportunity to "help herself" out of jail. Instead she held tight and never ratted her man out.

Uno, however, wasn't as thorough as he portrayed, and he ended up ratting her out to get a lesser sentence. He blamed everything on her and was out within three years while she wound up giving the state of Virginia ten years of her life. Not long after Uno was released, he was found dead on an old abandoned slave plantation in a guillotine, with his dick cut off and resting in his mouth.

Ruby was immediately indicted on murder charges. The DA claimed that she had the power and connections to have the hit arranged from prison. The state, along with the media, put her through a high-profile murder trial, dragging her name through the mud, so Ruby Lee Meedlepoint became a name that would never be forgotten. Since the charge was bogus, though, the jury returned within thirty minutes with a not-guilty verdict.

Ruby had been blackballed and her life ruined by the man she had loved so dearly. Although she was the victim and had suffered tremendously, no one ever regarded her as anything but a menace to society, simply because she had a weak man who couldn't take responsibility for his actions while she was woman enough to do so.

Ruby had thought that once she was released, her life would eventually fall back into place, but it never did. With her name ringing so many bells, no one would hire her. No one would give her a chance. The only place she could get a job was at Burger King, and that's only because she knew the manager. The manager paid her minimum wage and made her work the longest and crappiest hours. What else could Ruby do but accept it, which she did for a while. After working there six months, money started coming up missing, and she was sure it was the manager skimming money off of her register. Ruby knew if this ever surfaced, it was a free ticket back to the penal system. So she never returned to Burger King again, and the issue died.

Ruby's dream was to save enough money and move to a new place to get a fresh start. In the meantime, she lived with her mother, the only family she had. Ruby cooked, cleaned, and did all she could to make her mother happy, but it was never enough. Ruby's mother dogged her, always reminding her that she was nothing but a burden. It tore Ruby's self-esteem up to have to put up with her mother's verbal abuse, but where else could she go?

Bambi felt sorry for Ruby and always passed on clothing to her that she no longer used.

That day Ruby ran over to her smiling. "Hey, Bambi."

"Hey, girl, how you doing?"

"I am fine, but I need to talk to you. It's real important."

"What's up?" Bambi stopped.

"Look, I overheard Ms. Ellie telling Momma that you was starting your own business and that you hired Zonna."

Bambi didn't respond; instead she listened as Ruby said in such a sincere tone, "Bambi, I would never ask you if I didn't need it. I want to know if you would consider hiring me? I would do anything. Run errands, scrub the floors, clean toilets, anything. I need a job, and I need one bad. I am honest, and I got yo' back. If I don't know how to do whatever you need me to do, I can learn."

Bambi searched her heart but didn't know what to say, so she just listened.

"Bambi straight up, I need a job. I mean I'll work for the bare minimum. I just need to get out of this house every day. I know that as a business owner it might be hard to trust me or whatever, but Bambi, you know me and have known me your whole life. You—"

Bambi stopped her and said, "My business is still new. I don't know just yet what or who I will hire, but I promise I will keep you in mind."

"Okay, that's all I can ask, if you mean that! If it's from the heart."

"I mean it, and that's my word, Ruby."

Bambi went in and got the contract from Zonna and chitchatted with her for a while, and when she came out of the house, she saw Ruby sweeping the sidewalk. Ruby looked like she was still in the eighties. She wore an old checkerboard shirt with some Lee jeans and some beat-up, old, dirty Princess Reeboks.

Bambi called out to Ruby, "Ruuubbbeee, come here for a

minute." They met at the silver chain link fence that separated the two houses, and Bambi asked, "Were you serious about what you said?"

"Yes, I will do anything."

"Well, I don't know if you heard, but I was on home confinement for a while, and I didn't do a thing but lay in the bed. My house is a wreck. I straightened up a little, but it truly needs a thorough clean-up. Can I pay you to come and do it?"

"Yup, I sure would, broke as I am. You ready now?" Ruby said without one bit of hesitation.

"Yup."

They left, and Bambi took Ruby to get some cleaning supplies, and then it was on to her house. She explained that she had to go take care of some business but would be back.

"No problem, just show me where everything is and give me your cell phone number in case I need anything."

Before Bambi left, she planted two hundred and thirty dollars to see if she could really trust Ruby. Even though she had known Ruby for forever and a day not to mention she had much love for her, she had to know that she could trust Ruby beyond a reasonable doubt. And to her, a couple hundred bucks would be worth it to find out.

CHAPTER 8

The Predator
Becomes the Prey

Bambi stopped by the club to go over the contract with Disco, and the barmaid told her that Disco was on his way and that he'd said to have a drink on him. She sat at the bar drinking a virgin daiquiri and noticed a dude across the bar staring at her. The dude wore a Star of David around his neck with diamonds that were blinging from across the bar. Even from a distance she could tell that the diamonds were not crushed or unclear stones and that the price of the necklace could have been equivalent to a very late-model used car. She tried to ignore him, but he kept smiling at her. She returned a phony smile, which unfortunately he took as a sure cue for him to come and join her.

Damn, you smile at a nigga and now he wants to come over and talk you to death. Did I ask him for some company? Hell no!

"Is someone sitting here?" He pointed to the empty bar stool.

She never answered as he sat down. "Would you like another daiquiri?"

"No, I'm okay," she said dismissively, but he wasn't getting the idea.

The one-way conversation went on for about ten minutes. Then he finally said to her, "Pretty lady, I didn't catch your name?"

"Maybe because I didn't throw it," she said, resuming her phony smile.

"Bad day at the office?" He looked over her black Ellen Tracy business suit and her Dooney and Bourke briefcase, making the assumption she was at the club for happy hour.

She laughed a little. "No."

"I'm Smooth." He extended his hand out.

She almost shit a brick. Since Egypt's ordeal the word "smooth" made her stomach turn simply when used as an adjective. Here she was sitting face-to-face with her friend's predator. Her first thought was to run behind the counter, grab one of those bottles, hit him upside the head, and beat him unmercifully. But she managed to keep her composure, not showing one ounce of emotion, and smiled. "Oh, I like that name. It's different."

"I know. I think I'm probably the only guy in this town with the name Smooth."

Thanks for confirmation, you slimy dirt bag, she thought with a devilish grin, but extended her hand. "I'm Barbie."

"Damn girl, you's finer than any black Barbie doll I ever saw."

She smiled.

"Where yo man?" he asked.

"He broke my heart and left me."

"Damn, baby, that's some real ill shit, but don't worry 'bout it, cuz every dog has its day!"

"You're right, every dog does have its day," she agreed, nodding her head.

He glanced at her keys on the bar and noticed a picture on it that looked like it had been taken at a state fair. He picked it up for a closer look at her key chain and looked at the picture.

"This is your sister?" he asked, pointing to the other person in the picture.

"No." She shook her head and smiled. "It's my mother."

"Damn, baby, I can sho see where you get your pretty looks from."

"You come here a lot?" she asked, changing the subject.

"Umm, sometimes but not too much," he said.

Only when you're on the hunt for your next victim, huh?

Smooth's cell phone started ringing with back-to-back calls. Then his pager started to vibrate. He tried to ignore it, but he couldn't—it was about to blow up. He knew he had to answer so it would stop. He told her, "Look, I really gotta make a run right quick. But I don't want to leave if this means I will never see you or hear from you again."

"Oh, you will."

He finally answered his phone, having no idea that the phone volume needed to come down some because she could hear everything that was being said to him.

"Nigga, where da fuck you at?" she heard a high-pitched female voice scream. Bambi never gave any indication that she heard anything. She only smiled, batting her big brown eyes.

"I'm going to be on the way in a minute to come and get that." He played his role to the tee, acting like it was one of his homeboys on the phone.

"Yeah, nigga, you've been saying you on the way for three hours."

"Nah, for real, just make sure you have everything right when I get there."

The voice softened up a little bit, but Bambi could still hear her say, "I am naked waiting here so I can taste that sweet cum of yours in my mouth."

"I'm going to pass through there in a minute, so make sho' it's all good when I get there."

"Don't worry, it will be, baby!"

"A'ight den."

He closed the Startec phone, looked into Bambi's eyes, and tried to be sincere. She would probably have believed him had she not heard the whole conversation and also known what he did to her friend Egypt. "Look, baby, sorry . . . but ummm, I've gotta bust a move so I can get this cheddar for us."

Yeah, whatever, you lying-ass Negro, she thought as she smiled and said to him, "Oh, for real?"

"Yeah, baby, I'm straight feeling you, and I am trying to make you mines."

"Is that right?"

"Yup, that's right," he said, looking into her eyes. She was happy that she could smell his game a mile away. That alone was her advantage, because if she hadn't, she would have been up the creek with no paddle.

They exchanged cell phone numbers, and he promised to call her in a few hours so they could go to dinner and pick up their conversation where they'd left off. She agreed, knowing that he had fallen right into her trap.

When Disco finally dragged himself in so she could review the contract with him, she fussed at him, "Disco, this is business. You are almost an hour late. I can't do business like this."

She carried on for a minute, to let him know she was serious, and then once they got down to business he agreed to all her terms and conditions. It wasn't long before she was exiting the club with a signed contract in her hand—and a check for her first gig. As soon as she got into her car, her cell phone rang. It was Smooth asking her to meet him for dinner at the Outback Steakhouse. She agreed. As she drove to Outback, she looked at her missed phone call log. She had missed Egypt's and Zonna's calls and seven calls from Reggie. *Damn, can this dude just pleeeezzz leave me alone? Please!*

Five minutes had not passed, and Smooth was calling back. "Hey, baby, I want to talk to you until you get to me."

She smiled to herself and played along, listening to Smooth brag about how much money he was pulling down.

"I apologize for leaving you, but I had to handle my business. I'm going to try to stack as much paper as I can, because I can tell you like nice shit, trips, shopping sprees, fast cars, and big diamonds and shit, don't you?"

"Of course I do. I mean what lady you know don't like nice things?"

"I can especially tell that you do, and Boo, believe me, I ain't got no problem with that."

"I hear you talking. Shit, it doesn't cost nothing to talk, does it?"

"Yeah, baby, I got a spot in my life for a wife, and I feel the instant attraction to you. I know you're going to think this shit here is game, but I just had a dream about you, and then I come to the club and I see you. I swear I thought I saw an angel when I peeped you at the bar."

She listened as he continued to try to convince himself that his game was airtight. She didn't know his motive and really

didn't care, but she knew hers and wasn't going to give any indication that she wasn't falling for his lame-ass game.

"So when my phone was going crazy, I didn't want to make
the run, but I know you don't want to let that nineteen G's slip
through our fingers, do you?"

"Nope, I'll never stand in the way of you getting yo money,
especially if it's for us. But don't talk that 'us'/'we' shit if it's
really all about you."

"Baby, I can only show you better than I can tell you."

"Well, where is my cut?" she blurted out, not meaning for
it to come out like that, not to mention she had just pulled into the parking space beside Smooth in the Outback parking
lot. She tried to fix it up, saying, "I mean if you're going to
have to neglect me, make sure you play fair and compensate
me."

"Baby, I've been trying to tell you that I got you!"

"A'ight, we'll see," she said as she got out the car.

"Dammmmmnnnn, baby, you are really a black Barbie for
real, huh? Driving your red Corvette and everything? What am
I going to do with you?"

"Love me, that's all you can do," she said with just as much
game as he had been kicking. The only difference was he
seemed to be falling for hers.

He smiled and looked her over. There was no doubt about
it: Smooth was impressed. He had met his match, and he knew
it. He had no idea that Bambi wasn't taking him seriously any
more than she would the man in the moon.

Their dinner went well. They continued to stroke each other's
egos, but Bambi seemed to fondle his ego more, and Smooth
was falling so deep and fast he couldn't even catch himself. It
looked like he only had one thought: He wanted Barbie and

would go to east hell to get her. Whatever it took, Barbie was going to be his girl—and his number one at that.

As they exited the restaurant, his phone began to ring again.

"Damn, baby, I've got to get this money. I've been putting these niggas on hold all night. You understand, don't cha?"

"Yes, I understand completely." She shook her head, gazing into his eyes with disappointment written all over her face. He had to think of something quick, as he opened the door and she got in. He looked down into the car and handed her a wad of money.

"What's this?" she asked.

"Your cut. I told you when I leave you, I'm leaving to benefit us." He smiled and kissed her on the cheek and said, "Call me to let me know you made it home safe, and we gonna kick it on the phone all night, a'ight?"

"Okay." She smiled, knowing that her work with Smooth would be easier than she'd ever imagined.

Once Smooth turned and went in the opposite direction, she pulled over to the shoulder so she could count the stash of money. It was nineteen hundred. *Damnnnn, this psycho Negro is really strapped. I know it has to be more where that came from. It just has to be!*

She called Egypt and swung by her house and gave her half of the money.

"Look, don't ask me no questions. Just know I'm not doing anything illegal. Plain and simple."

Bambi didn't have to say it twice. Egypt gladly took the money and gave her friend a hug.

They talked on the phone all the way until she got to her house.

When Bambi got home, she checked her mailbox and pulled out a stack of bills. She was almost afraid to open up the credit card bills because she knew the damage that she had done while in her self-imposed exile was ridiculously high.

She could practically smell the bleach even before she reached her door. She opened the door and found Ruby in a recliner fast asleep. She was impressed by how Ruby had cleaned her house from top to bottom. All the boxes had been put away. She had rearranged the furniture, and the bathroom had never been cleaner since she moved in. On the coffee table was the two hundred and thirty dollars that she had planted, along with an additional ten-dollar bill and a bunch of change that Ruby had found throughout the house while cleaning.

Bambi woke Ruby and asked, "Ruby, do you have a driver's license?"

"Yup."

"Okay. Well, drive home and come and get me at eight o'clock."

She gave Ruby a spare key and a hundred dollars and walked her to the door. Before the door was shut Smooth had called her again.

CHAPTER 9

What Goes Around, Comes Around . . .

Bambi and Smooth talked all night long. Well, he mostly talked and sold her dreams. She listened and made him think she was buying them when Ruby knocked on the door. Bambi looked at her clock: 7:54 it read. Ruby was on time.

This is exactly what I am talking about, and they say good work is hard to find.

She ended the conversation with Smooth, promising to meet him later for dinner. She hung up the phone and opened the door. Ruby stood there with her hair in dire need of a perm. Her hair was styled in a semimushroom, her baby hair laid down with grease on the side of her face and some big yellow sunglasses covering her eyes. Ruby had on her Chic jeans with the cardboard crease, and you couldn't tell her nothing. The only part of her outfit that wasn't straight out of the early eighties was the pair of black Princess Reeboks she wore on her feet. Seeing Ruby standing there so confident in her eighties outfit made her smile.

"Hey, girl, come on in."

"You was still asleep?"

"Girl, I've been on the phone all night with this clown I met yesterday."

Ruby was getting ready to say something when Bambi's cell phone rang.

"Bambi, can we talk?" Reggie begged.

"Hell no! And what did I tell you 'bout calling my number from a blocked number."

"That's the only way you'll answer. Please don't hang up! Please!" Reggie whined like a little girl.

"All of a sudden I can hear the bitch pitch in your voice." Bambi was still hurt, but it made her feel better when she assassinated Reggie with her mouth.

As soon as she hung up, the phone rang again. When she reached for the phone on her table, she knocked her pocketbook off of it, and everything fell all over the floor. After she answered the phone, she began picking up all the items inside the pocketbook.

"Hi, can I speak to the lady that owns the red Corvette?"

"Who's speaking?"

"This is Paul, the mechanic from the other day. Are you the lady that owns the Corvette?"

"Yes. Why?"

"Because I was wondering what you plan to do with your car. I am prepared to take it off of your hands. I know being a woman and a single woman at that—I mean I don't know your business, but I didn't see any wedding band on your finger so I figured that you were not married . . ."

As she listened to the bull that the mechanic tried to lay on her, Ruby handed Bambi some of the items she had picked up off the floor for her. As soon as she took her personal belongings out of Ruby's hand, a bright idea hit her slam dead in the face. She cut him off. "So, how much you want to give me for the car?"

"Ummm, I'll give you six G's."

"Six G's? You mean to tell me all you can give me is six G's for my forty-thousand-dollar car. Are you crazy? Baby, you better come a little better than that."

This man must think I am crazy for real or either stuck on stupid. One or the other. But the joke is on him.

"Okay, I'll give you seventy-five hundred 'cause I may be able to get a used motor or rebuild the one you have up in there, but I got a lot to do to that car. I gotta get the parts, and Corvette parts are not cheap."

"Look, we can make this happen, but I need to at least get the payoff amount on the car," she stressed to him, although there was no loan to pay off. Reggie had paid the car off before she found out the truth about him. She continued, "The payoff amount is a little over eight grand, and then I need at least a G for a down payment on a new car."

Paul the Grease Monkey jumped right on it. "Okay, the best I can do is give you nine grand, and I am losing money doing that, but I see you a sister struggling trying to make it."

"Okay, you got a deal."

"When can I get the car?"

"When can I get the money?"

"I'll have your money for you this evening."

"Cash now, because I don't take checks."

"That's cool," he said.

Bambi thought of one thing that Reggie used to always say to her: "Fair exchange ain't never been robbery." Then she laughed under her breath.

"Ummm, so exactly what time are you going to have everything in order?" Bambi asked.

"Can you come by like around five, so I can still have time to run to the DMV and get some tags for the car? Because I am going out of town later, and I need it taken care of tonight."

"Ummm, I'll be at work, but I'm going to call my aunt and see if she can come through and handle that for me. So let me call you right back."

Paul hesitated for a minute, not wanting to let her off the phone, but he agreed, saying, "Now, don't make me go and get this money for nothing now."

"I won't. Give me a few minutes to get in touch with my aunt."

She hung up the phone, and Ruby was sitting at the table drinking a cup of coffee.

"Rue, you trying to get this money with me or not?"

"You know I am. Just tell me whatever you need me to do."

"I need you to go sell my car for me. You gotta act like I'm at work, but I'm going to be around the street in your uncle's truck waiting for you. He'll let you borrow it, right?"

"Bambi, I already told you yesterday that I got you. Whatever you need me to do, I got you."

"Okay, give him a call and see if we can use his truck."

Before Bambi could run down everything, Paul had called back two times. The second time Bambi told him, "Look, my aunt's going to ride out there with the title. Besides, the title is in her name anyway."

The title was still in the name of the person the junkyard had bought the car from. Since Bambi had come in the second day after the salvaged Corvette arrived at the junkyard, the owner had never had a chance to get the title transferred.

Paul agreed. Bambi and Ruby went over everything and agreed to meet back later.

Bambi went outside and cleaned out everything she had in the car. While she waited on Ruby, she ran to the 7-11 and purchased a prepaid cell phone. By that time Ruby had come back in her uncle's raggedy twenty-year-old pickup truck.

"Ruby, you drive my car."

They switched cars and headed to Ashland. Bambi purposely meant to be late, arriving at the shop at 5:40 instead of 5:00, knowing the DMV closed at 6:00 and was a good thirty-minute drive away. The shop was across the street from a grocery store, and Bambi parked across the street so she could blend in with the other folks as well as be able to see Ruby.

Ruby pulled into the shop's parking lot. Before she could touch the door, Paul the Grease Monkey walked out and said, "You must be the lady I been waiting for."

Ruby nodded.

"Can I take it for a test drive?"

Ruby looked into his eyes and asked, "Do you think that would be good with the motor in such bad condition?"

"You're right."

"I mean I took a chance driving it up here, and I don't want to be stranded on no country road."

He nodded and popped the hood. He looked up under the hood and said, "Tell Becky, Barbara, whatever her name is I'm going to give her eight flat for it. I can't see paying nine for this with this bad motor."

Ruby went into her pocket and pulled out the prepaid cell phone, "Look, this man is talking some lame shit, that he ain't giving up nothing but eight grand."

"What?"

"Yup. Here, you talk to him."

"Paul, I thought we had everything straight now. So why now when I get my aunt all the way up there, you switch up?"

"Look, I know what's up. I know my way around cars, and that's the best I can do."

This damn chump thinks he got all the sense, but little do he know the joke's on him.

"Look, just make sure you take my tags off and give them to her. Now, put my aunt on the phone, please."

He passed the phone to Ruby.

"Rue, just make sure you count the money twice before you come off the title, and make sure you get the tags off of there."

While Ruby counted the money twice, Paul was taking the tags off of the car. Once he gave her the tags, she signed off on the title and handed it to him. He smiled and exhaled. He was so excited that he stuttered when he asked Ruby, "H-h-h-how you g-g-gettin' home?"

"I'm fine. My friend is meeting me across the street at the grocery store."

Ruby strolled across the street with the bag of money in her hand. Once she got to the truck, she handed Bambi the bag of money. Bambi reached in the bag and handed Ruby a grand. Then she kissed Ruby on the cheek, and said, "Thanks, Rue."

"It was nothing. I would have done it for free," she said as she slid the money in her pocket.

They sat in the parking lot, and Ruby asked, "What's next?"

"Sit tight for a minute, because my work is not done here. Let's go get something to eat."

They sat inside the Ponderosa eating their hearts out, while Ruby went on and on about her prison stories. Night fell, and enough time passed so they could finish what they had started. The shop closed up, and Bambi looked from the window as Paul flew past in his truck. That was her cue to get to work.

Bambi ran over across to the shop, put her tags on the car, pulled out her extra set of keys, and sped off.

Ruby called once they got down the road. "I know you didn't just do what I think you did. Bambi, you wild as I don't know what."

"All I did is get my car from over there. There isn't any law against that, is it?"

"Hell nah, girl, but you gave him the title to your car."

"No, I didn't give him anything. You did, and that wasn't the title to my car. He don't have any ground to stand on. All he have is just that—a title, to what I don't know."

"Look, pull into that McDonald's parking lot right quick," Ruby said.

"Oh, okay, I know you still ain't hungry. We just ate."

"Hell nah, girl, I need to take a daggone dump."

"Oh, okay."

Ruby went in and came right back out with almost a whole stack of napkins. She held up one finger, motioning to Bambi to wait up a minute as she ran toward the woods. *What in the hell is that psycho Ruby up to?*

She was in the woods for every bit of five minutes. As soon as Bambi got out of the car and walked over to the woods, Ruby appeared. Bambi frowned a little.

"I was worried about you. What you go back there for?" she asked.

"What I tell you we stopped for," she said with no shame at all. "To take a shit."

Bambi could not believe her ears.

"What you mean?" Bambi asked. "I know good and well you didn't take no daggone dump in no woods."

"Why I didn't? Believe what I am telling you—that was one of the most best and peaceful shits I ever took," Ruby said.

Bambi didn't know if she should laugh or shake her head as Ruby kept talking. "Girl, don't you know I have shitted in stranger places than that? For ten years I had to squat and use the toilet in front of a thousand people, so I know you are going to let me take a shit in the woods."

"All I want to know is why in the woods? Why not in here?" she asked Ruby. Bambi opened up the door to McDonald's so she could go back into the bathroom to wash her hands.

"It smelled like death was on her period and threw up in there. I would've suffocated in there and died my damn self. Hold these," she said, passing another stack of napkins to Bambi. "Now watch the door while I go in here to wash my hands."

Ruby went into the men's restroom to wash her hands thoroughly.

When she came out, she grabbed another stack of napkins and headed for the door.

"Girl, what's the deal with the three stacks of napkins?" Bambi demanded to know.

"Shoot, napkins is a necessity in my world. Shoot, I am going to always need them, and I know damn well I ain't going to pay for no napkins when I can get these for free," she said.

Bambi smiled. At that moment she realized that Ruby was a thoroughbred. Never in her life had she met anyone who kept it so real with her, and although Ruby was common as all outdoors, it was *a must* for Ruby to be a part of Bambi's team. But without a doubt first some changes had to be made.

Over the next two days, Bambi put Ruby under total reconstruction from the crown of her head to the soles of her feet. When Bambi was done, Ruby looked like a whole different person. Her hair was cut into layers, and after the Hawaiian Silky perm was washed out of her hair, her hair was halfway down her back. Bambi didn't cut any corners when it came to Ruby. She even took Ruby to the eye doctor to get rid of her state-issued glasses and had her fitted for some contacts.

"Girl, I'm not going to be touching and poking my eyeballs. You know I am good and old-school. Can I just get me some glasses?"

"Here, what about these?" Bambi picked out some cute DKNY frames.

"Yeah." Ruby nodded. "They are cute."

As Bambi continued to bring her up to speed, she threw Ruby's 1980s clothes away and brought her into the present with her new clothes and shoes. She then realized that Ruby had been hiding her cute figure under her clothes. Bambi had no choice but to take her out and buy a bunch of cute underclothes, because she was embarrassed for Ruby when she opened up the dressing room door and saw Ruby had on holey bloomers left over from when she was in prison. Ruby practically danced with gratitude.

"Thank you so much. I can't stop looking in the mirror," she said.

"I know, you look so good! You are so pretty, Ruby."

"Thank you," she kept saying to Bambi. Even days later she continued to thank Bambi.

Though the clothes may have changed her appearance, all in all, she was still the same person inside: a true thoroughbred.

The next day when Paul got to the shop and discovered the Corvette missing, he reported it stolen. A few days later, he got a call from the police: "Mr. Waxx, we found your car."

"Where?" he asked.

"We found it across town at the junkyard."

"At the junkyard?" Paul said, puzzled.

"Yes, you can go pick it up any time."

Paul slammed the phone down after getting the address from the police. He went to the junkyard, saw that smashed-up red Corvette, and wanted to break down and cry. But he didn't. He sucked it up as a loss and tried to look at the bright side. He remembered all the other females that he had hustled out of their cars and felt it was just karma. . . . What goes around comes around. There was no need to try to get back at Bambi. He simply charged it to the game.

CHAPTER 10

When You Least
Expect It

Over the next couple weeks, Bambi continued to string Smooth along, meeting him for dinner and at the movies on a regular basis, but always making sure she had another appointment set up so he never managed to get any meaningful time alone with her. She was determined that none of their dates would end in a manner that could possibly lead to sex. She knew Smooth was intrigued with her and attracted to her, but before he got the chance to make any type of sexual advances, she would nip his move in the bud.

One evening when they were having dinner at Ruth's Chris Steak House, Smooth reached under the table, pulled her feet onto his lap, and gently rubbed them. Had it been anyone else she would have loved the gesture,

"Look, Smooth," she said, taking her feet back down. "You know I just came out of a relationship not long ago, and I'm feeling deeply hurt. So if sex is something you need right now, then maybe I am not the one for you. Truthfully, it's going to take me a minute to trust again. I want to get to know you, and I want to be courted and romanced by a real man like back in the day."

Smiling, he said, "I hear you, Boo, and I'll work on being patient with you. Just don't make me wait too long."

"I promise, Boo, I won't, but you can believe it'll be worth the wait."

Glancing at her Movado watch, Bambi thought, *It's 7:05 and I told Ruby to call me at 7:00, damn it. I can't believe she's late, and she knows time is of the essence.*

Bambi was surprised, because until then Ruby had never been late for anything. Just when the thought crossed her mind, her cell phone began to ring. "Excuse me one second, darling. Let me get this."

"Go ahead, baby. I know you's a businesswoman." Smooth settled back with his glass of Dewar's.

"Hello," she said after hitting the *talk* button on her cell phone. Smooth looked deep into her eyes, studying each word coming out of her mouth.

"Oh, for real? Girl, that is so messed up. Dag, I wish it was something I could do."

Smooth kicked her leg under the table, trying to get her attention, and then whispered to her in a low tone, so the person on the phone would not hear, "What's wrong?"

Ignoring him, she pretended to be deeply involved in her phone conversation and commented, "I wish I could go, girl, but I don't have any money for that and I definitely don't have my shit together to go anywhere. I really can't go, as bad as I want to. I don't even have any summer clothes to take, since I put on weight during that time I was laying around depressed."

Smooth looked at her face waiting for an answer, but she avoided direct eye contact with him, instead focusing on the design of wood grain in the table as she continued talking on the phone.

"Charge it? Girl, charge it on what? Every last one of my credit cards is through the roof. I'm looking for a li'l part-time job now to help me get through these hard times. You know that without ole boy my thing ain't the way it used to be and not to mention that nigga left me with a stack of bills."

Smooth whispered, "Hell nah, ain't no girl of mines gonna be working no two jobs."

She smiled at him, and just then the waitress brought them the alligator bites appetizers. She told the caller, "Look, our food just came, so I am going to call you back later. But keep trying to call around and see if you can find someone to go with you."

She hung up the phone, and just as she predicted, Smooth asked, "What happened?"

"Nothing really. My girlfriend had planned a cruise with another one of her friends. They were supposed to leave the day after tomorrow, but the other girl backed out at the last minute. With it being so late, my friend can't get any of her money back. She was trying to get me to come, but I told her I can't stand it right now."

"Well, baby, I think with everything you been through you deserve it."

"You ain't lying."

"How much is it?" he asked, putting a hand on hers.

"I don't know. But I know it's expensive because it's a Mediterranean cruise."

"I mean, what's expensive? Two, three, four G's? I mean what? Call her back and see and check on what it'll cost."

"No, because I don't have the wardrobe for a cruise."

"Well, I had planned to take you to Atlantic City in the next two weeks or so to let you do some shopping anyway, so why not now? I'll give you the money and you can buy yo'self what you need, pay for the trip, and have a little sumthin', sumthin' in your pockets to play with."

"Fo real? You'll look out like that for me?"

"Yup, I told you I play for keeps, and I want you to know just how deep I want to carry it wit you. Now, go ahead and call your girl so she can stop worrying." Smooth picked up a juicy alligator bite and took a bite.

Bambi smiled, picked up the phone, called Ruby back, and got the info the way they had already rehearsed.

After dinner was over, Bambi stopped in the restroom. When she came out of the stall, her friend Amy was standing there waiting for her with a big smile written on her face. Amy was gossip box number one, a.k.a. the Connie Chung of Richmond, Virginia, street life. She was into any- and everybody's business at all costs. It didn't matter whose or what, her job was to dip and to find out. Though Amy came off as a hater, 95 percent of the news she spread around town was true and looked on as the gospel. She took great pride in what she reported. It never mattered what it was, whose the baby was, who was sleeping in what bed, who got a big dick and who was riding it, who was snitching and who was going to jail, if Amy said it was so, most likely it was true. Her motto was, "I don't write no checks my behind can't cash."

"Hey, girl, what's going on?" Amy said with a hug.

"Nothing much. What's going on with you?" Bambi asked, heading to the sink to wash her hands.

"Girl, same ole same ole. Sorry to hear about your boy—or should I say yo girl," Amy said, trying to make a joke out of the situation.

"Oh, girl, it ain't no need to be sorry. I'm just glad I found out when I did."

"Well, I need to tell you something else," Amy said, looking at her intently. "I saw who you was with tonight, and that nigga Smooth ain't shit."

"Fo real?" Bambi said with a puzzled look on her face, but she said to herself, *Trust me you ain't told me nothing that I don't already know. I know for a fact the nigga is full of shit.*

"Yup, girl, I hope you drove your own car because he is psycho. He is sick fo real. You know I wouldn't kick no larceny-hearted stuff to you, because you my girl. We go way back to cutting class together, smoking cigarettes and shit in the bathroom back in the day. So I just want to put you down with the real."

"Let me have it then, instead of talking in circles."

"I know Smooth seem like he on top of his game, but girl, that nigga is crazy."

"Why you say that?" Bambi asked.

"Girl, he used to mess with this chick name Nita that I know, and I know her real good. So you can trust me when I tell you that this is from the heart right here—this here ain't no ghetto gossip. This is what I know for real. I promised that I'd never repeat it, but I gotta give it to you."

"Come on. I'm ready."

She had never seen Amy break any kind of gossip down like this. Amy usually couldn't wait to throw dirt on someone's name, but for this time Bambi could see that Amy was actually affected emotionally by the bombshell she was about to drop.

"Nita was messing with Smooth for a long time, and he would beat her like you beat an egg. At first he was cool, always throwing money at her, being her personal slot machine. But girl, by no means don't get it twisted. That nigga is Dr. Jekyll and Mr. Hyde fo real. He kept begging her to get pregnant, and after she did he told her he didn't want no babies."

"Girl!" Bambi said. "What did she do?"

"She asked him for money for an abortion. And all he did was keep putting her off. After missing four appointments, she found herself ten weeks pregnant. Leaving her with two weeks before it would be too late to terminate the pregnancy. Lying, she told him she only had one week left, so she wouldn't miss the deadline. He said he was going to make sure he got the abortion done for her. He wasn't going to pay for no abortion, though. Instead he began to fight her. She said he put the worst whipping she'd ever had on her. He kicked her in the stomach with his Timberland boots, and he didn't stop until his boots was covered with her blood."

Bambi just stood there dumbfounded for a minute. All she could say was, "Damn."

"Look, you do what you want to, but I am telling you the nigga ain't to be trusted. There's a few other episodes too that I could tell you about, but I think you get the picture. Now, you better get back out there before you trigger him," Amy said, trying to make a joke—but the look on her face was dead serious.

They hugged, and Bambi exited the bathroom. Smooth was waiting for her outside of the door, leaning against the wall with his arms crossed.

"I was sort of getting worried. I was wondering if you had fallen in," he said.

"I saw an old friend from high school, and we were just catching up."

"Oh, you look like you saw a ghost. You sure everything is okay?" he asked, concerned.

"Yup, I'm fine," Bambi said with a false smile.

Once they were outside of the restaurant, he gave her a wad of money and promised to see her the next day to give her some spending money for the trip.

"Look, when you get back, add up all your credit card bills and I'll take care of them, too, a'ight?" he said. He kissed her on the cheek and gave her a big bear hug, after which they went their separate ways.

On the way home, Bambi tried to analyze Smooth. She couldn't understand how he could be so nice and charitable to her, yet Egypt and Amy's friend had seen different sides of him for what seemed like no apparent reasons.

I need to get away from this animal. I cannot and will not fall victim to an abuser, Bambi thought. *It's only a matter of time before he shows me who he truly is.*

Although she'd told Smooth she was going on a Mediterranean cruise, she had actually booked a cruise on Carnival Cruise Lines in the Caribbean for herself and Egypt. The cruise was half the price for the two of them that it would have cost for just her alone on the Mediterranean cruise. When she called Egypt and told her that they were off to paradise, Egypt couldn't have been happier.

"Girl, how did you pull this off?" Egypt wanted to know.

"I just got a little bonus from my last event and thought we'd splurge," Bambi told her.

Early the next morning as she was about to go shopping, she met up with Smooth in the parking lot of Southside Plaza for five minutes to get the spending money. She got out of the car and went around to the driver's side and leaned in to talk to him.

"I hope you'll spend some quality time with me when you get back," he said, never looking up as he counted out the money.

She looked over his tight body. It was a shame how someone so handsome and sexy could be so mean and evil.

"You know I am. You oughtta take a break and come with us," Bambi said sweetly.

"You know I don't fly nowhere," Smooth said, shaking his head. "If God wanted me to fly, then I would have been born with wings."

"You wasn't born with wheels, but I see you got a car," Bambi said, pointing to his candy apple red Benz.

"Yeah, well, this car don't leave the ground either. Now, you make sure you call me every day to check in," he said, looking Bambi dead in the eye as he handed her the money, never letting go until she agreed.

"Okay, the calls are real expensive, but I'll call just to check in." She leaned in and gave him a quick kiss with the stack of money in her hand.

"Do you need me to take you to the airport?" he asked.

"No, my friend is just going to leave her car there."

"Well, I've been up all night, grinding, getting this money. So I'm 'bout to go home and get some sleep."

Before Egypt and Bambi knew it, the relaxing and fun-filled week passed by. They had snorkeled in the turquoise waters off Jamaica, shopped in St. Thomas, and lounged by the pool on the ship's deck, drinking piña coladas. All courtesy of Smooth.

When Bambi returned she decided to wait a day before she hooked up with Smooth to pay the cost for making a deal with the devil. Finally, she poured a glass of Pepsi-Cola, picked up the cell phone, and called Smooth.

"I'm baaaccckkkk," she said, as if she was happy to inform him of her whereabouts.

"Why you ain't call me yesterday?" he asked.

"I couldn't get a line to get through. Besides, I'm home now."

"So, when I'm going to see you?"

"Umm, whenever you want to," she said as she looked through all her mail that had accumulated while she was gone.

"You know me. I want to see you right now," he said. "I missed you so much."

"I missed you, too," she lied. *Like a hole in the head,* she thought, trying to amuse herself.

"Look, let's go get something to eat and hang out for the night. You know you gotta tell me all about your trip," he said. She knew he really wasn't concerned about hearing nothing about the trip; all he really wanted to hear was her moans when he put her legs in the air. He probably figured she owed it to him.

Once she agreed to the dinner date, he told her, "Meet me at the mall and we'll get you some real sexy lingerie."

Two hours later they were hand in hand strolling through the mall. Their first stop was Victoria's Secret. Forty-five minutes, two big pink-and-white shopping bags, and a receipt totaling $742.39 later, they left Victoria's Secret and headed for dinner.

As they were walking through the mall, Bambi remembered one of her mother's rules: "This is how you know you got him, when he takes you to the mall to buy one thing and you come out with what he wanted to initially buy plus at least one very costly item that you insisted you had to have." So right before they exited the mall, she saw some tall multicolored boots in the window of a small boutique.

"Ooooouuuhhh, we gotta look at these boots," she said. She pulled him into the store and picked them up. "I'd like to see these in a size eight, please?"

They were a perfect fit, and the saleslady cosigned by saying how nice the ugly boots were. Smooth didn't say anything. He just looked until she whispered in his ear, "Wouldn't you like me to fuck you in only these?" She looked into his eyes as if she was ready to jump on his dick right then and there.

He smiled and nodded. "They would go good with that brown thing we just bought for you, right?"

She nodded. Without any more hesitation, he peeled off the $2,600 for the boots.

Next they headed to the Wyndham Hotel. Smooth insisted that they drive one car, but she managed to convince him that both of them needed to drive.

"I have an early morning appointment, and after I'm done with you tonight I know you ain't gonna feel like getting up," she said, and ran a fingernail down his thigh.

He gave her the money and instructed her to get a room in her name. She did as she was told. She got the most expensive room they had to offer, pocketing the money left over. The desk clerk was so happy to sell the room, he didn't even ask for her ID. As soon as Smooth entered the room, he began walking around inspecting it.

"This is nice," he said, impressed with the surroundings.

She chuckled to herself. *It's funny how dudes sell more drugs than a little bit to be able to stack their money and live life to the fullest but in all actuality don't do anything to live it up. Like look at this clown—he's all impressed with this room. I mean it's nice for a room in Richmond, but nothing to get all like he's doing over the damn thing.*

She remembered trips she had taken with Reggie and the

world-class hotels they had been to in Vegas, LA, and Miami—
not to mention the five-star Plaza she'd stayed at with her mother
when she was younger.

*He got all this money and still ain't been nowhere but New York
on business and thinks he's really doing it big, bragging about bus
trips to Atlantic City. Hey, go to Vegas, high roller, and then holler
at me. But for real, the nigga is scared to fly yet he always bragging
about how he living large. Please, please, please! Step up in your
game and learn what it's like to be a real player!*

He fell backward onto the bed and motioned for her to
come over. She did, and he took her in his arms, whispering in
her ear, "I really missed you." Then he put her hand on his
manhood, so she could feel that it was hard.

"Look baby, I got something to tell you," Bambi said, gently
pulling away from him.

"I'm listening, and don't come with no bullshit," he said as
if he was joking, but she knew by the cold look in his eyes he
wasn't playing.

"Oh, I'm not. You know I haven't been with nobody in a
while, right, not since my ex," she said.

"Yeah, that's what you say anyway." He folded his hands behind his head and looked up at the ceiling.

"Look, I want this just as bad as a faggot wants a bag of
dicks! Trust me, but I just have a complex about something."

"What?" He turned to stare at her.

"I don't know how to say it."

His face grew serious. "Just say it."

"Straight up, I really can suck the skin off a dick, but at the
same time I will get turned off if it has the slightest odor." Before he could say anything, she told him, "Let me finish. I
know you don't stink, but I know you been out all day sweat-
ing a little bit. I'm just going to need you to hop in the shower,

and then I can get busy. This is really important to me. It's serious! Because if I go down there and I smell anything, no matter what you do, my coochie will not even get wet."

For a few seconds, he sat there stunned. He couldn't believe what she was saying. He looked at her a minute and then said, "I feel you! I can't do nothing but respect your wishes, because I know I want some of that bomb head of yours."

"I'm glad you understand, because I really want to please you," she purred.

"Go cut the water on for me and then come back and take my clothes off for me," he told her.

She did as she was told. But as soon as he closed the door, she listened until she heard a different pattern in the water. She knew he was in, and it was on and popping right then and there. There was no turning back from this point on. This was the moment she had been waiting so patiently for.

Bambi grabbed the two trash bags from her pocketbook and started moving around the room quickly gathering his clothes, jewelry, and every stitch of linen off of the bed. To put the icing on the cake, the layout of the room could not have been any better for her plan because the towels were on the outside of the bathroom, which made it easy to get them, too. She grabbed her pocketbook and dragged the trash bags in the hall. Once she was on the elevator, she stopped one floor down and set a pillowcase on fire in one of the trash cans, pulled the fire alarm, and walked off calmly. The alarm went off, the sprinklers came on, and she got the hell out of Dodge.

Just as she expected, Egypt's car was parked on the side of the building. Bambi had called her when she was on her way to the hotel. Bambi was out of breath when she hopped in Egypt's car.

"Girl, what the hell you doing?" Egypt asked. "You got beads of sweat rolling down your face. Who you running from?"

Bambi said in between breaths, "Hold on and just watch the front door. Just watch carefully now." Then she started beating on the dash and shouting, *"Drumroll!"*

"Girl, what are you talking 'bout?" Egypt asked with a confused look on her face. Bambi ignored her friend.

"Five!" she shouted at the top of her lungs. *"Four, three, two, one* and there you go, *surprizzzzze, baby!"* Bambi pointed to the door.

Smooth came running out of the hotel buck-bald naked with a towel wrapped around him, looking like he was a superhero or something. They both could see the frustration, anger, and humiliation on his face. He had no keys, no ID, no clothes, no money, and most of all, no way back in the room because the room wasn't in his name.

"Girl, how did you manage to pull that off?" Egypt asked, with her jaw about to hit the ground.

"I told you I was going to get him back, didn't I? It took everything in me to just play the role, but I had to, to get him to trust me. Now look at his dumb ass."

They both laughed, but not for long because they had to move before he saw them sitting there.

"Girl, let me get my car, and I'll meet you at the club later," Bambi said. "I hope you liked your surprise."

The next morning while Bambi was out getting her cell phone number changed, the technician answered her phone when it rang. When the technician passed her the phone, Bambi heard Smooth's voice. "That was fucked up what you did last night. I can't believe you did that shit!"

"Why can't you? It's the same shit you do. Haven't you ever

heard of that saying 'What goes around comes around'? Or 'Every dog has his day'? Well, you are the dog, and yesterday was your day! Charge it to the game . . . motherfucker!"

She pushed the *off* button on her phone and handed it back to the technician. She would always remember the sight of that no-good chump, standing in front of the hotel, his face screwed up in anger as he clutched the little towel around his butt. "Payback's a Bitch" was the song he sang.

CHAPTER 11

A Venomous Tongue

Tricia was listening to the "Clean up Woman" by Betty Wright and singing the song word for word as she moved around the kitchen dancing. She was preparing a gourmet meal for the new man in her life. He wasn't as rich as some of the other men she had dated, but he was so good to her that she thought she might change her ways and settle with just one man for a while. After all, she wasn't getting any younger. As she chopped fresh dill for the vegetables, she heard the doorbell ring.

Damn, she thought, *he's early and I haven't even gotten this started yet.*

"Ohhh, I thought I told you to call me before you came!" she screamed before she opened the door. But she was happy that he wanted to see her that badly. She opened the door without hesitation.

But it was not her new man standing on the colonial-style porch. Instead, it was the last person Tricia expected to see:

Reggie. Putting her hand on her hip she exclaimed, "What in the hell are you doing here, Reggie? Or maybe I should call you Regina!"

He haltingly said, "Look Ms. Tricia, may I come in? I . . . I ummm . . ."

Tricia looked around. She didn't want him to make a scene outside her door.

"Come in and make it quick. I've got company coming over, and by the way, it's Ms. Ferguson to you. Only friends call me Tricia, and you damn sure aren't any friend of mine."

Reggie took a deep breath. "A'ight, Mrs. Ferguson, please, I just really need you to listen to me. I promise I won't take but a minute of your time."

"One minute is all I got for your half-of-a-man ass." She returned to the kitchen, washed her hands, and began to cut some green peppers and put them in the pan. She wondered how he could have the nerve to stand here in her kitchen after what he did to her baby girl.

Reggie spoke slowly, as if he was trying to get his words right.

"Listen, Mrs. Ferguson," he said.

"It's Mizzz Ferguson," she interrupted him while looking into the refrigerator to get some butter.

"Mizzz Ferguson," he said to her, humbly watching as she put a thick sirloin in the pan, "I know I made a mistake, but the truth is I love your daughter."

"A mistake? How about a biiiig mistake? And did you say you love my daughter? Seems to me you claiming you love my daughter is the only mistake you made," she said as she sprinkled seasonings over the steak.

"Please, Ms. Ferguson, I am asking you to talk to her. . . ."

"Talk to her! For what?" she interrupted him.

"To let her know I love her and let her know I am sorry," he pleaded.

"Are you out of your mind? You made a fool of her and of me in front of God and everyone. The best thing you can do is get out of her life and never darken my doorway again. Sorry? You damn right, you're sorry. Now, go on and get out of my house. I got so much better things to do than listen to this."

She turned away from him. Damn, she'd left the oil going, and now it was too hot.

"You bitch," Reggie said. "This is your fault. You turned her against me."

Tricia didn't like the tone of his voice. She turned to face him, but when she did, he reached over to the stove and grabbed the pan of oil.

"What?" she cried out, but it was too late. Reggie had slung the pan directly at her. Drops of boiling oil splashed her face, her neck, her arms. It was like being cooked alive. She screamed out in pain.

Reggie lowered the pan.

"I only asked you to help me, you *bitch*," he cried.

But Tricia just kept screaming, the searing pain on her skin like the worst nightmare. Then she felt the pan crash against her skull, and the pain slowly dimmed as everything went black.

When Tricia woke up in the hospital room, she felt the pain all over again. She groaned.

"Momma, don't move," she heard Bambi say. "You've got third-degree burns all over your body."

As the tears leaked out her eyes, she felt the salty water trickle over the burned spots on her face. Oh, God, her face.

He had destroyed her. He might as well have killed her, she thought, before she slipped off to sleep again.

Weeks later when Tricia finally was able to look in a mirror, she wanted to scream. She wished she were dead rather than have lost her beauty. She thought of suicide but couldn't follow through. Her pretty face was her only asset, and now she couldn't find a reason to go on. She had no idea how she was going to survive. She was sent to Charter Westbrook mental hospital for a few weeks to try to cope with her injuries and to find some meaning to keep on living. She wouldn't accept hardly any visitors, so wrapped up was she in the loss of her looks. Only Bambi and Egypt were allowed to visit, and even their visits were limited as Tricia sank deeper into a depression. Reggie had been arrested for attempted murder and was in jail waiting to stand trial, but that didn't seem to make any difference to her.

Bambi looked at her mother's pill bottle.

"Mommy, stop taking so many pills," she said.

"The pills are the only thing that makes me forget."

Tears formed in Bambi's eyes as she thought, *Damn this is all my fault. I guess maybe I should have at least heard Reggie out a little bit, and now my mother had to pay. I wish it was me instead of her.*

"Ma, I swear to God on everything I love, this dude gonna get his."

"Don't you go out here and get yourself in any trouble. Let the law deal with him," Tricia said as she took another pill.

"The law?" She raised her voice a little bit and immediately realized that she didn't want to upset her mother.

Days later Bambi stopped by her mother's house to check on her, a daily routine that she had adopted since Tricia had been released from the hospital a few weeks earlier. That day she was dropping off groceries and got the shock of her life. As she entered the house, she called out, "Mommmeeeee." She listened, but there was no answer.

She approached the den and stood shocked when she saw her mother sprawled on the couch with her legs wide open. One leg was hung off the sofa, and there was an empty bottle of Belvedere on the coffee table. As she got closer, she could smell the liquor reeking from Tricia's body. Bambi was devastated. She knew her mother had been drinking a lot lately, but she'd always thought her mother would stop as she got better. She'd had no idea at all that the bottle was her mother's new best friend.

Every night Tricia went to the local bars for happy hour and to get pissy drunk. Sometimes she would get so drunk she couldn't remember how she'd gotten home. Since Bambi had begun doing events, she had become acquainted with most of the local bartenders. In turn, the bartenders tried to watch out for her mother as best they could. So it wasn't anything out of the ordinary for Bambi to get a call saying, "Bambi, I think you need to send someone to come and get your mother, because she's really out of it."

Most of the time, Bambi would drop what she was doing to go pick her mother up, and once she arrived, there would be no doubt Tricia was out of it. Bambi would graciously thank and tip the caller. Whenever Bambi saw her mother drunk, it shattered her heart. But she held her head up like a champ and dared anyone to make a negative comment. Bambi was always patient with her mother, never losing her cool. She sympathized with her mother's plight and vowed that she'd never look down on her or turn her back on her. After all, she felt partially responsible. On the few instances that she couldn't pick up her mother, she would send Ruby.

Her business continued to thrive, and she had just scored a big event—a bachelor party for one of Richmond's native NFL players. She was working on the plans when she got the familiar call. "Come get her, Bambi. She's gonna get herself in trouble." She hopped in her car and drove to Peenuckles, a low-rent kind of dive—the kind of place her mother would not have been caught dead in before her run-in with Reggie. She saw her mother slumped over the bar, her wig crooked and her makeup smeared.

"Mommy, come on now," Bambi said gently.

"I don't know why they had to call you and disrupt your business to come get the wrinkled-up old woman." Tricia's burns had healed, but an ugly scar was left on the left side of her face, and the burns on both of her hands were puffy and ugly as lobster claws.

"Because they know I love you, Mommy," Bambi said as she gathered her mother's keys and cell phone.

"Nope, 'cause them African booty sniffers is snitches! That's why. They know you gon' pay them for calling," Trish said, and nearly fell off the bar stool.

"Mommy, that's not why."

"Why you looking at my daughter? You like her little black ass, don't you? Well, she doesn't want you because she doesn't want a drunk," Trish shouted at some guy who was trying to mind his own business. "Her momma is a drunk, and she don't need two drunks in her life."

"Mommy, come on. Be nice."

"Only because you said so! I love you, girl, even though you black as tar."

Bambi always ignored the comments her mother would make about her dark complexion. She took her mother home and led her to the big king-sized bed with the floral comforter on top and helped her undress.

"I can't pay my electric bill, Bambi," Tricia slurred. "What am I gonna do?"

"I got it all taken care of, Mommy. I already paid that bill last week."

She heard the doorbell and went to let Egypt in.

"I got your message, girl. How can I help?" Egypt asked.

Bambi hugged her friend and thanked her for coming.

"Just stay with her for a while. I've got to go to handle my business. Oh, and here's some money for her in case she needs anything." She handed her friend a hundred dollars.

"She's just gonna use it to buy drinks, Bambi."

"I don't care. She's my mother, and I'd rather her have her own money than to get caught out dealing with a nigga and he have the nerve to think she owe him for some ten-dollar drink."

"I feel you."

The roles had reversed. Bambi now became the provider just as her mother had provided for her for so many years. Bambi busted her butt to make sure her mother never needed or wanted for a thing. She was the only thing that kept Tricia going, and she took care of her as if Tricia were the child and not her mother, and never complained. When Tricia was sober long enough to let everything sink in that Bambi had done for her, she hugged Bambi and said, "Thank you so much, baby."

"Ma, don't thank me. You're all I got, and I would rather die than to have you go without," Bambi said, and put her head against her mother's shoulder.

CHAPTER 12

In da Club

Lynx, one of the most well-known and biggest ballers in all of Richmond, sat at a table in Disco's club in Richmond and ordered another bottle of Dom Perignon. He had returned to town after having been gone for most of the past year, making deals and connections on the West Coast. Now he was back home, and things on his end were all good. Cook'em-up and three other members of his crew all sat at the table with him, catching him up on what had been happening since he was gone—who was doing time, who had rolled over, who was knee-deep in the money, who was broke, and who had gotten the most pussy.

Lynx felt like he had earned the spot in the Richmond gangsta scene that was once occupied by his father, Wild Cat, who was killed when Lynx was only nine years old. Cook'em-up used to be one of Lynx's father's little shorties and was always loyal to him. He stepped in to watch Lynx's back and give him advice from his many years on the street. The two men had known each other since Lynx was a little boy, and Lynx was about ten years younger than Cook'em-up. Ever since Wild Cat got killed, Lynx had vowed that one day he'd be a gangsta like his dad. Now he was.

Lynx looked around the club at all the broads and players, and suddenly he saw someone that made him stop and stare.

Lynx asked his homeboys. "Anybody knows who dat is?"

"Who, man?"

"Honey over there, the dark-skinned one with the big ole ass."

Cook'em-up, who looked liked a dwarf compared to Lynx, threw his hand up.

"Oh, man, that's Bambi, and that bitch—" he hesitated and shook his head—"that bitch ain't no earthly good. That bitch done damn near milked this whole town dry."

"Fo real, who she fuck with?" Lynx asked.

"Man, that chick just be straight catching cats out there. She be fucking with the niggas on the corners selling twenties all the way up to the niggas serving birds." Lynx listened as his man exaggerated. He could look at Bambi and tell she was about money, but his man souped it up. "Straight up, she is poison. Believe that, man."

The whole time Lynx listened to Cook'em-up give his synopsis of Bambi, he never took his eyes off her. "Do you know why she poison?"

"Man, that chick is straight-up wicked. Dope boys, stick-up kids, gamblers, gunslingers, NBA players, it don't make no difference—the bitch straight up don't have mercy on nobody's pocket. I'm telling you, man, that ho is wicked."

Lynx smiled as he watched Bambi mingling with the party-goers.

"Nah, man, I don't believe that. I think if she's like that, it's because she never had a real nigga tame her. That's why all dem cornball dudes is coming at her with their fake, weak game and she just play them like she do. I don't fault her. Shit, if I had a pussy, I'd get dem too," he said with a laugh.

"The only thing she got going for herself is the broad can throw a hell of a party and got a lot of game."

"Man, you can lay flat and bet, honey gon' be mines."

"Damn, man, is that you or the liquor talking?"

"It's me." He gulped down his drink and headed across the club.

When Lynx got up, his crew all got up and did the same thing. They acted as his security, and any one of them would kill for Lynx. Lynx himself was no wuss and had a few bodies under his belt.

Tonight Lynx turned to his crew and said, "I'm good. I need to do this myself."

Lynx strolled over smoothly heading toward Bambi. Having lost his dad at a young age, Lynx had gathered his decorous mannerism from watching actors like Superfly, Dolemite, Humphrey Bogart, and Victor Newman from the TV soap opera *The Young and the Restless,* as his mother sat him in front the television with her. As he made his way through the hot, musty, smoke-filled room, every person he passed, male and female, seemed to be checking his threads. He never noticed because his mind and eyes had locked onto one thing: Bambi.

"Would you like to dance?" he whispered in her ear. When he leaned over to whisper the invitation, he could smell the Laura Biagiotti perfume.

"Nope," she replied coldly, and turned her back to him.

He looked her over and simply said, "Well, if you ever do before the night's out, just holla at me." Playing it cool, he strolled back into the crowd. He was trying to figure out what he was doing. He didn't even like to dance, yet to get next to Bambi, he would have done the funky chicken, the robot, or the DC whop all night long for the privilege of her company.

Back at his table, he watched Bambi interact with the people around her. She never made any eye contact with him. She acted like she had the upper hand after she'd used her eyes to make him notice, her willing him over to ask her for a dance.

The DJ came on the mic and said, "All the real live niggas throw your hands up, throw your hands up, throw your hands up."

The whole party got hype, as did Bambi and her three girl-friends. They all started dancing. Lynx gazed at her as she moved rhythmically to the beat of the music. Cook'em-up saw Lynx studying Bambi's every move and said, "Don't you think it's funny that she ain't danced all night and as soon as 'All about the Benjamins' comes on, that money-hungry ho dancing like it's her theme song."

"Man, watch yo mouth."

"Look, man, I am just warning you. She ain't from the streets, and if something happen and the police come, that ho is the first one to start singing like a bird."

"Man, I ain't got her doing that. I got her holding strong, straight holding a gangsta down."

He looked over at her one more time and saw the black beauty moving so methodically, throwing her rump from side to side, moving her hair from over her eyes as she danced.

"Lordy, Lordy, look at shorty," was all he could say as he shook his head.

CHAPTER 13

Back in da Club

Bambi couldn't help but notice a man sitting at a table with his crew surrounded by buckets of Moët and Dom. Damn, who was this dude? Mr. Sexy was fine, with copper skin, teeth white as snow, with an open-faced-crown gold tooth on the side of his mouth. He was a little chunky. She couldn't put her finger on it, but something about him intrigued. She couldn't help herself. As much as she'd tried not to, she couldn't keep her eyes off him. She'd almost stared a hole in him. Amy had noticed.

"Girl . . . I see you looking at him. Ain't he fine?" she'd said.

"Yup, is he even from here? I don't remember seeing him around," Bambi had said. Amy leaned in close to her and spilled out his story.

"Chil' let me tell you." Amy took a sip from her drink and shook her head. "That's Lynx, and he ain't nothing to be played with, you hear me? Girl, I've been knowing him since I was a li'l girl and I know his whole family."

"What you mean?" Bambi had asked, and had motioned with her hands for Amy to bring it on.

"Lynx's dead daddy was a gangsta named Wild Cat. His momma, Lolly, is off the chain. She raised him and his brother up to be stone-cold gangsters, too. She's one of them mommas that pretends she is forewarning her sons against gold diggers and sac chasers, though it's all for her own selfish reasons. She knew her sons both would be rich one day, and she wasn't talking 'bout ''hood rich' either."

"For real?" Bambi had asked, wanting to hear more.

"To her the sole reason he was born anyway was to be heir to his father's throne on the streets, and as far as she was concerned, a son represented a sure meal ticket for her old age. And I'll tell you this, she isn't going to let any woman stand between her and her sons, and definitely not allow any skank ho take food out of her mouth."

"His momma ain't no joke, huh?"

"Girl, you betta know she don't play," Amy had assured Bambi.

"So how come I never saw him before?"

"He's been in California or Mexico, setting up deals. Wheeling-dealing from coast to coast."

People talk about big-mouth Amy, but I swear I am glad she is cool with me.

Later, when he had walked toward her to ask her to dance, she'd been mesmerized. She had tried to be coy and play off his effect on her, but she didn't have much success. When he'd come up into her space, she couldn't help but notice how fierce he was dressed. He definitely outclassed the partygoers, dressed as he was. He was wearing a bone-color cashmere suit with a purple raw silk shirt and tie and a matching hankie. And even though purple wasn't a color the average man could wear with any degree of style, this man pulled it off. That alone let her know that he wasn't an average dude.

When she'd looked down at his shoes, all she could say to herself was, "Damn, Hammer, please don't hurt 'em." His footwear were the Rolls Royce of cowboy boots: genuine Lucchese hornback gator boots. They were top of the line, and this confirmed what she felt from the first moment she looked into his eyes. She knew she had met her match. The clarity of the diamonds in his iced-out platinum bracelet, along with the Rolex he wore, broadcast that he was strapped in the money department, yet for some reason money wasn't the issue here. And that's precisely why she had turned him down cold. She damn sure couldn't afford to get her heart broken by this man.

The DJ got the crowd so hyped that four or five Southside dudes started throwing punches, chairs, and bottles, so Disco told the DJ to shut down. The lights came up, and the bouncers told everyone to get going. Bambi tried to sneak a peek at Mr. Sexy without him noticing. He walked out with his crew following him.

"You got a check for me, Miss Bambi?" the DJ came over and asked her. He had finished packing up his gear, and Bambi was almost done with the rest of her paperwork for the evening. The DJ left, and Bambi shut off the lights and locked the door behind her.

Once outside, she saw a flat tire on the rear of her new Mercedes. She'd had to get rid of the Corvette after dealing with Smooth because he would be looking out for that car. She must have run over something, because these were some good tires. *Damn, now what in the hell am I going to do? I don't know how to change a flat tire. Let me see if I can call roadside assistance.* Bambi checked in her purse and said under her breath, *Shit, I changed pocketbooks, so I don't even have my wallet to try to locate any damn info.*

Just as those thoughts entered her mind, a black Lincoln Navigator pulled up. A man asked, "You need some help?"

"It sure looks like it," she answered, then looked up to see Lynx's face.

He hopped out of the truck. "Pop the trunk." He opened the trunk to get out the spare.

"Thanks so much for helping me. I've never changed a tire before," she said in an attempt at casual conversation. When he got close to her, she could smell the sexy aroma of his Jean Paul Gaultier cologne. It sent shivers up her spine.

"Me either," he said, looking around for the jack. They continued to make small talk, and before she knew it, the tire was on and she was ready to be on her way.

"I know this dude at Merchant Tire who looks out for me. If you call me tomorrow, I'll take you up there to get a tire," Lynx said, wiping the grease off his hands.

"Oh, okay, thank you," she said modestly. "I'll give you my number and you can call me when you're ready."

She wrote her number down and handed it to him along with a fifty-dollar bill.

He gave the money back to her and said, "Baby, don't insult me. I'm not going to take away from you. If I can't add to your life, then you don't need me."

He took the number and hopped in his truck and pulled off.

Damn, he's smooth as hell, she thought. She could stand to be corrected when she was wrong, but she doubted very seriously if she was in this case. *That cashmere suit cost a good*

$1,500 and he got oil, grease, dirt or whatever that black stuff is all over it changing that tire for me even though I was rude as hell with him earlier. Hell, I wouldn't even dance with him, she thought. *I really hope he calls me.* And just then her cell phone rang.

"Hello," she answered, not even looking at the caller ID, wanting so badly for it to be Lynx although she knew better. He was too smooth to call a female on the first night. Once she heard the voice, she could have spit blood.

"Hey, baby, where you at?"

"Motherfucker, what the fuck you calling me for? And where did you get my number?"

"Bambi, always remember I got my ways. Did you forget a nigga is still getting money? And with money I got niggas and bitches that work places and can get me whatever I want or need," Reggie said calmly.

"Nigga, eat shit and die," she screamed into the phone and hung up on him.

He called right back; she never answered until the tenth time he called. "What?"

"Somebody told me you had a flat tire. Do you need me to come and help you?"

"Fuck *no!*" she yelled. *This sorry nigga must have got outta jail on bond, but he isn't staying out,* she thought.

"But I need to see you."

"And you will on Friday in court when they sentence yo sorry ass."

Bambi started up her car, and as she sped off, something clicked. *I bet Reggie was the one who broke the mirror on my Corvette and the one who probably flattened my tire thinking that I would call on him for help. But hell no, it damn sure ain't going down like that. I hope they lay his ass out to dry for that bitch-ass shit he did to my momma. I hope when he go to jail they gang-rape him time and time again maliciously with broom handles and everything else after what he did to my momma. He deserves whatever he gets.*

CHAPTER 14

Bagging Up

The next day Lynx and Cook'em-up were up bright and early, bagging up the work from the new shipment Lynx had just gotten in.

Although Cook'em-up had surrounded himself with lots of cats who stacked major paper, Cook'em-up never had been the type to get out and make it happen for himself. Truth be told, the only two things Cook'em-up had ever been known for was being a gunslinger and murdering someone at the drop of a dime, and his skill for cooking crack cocaine like a world-class chef preparing a soufflé in a five-star restaurant.

When Lynx was only thirteen, Cook'em-up had recognized his drive. He'd taken Lynx under his wing and introduced him to the life from all angles. With Cook'em-up's guidance, along with everything else Lynx soaked up, Lynx turned out to be one of the most thorough and wise young dudes to hit the streets of Richmond, V-A.

That morning Cook'em-up was trying to make light conversation with Lynx, but Lynx was distant.

"Damn, nigga, where yo mind at?"

Lynx just shook his head. "Man, I don't even wanna say," he said, as he added another stone of cocaine to what was already on the scale, trying to make the reading show an even four and a half ounces.

"What you thinking 'bout? That asshole full of money you 'bout to make off all that raw coke I just cooked up?"

"Nah, man, not even." He used a playing card, the queen of hearts, to take some of the powder coke off the scale.

"What's on yo mind then?"

"That honey from last night."

"You mean Money from last night?" Cook'em-up asked, trying to crack a joke.

"Nah, I ain't thinking 'bout no dude."

"I know, damn, I meant honey that's all about getting da money. The chick that throw the parties?"

"Yeah, man I'm straight into her. I am feeling her fo *real.*"

"Damn, it's like that?" Cook'em-up asked as he opened up another box of baking soda to continue to cook the coke.

Lynx nodded. "But she won't give a nigga the time of day. She made all my 'Excuse me, miss' lines look like two-cent checks. I was waiting for Sandman to come and get me."

"Look at you, man, you all to pieces. She got you all open up like that and you ain't even had the pussy yet. She something tough, huh?"

"Exactly."

"Look, man, I told you that ho ain't to be trusted. She ain't from the streets and don't know nothing 'bout the streets, and I don't trust the bitch no further than I can see her."

"Man, well, you ain't the one who got to deal with her, are

you?" Lynx shot back as he realized that something had happened to his plastic glove. "Shit I got a fucking hole in my glove. Hand me another one."

"A'ight man, I'm gonna back up, because you sprung, that's all. We've been through a lot together, and we'll get through this, too," Cook'em-up said and handed him another glove out of the box.

Lynx didn't say a word.

"Man, I hope I am wrong 'bout her. I hope she top-flight like you think. Because man, she really got you looking like Elmer Fudd, and that cartoon shit ain't cute. I know you ain't been no Casanova but, ummm, I know her kind. You gotta show her some real Romeo-type shit to finesse her."

"Man, I sell drugs not dreams. I gotta be real with her."

"Call the bitch then and see what she talking 'bout."

"I will, and watch yo mouth."

Once they were finished bagging up, Lynx decided to call Bambi. Shoot, he had wanted to call her last night as soon as he got her number, but he didn't want to seem like he was pressed. There was an unspoken notion to wait, not to call the same day one gets the number. With any other chick, he wouldn't care what they thought because he knew for a fact, right off the bat, they wanted him and it was a privilege to even receive a phone call from him. Bambi was different. He had to play his hand to the hilt with her. He looked in his pocket to get the number. It wasn't there. He checked his other pockets as well, but somehow he had lost it. He was upset, but what could he do? He didn't have the number and had no way to get in touch with her. He thought about calling her business to try to plan a party, but he didn't want to seem too pressed. So he sucked it up and remembered that they basically traveled in the same circles, and he knew he would see her again somehow.

CHAPTER 15

Lost da Digits

For a few days, whenever Bambi's cell phone rang, she hoped it was Lynx, but it never was, so she figured he was just another liar and player. Soon, she had other things to think about, like how to throw the biggest bash of the year—Tall Daddy's party.

Tall Daddy may have been confined to a wheelchair, but he was a very powerful man. Tall Daddy was involved with anything crooked in Richmond that made money: whores, guns, drugs, real estate, extortion, and loan sharking. Once a year Tall Daddy had a celebration—and when he had a party, he had a party. He cut no corners and took no shortcuts. Heavy hitters from all over—New York, Chicago, Detroit, Miami, LA, and all points in-between—traveled near and far to party with Tall Daddy. Even the ones who played the background and had no use to be seen on the scene would come out and bless him with their appearance. It was all about showing respect and supporting Tall Daddy. The gold diggers and sac chasers did whatever they had to do to get on the guest list and make this set. As soon as a confirmed date got out of Tall Daddy's gala, females started saving to ensure they had the money for extravagant outfits that would be sure to turn heads, because they knew that it was going to be nothing but heavy hitters and major players who would be in attendance. They were sure with the right outfit, this could be the night they could come face-to-face with their knight in green shining armor who would ride up and take them from poverty to paradise.

Every year Tall Daddy outdid himself, and by no means was he going to let Disco's little club parties outshine his. He hired Bambi to pull off this event and told her that she was the only person he knew of who could give the folks something to talk about.

Bambi had attended one of Tall Daddy's parties a couple years back with Reggie, and she knew what type of crowd would come out. She was excited that he'd chosen her company to put the affair together. She knew that this party could take her company to the next level. She charged him a pretty penny and intended to make sure it was worth every dime he paid and then some, but Tall Daddy had no problem peeling off the digits for her—especially after he met with her and saw what she intended to do with the Arthur Ashe Center, which he had rented for the affair.

Bambi worked around the clock for weeks to pull the party together. She promised herself that the day of the party she'd have at least the morning and early afternoon to relax and get herself together, because she knew the night would be a night of remembrance.

The day of the party she visited the Regency Square Mall to pick up a few last-minute items, including the perfect strapless bra to wear under the halter dress that she planned to wear to the party. As she passed the pet store, she saw a shiny black Persian cat in the window. Something about that cat caught her eye. Stopping in her tracks, she watched the cat sit all alone and show no emotion. The cat gazed at her but didn't come over to investigate; nor did he entice her to come in and see him. She'd never had any interest in having a pet, not even as a child, so she was surprised that something about this cat connected with her. The cat reminded her of when she was a little girl. She was pretty, so black, and most of the time left alone because she didn't fit in. The skin-color prejudices of her own black people made her feel like an outcast. The cat's shiny coat made her smile as she thought of the Vaseline her mother would put on her face, saying, "It ain't nothing worse than a black, ashy child. You might be black, but you'll never be ashy."

The cat's nonchalant attitude brought back memories of being left alone to play as a child because none of the white kids wanted to play with her either. Then she thought about the times that her own father didn't want to be bothered with her and seemed to showboat his other children by a light-bright-damned-near-white woman around town, never taking Bambi anywhere. To this day she had never ridden in her father's car. For the longest time, his neglect had taken a toll on her, affecting her self-esteem, but after a while she'd gotten used to it and trained herself not to care.

As she stormed into the store, she thought to herself, *I betcha them stupid people bought all the white cats and left him sitting there. It's all good though, because I am about to buy him. People make me so sick!*

Before the sales clerk could ask her if she needed any help, Bambi pointed to the front of the store and demanded, "Did you guys have any white ones?"

"Are you talking about the Persian cat in the window?"

"Yes." Bambi nodded.

"Ummm, we got those in about a week ago, and we got in ten white ones and two black ones. All the white ones are gone, and the other black one was sold to a family who had twins and they needed a way to differentiate the cats, so they got a black one and a white one."

Bambi cut the woman off. "Let me see him."

The woman reached into the window and got the cat. As soon as he was in Bambi's arms, he purred, and she knew he was meant to be hers.

"He costs four hundred and thirty dollars," the sales clerk informed her. She obviously felt the need to tell Bambi the price after inspecting her appearance. Bambi wore some blue faded and bleached tight-fitting jeans with strategically placed holes cut in them—only she had bought them like that. She wore a crisp white T-shirt that looked like it was a wifebeater without the ribbed material and some brand-spanking-new, white K-Swiss sneakers.

"Oh, okay, no problem. Is that all?" she asked.

The cat was so fluffy and cuddly. She hugged him tight before she handed him back to the lady. "Look, I want to pay for him now, and I'll come back to pick him up later. I have some shopping to do and don't want to lug him around the mall with me."

"As soon as you pay for the cat you have to take him," the clerk told her.

"Well, will you hold him for me, and I'll be back for him in about an hour or so?" Bambi asked.

The clerk agreed. Bambi took one last look at the cat, whose eyes were filled with disappointment at her leaving.

"Baby, don't worry. Momma will be back for you, okay?" she said as she turned to leave the store.

Once she found the bra, she stopped in the food court. She knew this would be the only time she'd be able to eat. She sat at a table eating a piece of greasy Sbarro pizza when someone walked up with some food from Chick-fil-A.

"Hey, miss. Lady, can we share this table?"

She looked up. It was Lynx, looking scrumptious even in his khaki pants and a khaki uniform shirt. Bambi remembered that Amy had told her Lynx owned a few businesses, but that crisp khaki outfit didn't look like he had been doing any kind of strenuous work.

She rolled her eyes and said, "I don't usually share tables with liars."

"So that must mean yes, because I may be many things, but a liar ain't one," he said, and sat down across from her.

"I can't tell."

"Oh, if you talking about me not calling you, I lost your number."

"Come a little better than that, baby. Give me a new and improved line, because that is the oldest line, or should I say lie, in the book."

"For real, look a here, I looked high and low for that number. You going to give it to me again? I promise this time I'll guard it with my life."

"Sorry, Boo, you got a better chance getting it from the Psychic Network than from me." She looked at her watch as if she had somewhere to get to.

"Damn, baby, tell me how someone so beautiful could be so cold."

"I am not cold, but a brother makes me sick when he talks the talk but don't walk the walk, know what I mean? Keep it real with me. I'll keep it real with you."

"So that's what you want—a man who can keep it real."

She nodded and smiled. "Yup."

"Okay, then my question is, are you sure you can handle a man who'll keep it real? Remember what they say: 'Be careful what you ask for.' 'Cause, babygirl, I'm as real as they come. I don't play games. Hell, I quit school in kindergarten because they had recess."

"Please. Baby, if you for real then I'm wit it 'cause I'm a true sister all the way in all ways."

"We'll see." He smiled a big smile and then leaned over the table and whispered, "You got a big-ass booger hanging out of your nose! You better kill that sucker, because he sho is riding hard."

Her smile turned to a frown, and the frown was converted into a look of embarrassment. When he saw that look, he moved in for the kill.

"See, I like you for you even with a booger in your nose," he said, and casually handed her a napkin. He added, "I can get it for you, if you want me to."

"No thanks."

She went into her pocketbook and grabbed her handheld mirror, and lo and behold, Lynx wasn't lying. Lynx changed the subject while he put her trash on his tray.

"I heard you doing my man's party tonight, and they say you're doing it big."

"You heard right." She smiled timidly, still embarrassed. "So you going to be at the party?"

He nodded.

"Well, I'll see you there. I got a big night ahead of me and still have a lot to do in preparation for the gala affair."

He smiled and walked off. She had never been so embarrassed in her whole life. She pulled out her cell phone and called Egypt to vent. Egypt tried to convince her that it wasn't all that bad.

"Girl, at least he told you. What if he wouldn't have said anything and then you would have found out later?"

After talking with Egypt and feeling marginally better, Bambi continued to shop, stopping in a couple more stores before heading back to the pet store. When she approached the shop's window, she saw that the cat was gone, and she saw a sign in the cage that said SOLD. That indicated to her that the Persian was waiting for her inside.

She strolled in and told the woman, "I'm going to put my other bags in the car and will be right back. I'm parked right out front."

The clerk looked surprised to see Bambi back, as if she had been convinced that Bambi didn't have $430 plus tax to spend on a cat and wouldn't be back.

"Miss, you said an hour or so, and it's been almost two hours," the clerk informed Bambi.

"So what are you saying?" Bambi asked suspiciously.

"You're too late. Someone just purchased the cat, and he's gone home with his new owner," the clerk said, with an apologetic glance at the empty cage.

Bambi went off, cussing and fussing until the woman demanded that she leave before she called the police. Bambi was convinced that her day had been jinxed. First the booger and now her cat. What else could go wrong?

Bambi walked to her car, parked as always in the "expectant/new mother's" designated parking space, and saw that someone had put a big box on the car and what looked like a parking ticket under the windshield wiper. The first thing she thought was, *Someone had the nerve to leave some damn trash on my car.*

As she got closer, she heard meowing and the sound of scratching in the box. She opened it and found the shiny black Persian cat. She couldn't have been happier. Her day was turning around. "Where did you come from?" Bambi cooed.

She didn't care. She hurried and put the cat in the passenger's seat of the car and prepared to pull off. If someone had left the cat, oh well, finders keepers, losers weepers. Once she was down the street, she realized that the parking ticket under the windshield wiper was actually a note. She pulled over and grabbed it. Opening it she read: "I've been checked for fleas, ticks, and boogers, and now I am ready for a good home!"

She smiled. Now she was really looking forward to the party. This time when Lynx asked her to dance, she'd have a different answer.

CHAPTER 16

The Freak of the Week

That night when Bambi arrived at the Arthur Ashe Center, she was informed that flowers had been delivered for her. They were her favorite—sunflowers. The enclosed card read: "To the best party planner this town has ever seen. Use this night to shine. "

There was no mistake about it: Tall Daddy's party was definitely the place to be. The line to get in was wrapped around the building. Inside, the party was jumping; the music was by DJ Clue. As Bambi looked around, she happened to catch a glimpse of some light-skinned girl all up in Lynx's face. The girl's name was Unique, and she had many aliases—"the freak of the week," a.k.a. "straight skeezer", a.k.a. "the greatest hood rat of all time"—but she was best known around the town for holding the champion title for her state-of-the-art blow jobs. Bambi knew if Unique ever got her mouth on Lynx, it would be over—such was Unique's reputation when it came to giving head! Bambi had never felt threatened by any woman. Still, she knew Unique had one up on her: her freak game.

There was no denying Unique's attractiveness, but it was the way she carried herself that made her ugly. Unique had a light complexion with long hair and cat eyes. Her shape was fierce, and she always dressed in form-fitting clothing. Unique's man, Took, had spoiled her until he went to prison, leaving her with what was rumored to be a nice stash, about forty or fifty grand, which she let run through her hands like water. Once she realized that she had no money coming in, she became a straight hood rat. After Took's arrest she went from being a hustler's wife overnight to being a bona-fide nickel-and-dime ho.

Bambi knew that Unique was on the prowl, and she wasn't having none of it now that she'd set her sights on Lynx. *Oh I know that ho Unique is not going to get her claws into Lynx, and she needs to know it. I got something for her, if I have to take this dude home tonight myself. I know one thing for sure, two things for certain. . . . Ms. Unique won't be putting her slobbing lips on that, not tonight anyway. Where the hell is Disco? I know his ass is around here somewhere trying to scope out his competition. Shit, I'll give Disco a hundred dollars to pay that ho to fuck him. I know that nickel-and-dime two-bit ho will definitely go for that.*

Just then Tall Daddy rolled up in his wheelchair, smiling. "You did it up, baby. You dat bitch fo real!"

Strobe lights pulsed over the room, and the best East Coast rappers were on the stage tearing it up in a freestyle battle. Bambi looked around and didn't see Lynx or Unique anywhere. The party was in full throttle, with aproximately two thousand people dancing and going wild. The crowd pressed against her, but she kept searching for Lynx.

Finally, she thought she saw Lynx's man Cook'em-up. But

as she started over toward him, the fire marshal came in and shut the whole party down. Just like that, lights were out and the party was over. Bambi was upset until Egypt told her, "Girl, you daaaa shiiiiit when the fire marshal comes and shut yo shit down."

"You really think so?"

"Yup, girl. I am telling you, if the fire marshal say it's too many ma'fuckas in a place, and the place is as big as the Ashe Center, girl, you's a bad bitch if you can sell out this place. Mark my words, I betcha a whole bunch of other folks be calling you to do their parties now," Egypt assured her friend.

"I hope so. You are such a good friend. Thank you so much!" She hugged her and then changed the subject. "I thought you would have been long gone. Aren't you going to the joint in the morning?" Bambi asked her friend. "Or did you change your mind or something?"

"Don't be funny! You know I'm going."

Bambi knew that was right. Even if her friend stayed out and partied all night, it wouldn't stop her from getting to her destination in the morning. After Egypt's run-in with Smooth, she had decided she wasn't going to pick up any more men in the clubs. Egypt had promised herself that before she'd even go out with a guy she'd get to know him inside out. She wanted to talk to guys for months to scope out their game. Most of the guys she ran into on the streets were not having that telephone love. After a few times on the phone, they wanted action, and when the action wasn't jumping off, they lost interest.

But one day Egypt had answered her telephone: It was a wrong number, a collect call from a federal prison. Thinking that it was someone she knew calling, she accepted the call. Once she found out it wasn't, *I ain't really got nothing else to do, so let me see what this dude is talking about,* she'd thought. After carrying on a conversation for a few minutes, at that moment her whole grind changed from gold digging drug dealers to hustling the major players in the penitentiary. Her whole existence revolved around finding love on lockdown.

Bambi had gotten a whiff of this one day when she called her friend to chat.

"Hey girl, what's up?" she'd asked.

"Is it something important?" Egypt had said. "If not, I gotta call you back."

"Damn, what you doing?"

"I am online trying to do some research."

"Research on what?"

"This dude I'm about to holla at."

"What dude? Where did you meet him?" Bambi had wanted to know exactly why her friend hadn't told her about the mystery man before.

"I haven't met him yet, but I'm 'bout to," Egypt had said.

"What you mean? Give it up, you know I can't take it. I want the whole four-one-one."

"Girl, I'm almost ashamed to say."

"I'm your best friend. If you can sit and tell me how you bleeding like the damn blood bank and every other thing, telling me about some dude shouldn't be no big deal. Now come on, give it up," Bambi had demanded.

"Girl, the dude is in jail."

"What? Jail?" Bambi had said.

"Yup, girl, but hold on before you start trying to give me a damn speech. A speech that I don't need or want to hear either."

"I'm listening," Bambi had said, smiling at how her friend

knew her so well, because the truth of the matter was that she had been about to give her a sermon as sure as her name was Bambi.

"Girl, he just ain't your average dude doing time, needing me to send him some commissary money. He's a paid-ass nigga with an asshole full of money and a stash, too."

"For real? And how you know all of this?"

"Girl, please if the feds took a reported four hundred thousand from him at the pickup, then trust me it's more where that came from," Egypt had informed her friend.

"Oh, okay. But how you know that wasn't all he had?"

"Because dude been in the game for a while. He ain't new to this, and just from reading up on him, I know he got a stash."

"And if he do?"

"Then if I play my cards right, I know I'll have a stash, too."

"And what if he doesn't have a stash?" Bambi had asked.

"After reading up on him, if he don't have one, I'm sure he know plenty of dudes who do, and you know what? It's only one way to find out."

"Oh, okay, but how you going to meet him? You still haven't told me that yet."

"Don't worry. I'm going to get his address and send him a letter. Tell me what dude in jail don't want somebody to show him love? Every dude in jail want a letter, a card, a picture. Shoot, that's the highlight of the day in jail: mail."

"Shit, you ain't lying. I remember when bitch-ass Reggie had that little bid to do. He would stress me out for mail every single day. And if he didn't get anything on mail call, trust me girl, all hell broke loose! Then on top of everything, girl, he used to talk to me every day on the phone. So yup, I agree, dudes do want all the pen pals they can get."

Since then, men in jails all across the country had become a major part of Egypt's bread and butter. Whether the money came directly off of their inmate account or they had their homeboys sending her money, the money came and it came faithfully and regularly.

As people left the Arthur Ashe Center, Bambi gave Egypt a hug, and Egypt promised to call Bambi when she got on the road the next morning to go visit her convict friend.

After Tall Daddy rolled out of the party with his boys, he promised her that not only would he be having her plan all of his future parties, but his boys would too. Bambi got all her paperwork for the caterer and the decorator and everything else in order and headed to her car. As she approached her car, she saw Lynx standing next to it talking with Cook'em-up. They were drinking Heineken beers.

"May I help you with something? Do you need a ride or something?" She tried to be sarcastic, but her grin betrayed her true feelings. And she was especially happy that Lynx wasn't somewhere laid up with Unique.

Cook'em-up looked at her up and down, and instead of acknowledging her, turned to Lynx and asked, "Man, you a'ight?"

"I'm a'ight now that my baby is here." Lynx gave Cook'em-up a pound and sent him on his way.

"I was just waiting for you so I could make sure you got to your car okay. I heard the dudes up Broad Street got to shooting up the Seven-Eleven. I knew you'd be coming out late, so I wanted to make sure nobody snatched you or nothing."

"Oooh, you're so sweet. Thank you! And thanks so much for the cat. I love it," she said, but the whole time she was looking at his manhood bulging out a little bit through his tailor-made Armani linen suit.

"Yeah? I hope in the same way you'll grow to love this cat." He smiled, pointing at his chest. Then his cell phone rang. Instead of answering it, he reached into his pocket, cut the phone off, and threw it on the seat of his truck. For Lynx to shut his phone down meant that only she had his attention, and Bambi liked that. He finished his Heineken and tossed the empty bottle into a trash can.

"Look, all I am asking is that you give me one more chance," he said.

"And if I do and your chance falls through the floor, then what?" she asked, jingling her keys, trying not to seem nervous.

"Then I'll pick up the pieces of my heart and ego, and I'll bounce. Now is it a deal?" He extended his hand for a handshake.

She shook his hand. He was looking at her, admiration in his eyes.

"Now can I ask why you are looking at me like that? Do I have another booger on my nose?" she asked.

"Naw, you just soft on the eyes, that's all," he told her as he reached into the cooler in the back of his truck and pulled out two beers, offering her one although he knew she would refuse it. He opened it and took a sip.

She watched him and made up her mind that she was going to test him until he dropped. She said, "Look, man, you got to stay focused if you want to mess with me."

"What you talking 'bout? I am 'bout one of the most focused-on-point dudes you'll ever meet."

"Well, look," she said, looking at her watch, "it's three a.m. and you out here drinking and got a cooler filled with beer. Now, to me that isn't being too focused. I'm offered beer all the time, but I refuse it because in my line of work I need and want to be focused. I know one slip can cost me. I know we have different professions. Still, I'm sure a slipup can cost you your life. Right?"

"I feel ya," he said, and threw the bottle across the parking lot into the woods.

"Well, good night, Lynx, and thanks for the cat. I named him Snowball."

"Look, can we hook up and do lunch tomorrow?"

"Yup, we sure can. I'll get with you tomorrow. Good night and stay focused," Bambi said as she got into her car and pulled off, leaving Lynx standing there.

They still had not exchanged numbers, and he had no idea how she was planning to get in touch with him. Things weren't exactly going his way. Well, not the way he'd planned anyway, or it hadn't so far, at least when it came to Bambi. As far as he was concerned, it always seemed like Bambi had more hold than any point guard, never turning the ball over and always crossing over at the right time, leaving dudes for broke. Most dudes would've been intimidated by Bambi, but not him. Lynx knew for a fact he was not outclassed. After taking all those things into consideration, Lynx wasn't trying to get her on his team. Instead he had to be on her team. In his mind Bambi was the franchise maker, the star of the squad, and it would be a privilege for him to squad up with her. He knew that with her he couldn't lose. Being mindful of that, he was willing to play his position.

He thought about her last words as he drove home. *Stay focused.*

CHAPTER 17

Unexpected Guest

It was 11 a.m., and Cook'em-up was at Lynx's house making BLT sandwiches when someone knocked on the door. He got his pistol because he knew Lynx didn't usually invite anyone over. He asked, "Who is it?"

"Bambi," she said sweetly.

He opened the door and rolled his eyes at Bambi. "You better be glad you identified yourself, because I was about to shoot first and ask questions later."

"Oh, my! I am glad you didn't act on impulse. Is Lynx here?" she asked, batting her eyes.

"He still asleep. Go on upstairs and wake him up." Cook'em-up didn't think twice about Bambi coming over. He was sure if she was here it was because Lynx had told her to come. No broad would have the nerve to come over without an invitation.

He watched her sashay up the stairs in her baby blue Iceberg capris with a matching tee. The whole ensemble looked like it was painted on her. He shook his head, trying to figure out exactly what his main man saw in that high-priced whore.

Bambi knew that this was the house she had followed Lynx to, but she had no idea whose house it was. It was in one of the nicer, secluded communities in Richmond. It had a finished wood stain on the outside. The interior of the house was like something out of a magazine: high, vaulted ceiling, skylights, sunken den and living room, and a three-car garage. All the furniture was white throughout the downstairs of the house, from what she could tell.

She reached what she figured had to be Lynx's room because it was the only room with a closed door. Without even knocking she slowly opened the door and peeped in. The large colonial-style California king-sized bedroom suite didn't even take up half the room. Neither did the chaise chair and theater-sized television. *He had to have a wall or two knocked out to have such a spacious bedroom,* she thought. She loved the crisp white linen on the bed and the custom-made drapes to match.

The furniture and unique architecture of the house was a visual appetizer. Now her eyes really took in the main course. Lynx was asleep on the bed naked. She stood over him, admiring the total package as he snored lightly. Lynx had the prettiest dick she had ever seen in her life. While she watched him sleep, she decided that she'd call Egypt to see if she'd made it to the penitentiary yet. She was expecting to leave a message, but Egypt picked up.

"Hey, girl," Bambi said.

"Hey, girl, what you doing?"

"Girl, I am at Lynx's house in his room, watching him sleep. You haven't made it there yet?"

"I've just left there."

"What happened?"

"Girl, you don't want to know," Egypt said with a sigh.

"I can only imagine, but tell me." Bambi was more eager to know than she let on.

"Girl, got all the way up there and almost got busted."

"What? What you mean 'busted'? How in the hell you gon' get busted at the damn slammer jammer?"

"Girl, listen, you know I be going to see Moe up Powhatan, right?"

"Right," Bambi said, wishing Egypt would hurry up and get the story out.

"Well, today I was going to see Jay. He's up in Coffeewood."

"Right?"

"Well, when I got up there, it was packed like sardines in a can. So, I had to ride around the parking lot to try to find a parking spot. Girl, and guess whose car I saw?"

"Whose, girl?" Bambi said.

"That gotdamn motor mouth Amy, and you know like I know that bitch will blow anybody's spot up at the drop of a dime. And Moe is up in Powhatan with Amy's cousin, too. I knew before I could get back to Richmond, Amy would have already gotten word to Moe through her cousin that's locked up with him. By no means am I trying to fuck up the money I get every month from Moe. So I busted a U-turn and sped out the parking lot, and now I'm on my way back to Richmond."

"Girl, you are crazy, but I am not even going to lie. I would have done the same damn thing."

"Girl, but that ain't even the funny part," Egypt said with a laugh.

"What else?"

"Okay, there's this man who circles the prison like every two minutes—I guess patrolling the perimeter—in this white state-issued pickup truck. Right?

"Okay."

"Girl, when I saw Amy's car, I put the pedal to the metal and got the heck out of Dodge."

"Right. Right." Bambi was waiting for the funny part to come.

"Well, how about the rent-a-cop dude had the nerve to try to come behind me to pull me over. I kept going until I couldn't see the penitentiary, and then I pulled over."

"What did he say?"

"Talking about I was speeding and I could get in a lot of trouble. So, you know me—I asked him what kind of trouble. He gon' tell me he can take my visits. I told that fake-ass cop, I don't give a damn. Take them ma'fuckas because you won't see me up here anymore anyway and sped off again. He put the siren on this time. I didn't even stop. His truck couldn't keep up with me, and by then I was off the prison property."

"Girl, let me find out you was on the high-speed chase from a rental cop."

They both laughed, and Bambi's laughter woke Lynx up. He saw her, and for a minute thought he was dreaming. Then he focused and realized that it was actually Bambi in the flesh. Without saying anything, he got up and went into the bathroom to take a dump, brush his teeth, and wash his face. When he returned Bambi brought her conversation with Egypt to an end and turned her attention to him. For a second her heart began to pound. She didn't know whether Lynx was angry or what for her showing up at his house unannounced.

"How you find out where I live?" he asked.

"Well, I'm happy to see you, too."

He looked at her coldly, and she knew he wanted an answer. "If you were focused, then maybe you would know."

"If? If? If 'if' was a fifth, we'd all be drunk. Now I'm asking you again, how you find out where I live?"

She didn't know how to read the expression on his face. She responded nervously, "Ummm, let's just say, let's just say, I saw to it that you got home safe last night."

He looked at her and then said, "Come here.

"You look nice," he said to her as he took her in his arms, hugged her, and kissed her on the forehead.

Though the hug lasted only about five seconds, it had her all to pieces. It had been so long since she had been hugged by someone she actually liked that she had forgotten what it felt like. When he let go, she wanted another but wouldn't dare ask for one or initiate one; she didn't want to seem too mushy.

Bambi and Lynx hung out all day. They stopped at Kentucky Fried Chicken and had a picnic at Maymont Park after walking through and checking out all the animals. They sat on the little blanket and talked for hours, getting to know each other.

She felt a little awkward because when they were inside KFC, a guy Bambi had seen at a lot of her parties spoke to Lynx.

When he thought Bambi wasn't paying attention, he asked, "Are you with her?"

"Yup, that's my baby," Lynx responded.

"Damn, man, I didn't know that. Just watch yo'self because I heard she will trick you out your money," the guy said. Bambi was getting ketchup for the french fries, but she could hear plenty.

"Only if a nigga let her. I'm too smart for that, but good looking out, man," Lynx said. Bambi joined Lynx and pretended she hadn't heard a thing, but she felt bad about her rep. Maybe some of it was true. She had taught a few so-called players a valuable lesson about messing with women in the months after she had schooled that rattlesnake Smooth. But a lot of it was just haters talking about shit they didn't even know, who wished they could see firsthand what she was about.

Later that night they went to Lynx's house, and he invited her in to watch the movie *Rush Hour,* which he'd purchased earlier that day. They went to his bedroom, and he took off her shoes and told her to get comfortable. As she lay across the bed, he began to give her a massage. He unsnapped her bra, telling her to turn over, and when she did he put her perky chocolate breasts in his mouth and began to suck on them. She wanted to tell him to stop, but she couldn't make her lips say it.

What if I told him and he really did stop? Damn that shit feels good as hell. I ain't going to say a word. I am just going to ride the wave.

And that's what she did. She rode him like a cowgirl. The only thing was, she didn't have a lasso. Though she was in excruciating pain because of his size, she took it like a real woman. The next morning her whole body was so sore she felt as if she had run in a marathon. Lying in his arms, she realized that this was what she had been missing. Sure, she had a box of vibrators that could make her come as many times a day as she wanted, and without a doubt, they did a damn good job. But it was not until she lay in Lynx's arms that she realized she had missed having a warm body to comfort her.

She spent the next few weeks making up for what she'd been

missing. She and Lynx tried different restaurants, went to the movies, museum, and took walks. They enjoyed one another's company and easily made the transition into one another's lives. They both had respect for the other's hustle, neither questioning the other about what he or she really did. They were seeing each other exclusively, but neither had made a formal commitment.

After a few weeks of going out to various restaurants every night, they both agreed to try their hand at cooking for one another. Neither one of them was even close to being a world-class chef, but together they did their best. One morning Lynx lay in the bed as she fed him a meal of scrambled eggs, Canadian bacon, fried potatoes with onions, toast with marmalade, and coffee. She felt proud of having prepared it for Lynx, although half of it was pie-cooked and she only had to heat it up in the microwave. *Damn, I literally have him eating out of the palm of my hand,* she thought.

They were making small talk when she blurted out, "Lynx, I don't want your money."

"What?"

"Look, I heard what your friend said about me that day when we were in the KFC, and yes, I do like money. Shoot, I love money, every dime of it I can get, but"—she looked into his eyes and told him—"I don't want or need your money, for real. You seem cool, and I don't want you to treat me a certain way because of what people say."

"Listen, I'm my own man, got my own mind, and make my own decisions."

She cut him off. "I see that, but I want you to know that I have my own money. I have a very successful party-planning company that I built from the ground up. I also have another field of prey, and that's pussy hounds. That's kind of a side job.

When a chump sticks his head out there, I cut it off and put his ego in his pocket, and when I'm done with him, he never wants to see a bitch like me again. I mean, shit, it's not like I'm giving up any pussy or anything—shit, the nigga really be just plain playing himself. So, am I wrong?"

He smiled, respecting her honesty and hustle even more. "That's gangsta! I can live with that. I ain't no weak nigga, and I appreciate you running your game by me. Anything I give you, it's 'cause I want you to have it, not because you whine for it or anything like that. It's simply because I choose to."

"Well, now you know what I do on a regular. Now give me the four-one-one on what you do."

"Baby, I'm just a dope dealer. Ain't nothing fancy about that. Your job is way more complicated than mine. I can handle that and what's to come. Basically, I don't want to get into it too deep with you, because if they ever come for me, I don't want them to come for you, too. If you don't know nothing, you can't tell nothing, right?"

"If I knew I wouldn't rat anyway," she said, trying to convince him. "I respect what you saying, though."

He hugged her tight and gave her a long wet kiss.

CHAPTER 18

Captain Save-a-Ho

Bambi sat on Lynx's boat, paging through his *Don Diva* magazine as he fished. She had already paged through all of his car magazines and damn near every other male magazine he had bought. "I can't believe I left my bag with all my entertainment," she said. He knew for sure that she really cared for him because she was out in the middle of the Chesapeake Bay on a boat that wasn't a cruise ship or party boat.

"But it's all good 'cause it gives us time to talk while we're out here," she said. "Other than the little stuff you tell me about your brother, and I hear your mother call your cell phone asking you for money, I know nothing about your family. Tell me about your childhood, your family."

Lynx took a deep breath, opened up, and filled her in on all the details about growing up. When Lynx was young, he'd watched his mother, Lolly, time and time again swindle man after man out of money to pay their bills. When she knew her two sons were watching, she'd told him and his brother Cleezy,

"This is how women will do you. Never trust them or a word they say because all they want is yo money and anything else you'll give them."

Lynx explained to her that he'd never cared about women or what his mother had to say about them. He'd had his own mind, and all he'd wanted from his mother was one thing. He'd begged and pleaded with her: "Ma, can you teach me the game? Ma, please teach me to be a hustler just like my daddy. Daddy had a lot of money and took care of you and a lot of other people. I want to make a whole bunch of money and have the respect of a lot of people, too."

He and his mother would have this conversation over and over again. She never quite knew how to respond to her son. She really didn't want her son to follow in his dad's footsteps, at least not at such a young age anyway. When Lynx turned eleven years old, she couldn't ignore the questions any longer and decided to tell Lynx everything about his daddy, so that Lynx would not make the same mistakes his father had made. He wouldn't be much good to anyone if he was in jail or dead.

"Dang, that's deep." She searched for more words to say to comfort him, but just then he hooked a big fish and the conversation switched to the fish.

Later that night at Lynx's house, they lay in the bed.

"I gotta holla at you 'bout something."

"What, baby?" Bambi asked.

"You told me that you'd give me one shot, and I think I have proved myself to you. Listen, we've been kicking it for a minute and seems like we get along. I want you to be my lady."

Now he wants to go and mess things up. It seems like everything has been going well, but as soon as we make a commitment, the bullshit comes. I really like him, and I don't want to mess things up between us.

"Honestly, I don't see nothing wrong with the way we are now. I'm comfortable," she told him.

"I feel you. I like it, too, but I really feel like I want you to be my girl," he said, sounding just like a little boy.

"Me and how many others?"

"Just you!" he said as he looked into her eyes.

"Yeah, right, I saw that ho Unique up in your face at Tall Daddy's party looking like she was about to drop to her knees and give you some head on the spot."

"Man, please. I know her man, Took, that's locked up," he said to her, gazing into her eyes. He was surprised that she still had Unique on her mind. The party had been months ago.

"So what that mean? That ain't never stopped that ho before."

"Look, I am not on that type of time with her. She was telling me something about how she was struggling, about to lose her house, and how Took wanted to know if I could help her."

"What? So you are Captain Save-a-Ho now?"

"I had just talked to Took, and he didn't mention anything about her conniving ass. I know her story and her stello, so don't worry. Baby, listen," he said as he lay on top of her, kissing her face and gazing into her eyes. "Look, she got a better chance giving Jesus Christ some head than me, and that's on everything I love."

She fell out laughing.

"You are crazy," she said to him as he moved and lay beside her, still looking in her eyes.

"Nah, I'm for real. Right now it ain't nothing none of them chicks can do for me. I'm trying to be with you exclusively. I done had plenty of pussy and head. Half of them would fuck me and then my crew or, shit, would fuck half of Richmond. I never even claimed to love any of those chicks, never even spent the night with none of them hos. Yeah, I took them to the hotel, but soon as I finished, I left. And that coming over to my house, laying up in here, that shit is dead! You da first girl that ever even been over here before. I don't play that shit."

"I hear you talking," she said nonchalantly, but her ears were wide open listening.

"This ain't talk. I'm just keeping it real. I am not going to lie. There have been times when I called my comrades and told them to go up to the hotel room and hit a chick I just got finished knocking off. They'd go up there, and for a few dollars the chicks would give it up. That's how much I cared for them. I didn't love none of them hos. Yeah, I gave them a few dollars, but that's why I gave them money so I won't have to see them until the next time. It's a business move. I never even kissed them hos, hugged them, or nothing. Broads think I'm cold, but I'm not. I just don't need them to feel attached to me in no kind of way."

"Is that right?" she said, smiling, joking on him for being modest.

"Look on da real, I don't have to campaign for no girl. Shit, I'm one of Richmond's most wanted niggas. But I don't want them. I want you! I wanna be here for you. I want to try my hand at this relationship-type shit wit you."

"Look, all that sound lovely. I mean that whole spill is big, but I don't know if I can let a nigga have my heart. I promised my mother about two years ago that I would never let another man have my heart."

"What is it? I mean, what is the big deal? Do you hate men? Shit, do you need to tell me you bi or something?" he asked.

"*Helllll nahhh,* it ain't shit gay about me! I am strictly dickly!"

"Well, then what is it then? Let a nigga know what time it is, 'cause this cat-and-mouse shit, I ain't feeling."

Bambi was quiet for a while. He gave her a cold look, and she said, "It's just . . ." She took a deep breath and continued. "It's just every single man I've ever loved, every man I let get close to me, has wound up hurting me. It's been like that my whole life, it seems, and I don't want to take another fall."

"Damn, baby, tell me all about it. I'm going to show you that I'm going to be the man you need me to be. Whatever those dudes lacked, I got."

"I hear you talking. Shit, you must plan to fill some big shoes, then."

"Tell me about every dude that ever crossed you, then."

"It's too much to get into."

"Well, I got years to listen to what you got to say, because I am not going anywhere."

She inhaled and was silent for a minute.

"Well, first it was my dad. He made up all kinds of excuses why he doesn't and won't claim me. He feels my mother trapped him."

"That's some ol' cop-out type shit," Lynx said after smacking his lips, sympathizing with her.

"I know, but it was also because he had a wife and kids when he got my mom pregnant, and he's always said his wife would never accept me. But I'm like, what kind of woman wouldn't accept an innocent child?"

"A weak, insecure woman."

"When his wife did finally find out about me, she told my dad that she would make it a big scandal if he ever had anything to do with me. He was soooo concerned with his career that he never had a thing to do with me. He only sent checks, but other than that he was never a part of my life. There was never any father-and-daughter picnics that I could attend. He never came to pick up any of his Father's Day cards that I would make for him. I never got to go for ice cream with Daddy Dearest. I never had my daddy to lean on, to protect me from the mean world, or to school me when niggas tried to play me, nothing! I mean, I didn't turn out bad, but I bet I would have turned out better had my dad been a part of my life."

"Well, baby, don't worry, because I'll claim you. If I have to, I'll rent the Goodyear blimp to let the whole world know you're mine! I'll be a crutch when you need me to lean on. We can go get ice cream. I'll protect you from the evils the world tries to send your way. I'll school you to whatever game you need for the outsiders. Next . . ."

His promises made her feel good, but could he keep them? Or more importantly would, he?

"Next, there was Douglas 'the Doo-doo' Dames."

"What did he do?"

"He used to live up the street from me when I was a kid, and our moms used to carpool together every since we were in nursery school. He used to come over my house to play and act like he was my brother, but whenever we were around the other children at school, it was a whole 'nother story. He was mixed, and he fit in with those white kids better than I ever could. Once we got to school, to score his own brownie points he always cracked on my dark complexion: 'She so black she sweat tar' or 'She so black that she could show up buck naked at a funeral and no one would ever know she was there' or 'She so black that when her momma put Vaseline on her, she looks like patent leather.' He would just go on and on, embarrassing me in front of the other kids with no shame."

"Baby, fuck him, the blacker the berry, the sweeter the juice."

"Yeah, that's what my grandma always told me."

"You know you my Black Beauty, right?"

"I hear you, baby," she said with a smile. "One Halloween we wore our costumes to school. He painted his face all black and drew some real big red lips and told everyone he came as me."

"If we ever see that nigga, I'm going to smack the shit out of him just for picking on my baby. "

She chuckled. The thought of someone wanting to get Douglas back for all the years he'd antagonized her made her feel better.

"Nah, I don't even know where he is now, but I have heard he is some bigshot in the military," she said.

"Baby, look, I want you to know that I care about you whether you are black or blue. Baby, you are so beautiful. Now, who else crossed you?"

"Then there was my ex, Reggie."

"What did he do?" he asked. She figured he had heard a few of the rumors about Reggie circulating around town, but he needed to hear it from her.

She exhaled and took her time. "I don't even want to talk about him, because I'll break down and cry."

"Didn't I tell you that you got my shoulder to cry on?" He could see the pain and hurt on her face. He took her in his arms and held her tightly as she burst into tears. He kissed her on her forehead and wiped her tears away.

"He made me into the person I am today. He hurt me the

most." She sniffed as she took a few minutes to get herself together. He continued to comfort her.

"First he introduced me to the street life. I mean, don't get me wrong, I wanted to know about it, but he had me living it, flipping birds while he was in prison. I held him down and believed in him like no other could. You hear me? I gave him all of me. I hustled for him, kept his money together, never jerking off a dime of it. I knocked the doors down to visit him while his ass was doing a funky-ass ninety-day bit. And instead of him giving himself to me, he gave himself to another man. The nigga turned out to be a homo-thug. Had me looking all stupid and shit, got me running down the jail seeing him every visiting day. Even convinced me to let a guard look down my shirt so I could get in to see him every visiting day, and the whole time as soon as he leaves the v-room . . . he probably went back and fucked Tom or Thomasina or whoever. Oh hell nah," she said.

"Baby, I feel you. That right there, you damn sure ain't got to worry about as far as I'm concerned. And if it makes you feel any better, a bunch of dudes do that shit. It's just that the girls don't ever find out," he said, trying to ease her pain a little.

"I didn't find out until I was at my engagement party. Shit, I loved this man and was ready to give my life to him. I was the last person to find out he was a faggot."

"Baby, some chicks never find out or find out when it's too late and they got AIDS. So be grateful for that."

"Oh, I have been tested. But check this out, you haven't heard the worst. He might as well have killed me, because I have to live with the fact that he almost killed my mother."

"What? What do you mean he almost killed your mother?"

"Well, you might as well say you killed her. He stripped her of the most important thing my mother felt she had to offer: her beauty." Bambi broke down and cried, whimpering while trying to explain the attack to him.

"So, where is he now?"

"He's doing time, but they got him on all this medication talking about he ain't right. But what is jail? Shit, he's free for real. A faggot in jail with nothing but dicks floating around—shit, he's in heaven."

A look of anger passed across Lynx's face, and that touched Bambi. She felt safe with him, as if he could be her knight in shining armor.

Just then her cell phone rang. At first she didn't answer it because she didn't want to interrupt the mood. But it kept ringing, so she finally answered it. A bartender informed her that her mother was drunk and had passed out in one of the bathrooms. She hung up the phone and gathered her clothes, saying, "Look, I've got to go take care of something important."

"At this time of night? I'm going, too." Lynx sat up in the bed.

"No, you can't."

"Yes, I'm. I'll drive you." He got up and slipped on his jeans.

"No, you can't go, Lynx, for real. I've got too much drama, and I don't want to drag you in on it."

"Baby, I already told you. Yo drama is my drama. You got beef, I got beef. If it's with a bitch, then we'll double-bank that ho," he assured her as he slipped on his Prada sneakers. There was something about Lynx and the way he handled her that made her want him more. He listened to her, he comforted her, and he accepted her for who she was. And when he had to put his foot down, he didn't hesitate to do so.

She sat down on the bed. "Look Lynx, I never finished telling you. After my mom was burned, she turned to the bottle."

Lynx looked at her. "Okay."

"I mean she drinks like crazy and doesn't know when to stop. Like now I have to go pick her up. She's passed out in the bathroom at Terry's Lounge."

"Well, what are we waiting for? We need to go and get her. Come on."

Lynx was everything she needed. Right then and there she made up her mind that she was going to give him the chance he asked for.

After they picked up Tricia from the club, Bambi decided to spend the night at her mother's, and Lynx stayed with her. The next morning she told Lynx, "You can leave if you want. I know you got stuff you need to do."

"Nah, baby. I got workers and employees just like you do. I can be away from the fort for a couple days if I need to. I'm here for you. I love your momma like she pushed me out her womb. And if you need to make any runs, I'll be right here for her until you get back."

She thanked him with a long, passionate kiss. She wondered if he knew that the way to a girl's heart is through her mother. *And damn,* she thought, *he done stole my heart in a big way.*

Lynx, Bambi, and Snowball spent the next two days with Tricia, who was an excellent cook and made dinner for all of them. Then Lynx stayed up half the night, playing cards with her and listening to Tricia tell childhood stories about Bambi. Tricia got to know Lynx, and for once she actually approved of a man who wasn't a doctor or a lawyer.

When Lynx finally left to do some business, Bambi asked Tricia, "Mommy, what you think about him?"

"I think he's a keeper, and he's worth you breaking our pact.

I am pretty sure your heart may be safe with him." Very surprised at her mother's comment, she knew that the misfortunes in Tricia's life had made her lighten up a little. Tricia realized for the first time in her life that money isn't everything. It's more important to have love and happiness.

Bambi hugged her mother. Maybe their luck was finally changing.

CHAPTER 19

Disappearing Act

After Bambi and Lynx left Tricia's house, they both agreed to spend one more day together away from everyone and everything. In the morning when they were in the shower, Lynx got down on his knees and lightly kissed Bambi on the butt, saying, "Don't ever tell me to kiss yo ass, because I already did that."

"Don't ever give me what you gave another, because I want what we have to be special," she said to him, astonished at how sweet he was.

Lynx walked Bambi to her car and kissed her on the cheek before allowing her to pull off. She rolled down the window as he strolled over to his truck and said, "Tonight you can come and stay over at my place."

"What, finally I get to come to your house?"

"Well, my little humble apartment. I moved out of the house when I left Reggie."

"Well, I don't care if it's a one-room shack. As long as I'm with you, I'm cool."

"I'm going to call you later and give you the address and directions."

"Call me when you get to work," he instructed her.

"I will, but I gotta go home first; then I am going to the office."

Three hours later Bambi headed to the office, and when she arrived Zonna came to the door. "Girl you've got a big-ass vase of flowers in here."

"For real?"

"As a matter of fact you got two dozen roses in one vase, and then about an hour later another delivery came for you with another dozen."

She ran to the phone to call and thank Lynx, but it went straight to his voice mail. For the rest of the day, every hour on the hour, flowers continued to arrive. Not just roses, but violets, forget-me-nots—heck, the office began to look like a florist shop! She continued to try to call Lynx, but all she got was his voice mail. When the eighth delivery arrived, the card read: "The eight weeks we've been together have been nothing but the best . . . simply because I have spent them with you. I've got something big planned for us tonight!"

She read the card three times before she tried to call him again. This time when she called, the voice mail was full. She waited and waited for his call—but it never came.

After a week she tried to call again, but she still got no answer. She was sick to her stomach from missing Lynx. She had no choice but to crowd her days with things to try to keep her mind off of him. But that didn't work. After a few days of his phone going straight to voice mail, she began blocking her number when she called—and still it went to the voice mail. Finally after a month went by, his phone was disconnected. She rode past his house, but his truck wasn't there. She was convinced that karma had finally kicked in. Lynx had played her.

Why am I kidding myself? I've got to chalk this up as a lesson. He got me. I guess this is my payback from all the dirt I've thrown, playing niggas for weak. I guess the saying "What goes around comes around" is true, after all. Damn, what the hell was I thinking? I slipped up again. I gave this nigga all of me. I believed in him, and he only looked at me as "a wham, bam, thank you ma'am." Shit, I might as well give myself a quarter, because I played myself.

Again Bambi's heart had been shattered. Even though they had only spent eight weeks together, she had been without a man so long that she had let herself get used to Lynx being around. That alone injured her the most.

She looked at the caller ID for the next few days as the phone rang and rang, but she never answered her friends' calls. She didn't feel like explaining to them that she had been left high and dry. She knew they would understand, but she felt too embarrassed to tell them. At first she couldn't sleep at all, tossing and turning missing Lynx. Then for the next few nights she took Tylenol PMs so she could get to sleep. Snowball could sense that something was wrong, so he cuddled with Bambi. As much as she wanted to cut all ties from Lynx, Snowball was the only connection she had to Lynx, and she treasured him.

Finally a few days went by, and she checked her messages. She heard Egypt: "Hey, girl, I know you are probably hanging out wit yo dude, and I ain't mad at cha. But holla at yo girl. Give her some details of how life is with the real thing instead of a big ol' dildo."

She wanted to smile, but she only cried, and somehow she dialed Egypt's number.

"Getting away from good dick ain't easy?" a happy Egypt answered the phone. She saw it was Bambi calling from the caller ID.

"Hey." Bambi could barely get it out as she broke down and started crying.

"What's wrong?" Her joking manner turned serious.

"He left me . . . ," she managed to get out in between whimpers.

"What happened?" Egypt asked.

"I . . . I . . . don't know. He just left me."

"Hang up. I'm going to call you from my cell phone. I am on my way over there."

When Egypt arrived at Bambi's house, she was wearing some short-short Levi's cutoffs and a T-shirt that she must have spilled bleach on somehow. The T-shirt almost covered her shorts, making it look like she had nothing on under the T-shirt. She had on some white slouch socks and a pair of wheat-colored Timberland boots. She barged through the door.

"Get yo shit on! Take me over this nigga's house. We 'bout to double-bank his ass. I don't play when it comes to my friend, and nobody asked him for his lies. Lying-ass nigga," she said, tying up her shirt in a knot on her stomach.

Bambi smiled a little and wiped her tears away.

"Girl, I am not playing. I'm tired of playing with these men-folks. You hear me? As soon as he come to the door, I am gonna hit him dead in the lip," she said, throwing a punch into thin air as if she was practicing how she was going to hit Lynx. "And as soon as I pop him, you come and kick him right in his balls. And he'll fall over, and when he do, we gonna get him on the ground and start stomping the shit up out of him. I am dead serious."

Bambi laughed, but Egypt was serious as a heart attack.

"You were fine. He pried his way into yo life and he want to do a disappearing act. He don't decide when he wanna give somebody the boot. We gonna give him the boot—this Timberland boot right up his ass," she said, kicking into the air like she was playing kickball.

Egypt had Bambi hyped, and she too slipped on her Timbs. They drove over to Lynx's house and banged on the door. Of course, they didn't get an answer, but it made Bambi feel a lot better. She realized the longer she didn't hear from him or ride by his house to see if his car or truck was there, the faster she would get over him.

I guess the principles of drug rehab apply here. You have to go cold turkey. You have to just leave it all alone. You can't just dip and dab and think you'll get over it.

Two months later at the office, Bambi interrupted a conversation she was having with Egypt to head into the bathroom. She leaned over the toilet and threw up her breakfast. What was going on? She didn't feel like she had the flu, but this was the third day in a row she couldn't hold anything down.

"Girl, we're going to da drugstore right now," Egypt said, holding Bambi's pocketbook and keys when Bambi came out.

"What for?" Bambi asked, trying to act as if she felt fine.

"What for? What you think? To get you a EPT test," she said as she held the door for Bambi to come out behind her.

They got the kit that day, and the little stick came back blue for "baby." Bambi wanted to crawl into bed and never come out. She knew she must have fallen hard and deep when she realized she'd actually been having unprotected sex with Lynx. She beat herself up mentally with her head laid on the table crying. No matter how much she tried to get him off her mind, the only words that she heard were the lyrics of DMX's song, "I'm slipping," playing over and over in her head.

If she went through with this, who would help her raise the baby? Her mother was too busy hugging the bottle to play Grandma. She saw her mother's struggle and decided there was no way she was going to put her child through the life that she had endured without a father. No, she knew if the saying "A girl's gotta do what a girl's gotta do" had ever been true, it was right then and there. She got on the phone that day and made a doctor's appointment.

Three days later Egypt went with her to the doctor's office. In the car, Egypt tried to say whatever she thought would stop the tears from rolling down her friend's face, but nothing seemed to work. They sat in the parking lot of the clinic for fifteen minutes as Bambi pulled herself together.

The nurse asked her if she needed anything to help her relax, but Bambi said no. She just wanted to get it over with. She hadn't expected the abortion to be painful, but it was. She had no idea if it was from the pain of the actual procedure or the hurt in her heart. Egypt took her back to the apartment—the apartment that Lynx never did get to visit. Bambi wondered if he was off with his crew, laughing about what a fool she had been and about how he had played her before she played him. Well, she had indeed learned her lesson. When it came to men, the only business she had to tend to was waiting for them to slip, and when they did, she'd bankrupt them.

That night she slept, but she woke up about 3 a.m. with cramps so bad she thought she'd have to go to the ER. She took some Tylenol and it got a little better, but the next day she woke up in a pool of blood. When she took a shower, big clots of blood fell on the shower floor. Something had to be wrong; she was bleeding uncontrollably.

"I'm sorry, but you're going to need a partial hysterectomy," the doctor told her when she finally went in to see him. "You won't be able to have children." He said it bluntly and coldly. The average person would have gone into some kind of emotional breakdown, but Bambi wasn't the average person.

Bambi nodded. Maybe God was punishing her. Maybe she should have had the baby anyway. She didn't want to struggle to raise a child without a father around like her mother had done. But if that was the case, she'd take her punishment like a woman. I don't want to bring any kids into this fucked-up world anyway, she thought.

"All right," she said to the doctor. "When can we do it?"

As soon as Bambi left the doctor's office, her cell phone rang. It was Amy. "Girl, you heard what happened to yo boy Reggie, down in the jail?"

"Nope, what happened?" The thought alone of something—anything—happening to Reggie down in the jail was like music to her ears, and she needed some good news right about now.

"Girl, this is fresh off the press. Your boy, or your girl should I say, was stabbed in the neck while he was in line in the rec yard. Don't you know they broke the shank off in him."

"For real?"

"Yup!"

"Is he dead?"

"Yup! And you know they don't give a shit who did it."

"Good for that nigga."

Bambi hung up her cell phone and got in her car. Reggie's death didn't faze her. She had lost her baby, and now Reggie's momma had lost hers. It was just another day in the jungle.

CHAPTER 20

One Hand Washes Another

Tricia sat at the bar in the Radisson hotel getting her drink on. With the liquor poured on demand, she did what she did best—sipped her Paul Masson and talked trash. She cracked jokes without thinking twice about anyone's feelings and said whatever she felt like saying. Although she was loud and boisterous, the bartender didn't dare have her removed. After all, she was his best tipper.

A sexy dude young enough to be her son sat beside her at the bar. He looked like he was in need of a laugh. He had a frown on his face and tapped his keys on the bar like he was thinking about something. Tricia leaned over and slurred, "Young gun, what's wrong with you? Pick yo lip up off the floor and tell the old lady who the heck is messing with you?"

He smiled at Tricia for trying to sympathize with him.

"You ain't no old lady," he said in an attempt to give her a compliment.

"Boy, I'm old enough to be your momma," she answered,

and clinked the ice in her glass, looking for the bartender. He was over at the other end of the bar messing with some ugly chick and she couldn't get his attention.

"Damn, I'd never believe that."

"I got a daughter your age."

His cell phone rang, and the young dude pulled it out of his pocket.

"Yeah," he answered. As Tricia eavesdropped on his conversation, it was apparent he'd become frustrated with the person on the other end. "Look, get me off. I can't stand an indictment for no bullshit-ass charge like that. Just tell me, are you going to be able to beat the charges if they indict me? Man, this is some bullshit. Look, man, get this mess straight. I'll pay whatever," he said as he hung up the phone. He shoved it back into the pocket of his Pelle Pelle leather jacket.

"Whoever it is messing with you, do you want me to go jack them up? Because you know I will," Trish said with a sweet smile as she picked up her keys off the counter like she was ready to go and fight the people for him.

"Nah, I can handle them," he said, sounding disgusted.

"Well, you want to tell me about it? And we can just talk shit and dog them out together."

He finally smiled and said, "Yo, Miss Lady, you wild as hell."

"You say you don't want to talk, you don't want me to fuck 'em up. Shoot, I was trying to help your pitiful-looking ass out. I could have given them the look of death, if you wanted me to. Lord knows I got it. All I got to do is look at them, and they'll back off."

"No, you don't! Beauty is in the eye of the beholder, and yo personality is genuine." He smiled at her. "Miss Lady, you cool as shit. I'm gonna be all right."

He looked at her key chain as she threw it back on the bar

and became puzzled and asked, "Who is this with you, yo sister?" He pointed to the other person on the key chain picture.

Tricia gazed at the key chain and said, "No, that's my baby."

"Yo baby?"

"I told you I was old enough to be your momma," she said, and gazed at the picture. "Pretty, ain't she?"

He shook his head with a devilish grin as his cell phone rang again. He talked briefly for a minute and hung up.

"Yo, bartender," he called out.

As he waited for the bartender she looked at his chain.

"This is a nice piece you got around your neck." She nodded her head, looking at how clear the diamonds were. "Star of David, huh?"

"Yup," he said with a smile. He seemed mighty proud of that necklace.

"Young 'un, what you know 'bout the Star of David?"

"Nothing. I just saw it and wanted it."

"Look, let the ol' gal school you. . . . The Star of David symbolizes the shield of protection for David. He used it to show God was protecting him from all directions. So it's supposed to protect you."

"Damn, you learn something new every day," he said, shaking his head.

"In the future you might want to research religious pieces before you buy them."

"Why must I do research when I can meet you for drinks and you'll just school me?" Just then the bartender walked up. The young dude went into his pocket, pulled out two one-hundred-dollar bills, and said, "Look, her drinks are on me tonight. Just take real good care of her."

"Why, thank you," Tricia said, pleased to know she was set for the night. "I'll get you next time."

"No, it's no problem. I've got to go make a run, but I'm always in and out of here, so I'll definitely see you around. Maybe even later tonight." He winked at her and walked out the door.

Tricia continued running her mouth, talking about every single person that walked through the door. She realized she had to pee, so she stumbled to the bathroom, but didn't quite make it in time and pissed on herself.

"How 'bout you let me call you a cab?" the bartender said when she came back and ordered another drink.

"Hell nah," Tricia said, looking around for someone to cuss out.

"Then I'm going to call your daughter," he said, and turned to the phone.

"That's right. Call Bambi. Tell her that her old drunk momma has pissed herself and needs to go home. And gimme another drink to go. You little snitch! You know what snitches get? Snitches get stitches."

The bartender shook his head, but fixed her one more drink after he called Bambi to come get her. Tricia took the drink and her purse and started toward the door. She tripped and spilled the drink all over her pale yellow silk shirt.

"Guy dammit!" she screamed.

Just then a strong hand reached down and helped her stand up.

"Hey, Ms. Lady, let me help you."

Tricia looked up and saw the young gun holding on to her arm.

"I thought you was gone somewhere," she said.

"I finished my business and came back. Why don't you let me help you to your car?"

"I don't need any help," she screamed, pulling her arm away from him.

"I know you don't need no help," he said. "Still, at the same time, maybe it wouldn't be a bad idea for me to just help you make it to your car."

"I ain't no gotdamn fool. I ain't driving in my condition. My daughter is coming to get me, and she need to hurry up. The li'l black heifer."

"Look, I just want to help you like you wanted to help me when people was messing with me. You know one hand washes another," he explained in a calm voice as he led her to a chair. "So, sit right here. I'm going to get some napkins so I can help you clean this spill off your blouse."

Tricia sat in the chair, feeling the place slowly whirling around her. She wondered where Bambi was. She didn't stop to think that it would take at least twenty minutes for Bambi to get there from her place.

Quickly returning, he said, "Look, is your daughter name Barbie or something?"

"You mean Bambi," she said.

"Well, I just talked to her, and she told me to get you out here. I'm going to take you to meet her. She don't want you around here. You know how she feel about you and how much she love you, don't you?" he said in a charming voice.

Tricia never thought twice. As the young man helped her into his candy apple red Benz, she noticed something dangling from his neck.

"What the hell is that?" she asked. "Are you a Jew?"

He just smiled and said, "That's a Star of David. You told me that, remember?"

Tricia shrugged and mumbled something as the helpful young man shut the door.

The next day around noon, Tricia was awakened by a cleaning lady knocking on the door. She had slept through the night and chalked it up to the fact that she must have passed out. When she opened her eyes, she could not believe what surrounded her—on the walls, on the ceiling, on the mirror, everywhere. There were photos of her that were so horrible, she froze. She finally peeped out the door and told the woman, "Please, my ride is on the way. Just let me stay here for another hour. I promise I will be out. My daughter will pay you extra when she gets here."

She picked up the phone.

"Bambi, it's Momma," she slowly said.

"Hey, Ma, we came looking for you. The bartender told me you went home with one of your drinking partners."

"No, I had a date, and the date left me for whatever reason. You need to come get me. Now."

"Ma, I'm on the way. Just tell me where you are."

She looked on the phone for the address to the hotel as she tried to get the pictures down with her in the compromising positions, but after she tried to pull them from the wall, she realized that they had been glued. Disgusted, fed-up, and angry with herself, with the young dude, and most of all with drinking, she couldn't get her mind together. She lay back down. As she lay on the bed crying hysterically, flashbacks came to her of the many men she had played, swindled, scammed, or hurt. At that moment she realized that truly what goes around comes around.

Tricia was more than sixty miles away, and Bambi burned up the road to get to her mother. When Bambi arrived, to her surprise, her mother had a bald head. "Ma, what happened to yo hair?"

"Look, don't come in here. Wait outside until I am ready."

Bambi pushed her mother aside and forced her way in. She was shocked by what she saw.

"I don't believe this shit!" she screamed. "Oh my God, I am going to kill this nigga. How could someone be so fucking cruel? Who was it, Ma? Tell me his name!"

Tricia shrugged her shoulders because she didn't know. She knew she had met him in a club, but she'd never asked his name.

"He gonna get his. Damn!"

Bambi paced the floor as her mother sat crying.

"Baby, I am soooo sorry. It's all my fault," Tricia whimpered.

Bambi hugged her mother. "Mommy, you've got to stop this drinking. I know you hurting and rightfully so, but Mom, drinking is running away from your problems, not solving them."

Tricia blew her nose and nodded her head.

"Baby, I promise you, I am going to stop," she said.

Bambi got up and began peeling the poster-size pictures from the wall. It turned her stomach to see her mother in such compromising positions, looking nothing short of a ten-dollar whore. When she walked in the bathroom, she saw that someone had taken her mother's mocha-color lipstick and written NO HARM INTENDED TO YOU, BUT TELL BAMBI PAYBACK'S A BITCH!

Bambi then looked at her mother's forearm and saw a tattoo,

which was something that her mother had always considered disgraceful.

"Mommy, what happened? When did you get that?" she asked.

Tricia had been too busy feeling sorry for herself to notice the large tattoo that covered the majority of her forearm. It was a crown with a heart that read SMOOTH, MY KING; ALWAYS AND FOREVER.

Nothing could describe Bambi's anger at the moment. She hoped that karma really did exist and that one day Smooth would get his.

"He only did this to you to get back at me. He's crazy," she told her mother.

Tricia looked up at Bambi dumbfounded.

"What do you mean, to get back at you?" she asked.

"Mommy, it's a long story, and I don't feel like getting into it."

Bambi finished getting the rest of the photos down and took her mother home. As she drove, she knew that Smooth would just keep bringing the noise, doing everything he could think of to hurt her. So at that point she said a silent prayer, asking God to take care of Smooth for her.

That day Tricia poured every bottle of wine, beer, and hard liquor right down the drain, and Tricia never had another drink. No rehab, no AA, nothing. She kicked it cold turkey.

CHAPTER 21

A Sucker Is Born
Every Day

Bambi sat in the first-class section of the 757 on her way to Dallas, Texas. As she looked down at the little houses and patches of ground below, she thought how lucky she'd been to get this contract to arrange events for Ted, a young man whom she had met at Tall Daddy's party. Ted was very connected and was heir to his parents' Texas Royce dealerships.

On her first night there, Ted took her to a fancy steak restaurant. She walked inside and saw what looked like young rich men and even richer old men.

"Damn, I know for a fact I can find three or four black J. R. Ewings in this place here. Can a bitch be Sue Ellen or something?" she said to herself as she handed her silk jacket to the maitre d'.

After they ordered, Ted escorted Bambi to the ladies' room. A deep male voice call out her name. "Bambi."

Who could that be? No one here in Texas knows me.

"Bambi Ferguson? Is that you?" The voice got closer.

Bambi turned around and at first didn't recognize the attractive guy in the army uniform, decked out with numerous campaign ribbons. She zeroed in on the nametag that read DAMES. It was Douglas Dames, the guy who had tortured and bullied her as a youngster.

"Small world, huh?" he said, grinning down at her.

"You got that right."

"What are you doing in this neck of the woods?" Douglas made conversation as if they were indeed old friends.

Bambi hesitated. "I'm actually here on business, and you?"

"Well, believe it or not, I'm now an army captain, actually a pilot, and I'm stationed at Fort Hood, which is a couple hours from here. I'm leaving in a couple days for Korea, where I'll be stationed for about three years." He said this with his chest stuck out in an attitude of undisguised pride.

"Oh, really," Bambi said. She wanted to cuss him out, but she did not want Ted to see her lose her cool or act unprofessional.

"Bambi, you are so beautiful. You look so good. The years have really been good to you," Doug said.

I know this; you don't have to tell me, she thought, but she said, "Why thank you so much. That means so much coming from you."

"Listen, let's keep in touch. I'd love to write you while I'm in Korea. Letters from anyone from back home are always a great pleasure."

Motherfucka, I know you don't want black-ass Bambi to write you a letter. Not the girl who is so black that she showed up at night school and was counted absent, let you tell it. Today is your lucky day, because if anyone but Ted was standing right there I would have royally cussed your half-breed ass out. Do you know how much pain and anguish you caused me, how insecure you al-

ways made me feel? And you got the nerve to ask me can you write me?

These thoughts raced through her mind, but she only smiled and said, "Oh, okay," and handed him her business card, and then introduced him to Ted.

"Make sure you write to let me know you had a safe arrival," she said as she walked off and entered the restroom.

Ted stood outside the door, continuing a conversation with Doug. When Bambi returned, Doug promised to call and returned to the table with his military buddies.

"He seems like a nice fella. He's a captain, and at such a young age. Very impressive. Wow! He must really be gung ho. He certainly speaks highly of you, Bambi."

I think I am about to throw up, she thought.

Back in Richmond, Bambi juggled planning all the parties she had contracted there while continuing to work her butt off putting Ted's birthday party together in Texas. During this time she received several letters from Douglas—letters she made no effort to respond to in any way. One letter stood out and caused her to wonder. It began,

> *Dear Bambi,*
> *I am not sure if you received any of my letters. I have written you a few over the past two months. I know you are busy and probably have been traveling a lot, but please write me back because I am getting a bit worried not hearing from you.*

Yeah right, you wasn't worried about me when you were teasing me, were you? she thought as she continued to read the letter.

*Anyway, well, things are going great for me. It's very differ-
ent here for me. I wish you could come and visit. There is so
much shopping for a woman to do. I see some things that I want
to ship home—furniture, etc.—but I won't do that for a while.
I usually just go to work and shop at the PX. I like being here
because of the extra pay, and there's really no need in me spending like I would if I was in the States. So basically the money
that I am making is just sitting in my account adding up,
which is always a good thing.*

"Not for long, old buddy!" Bambi said to herself. "Because
you reap what you sow!"

At this point she stopped reading his letter. He had given her
all the information she needed. She grabbed a pad and pencil
and began to write Doug a sweet letter, pouring every ounce of
her charm in it. When he received her response, he was over-
joyed to hear from her. This started an exchange of letters, pictures, and cards on a regular basis. Bambi put Ruby in charge
of souping up the letters after she dictated them to her. Writing
was Ruby's specialty after being in prison for so long, and de-
ception was right up her alley.

Doug's mother had passed away a few months before he and
Bambi had run into each other in Texas, and he was her sole
beneficiary. With this money and his pay from the military, he
was in a pretty solid financial state. Bambi told him that she
knew of some good investments, and he began faithfully sending Bambi money. Soon he had filled out a form that allowed
money to be transferred directly to her account on his paydays.
When he got paid, Bambi was paid.

It wasn't long before Douglas was sprung. He lived to receive
Bambi's letter. He told her that all his thoughts were of the two
of them together. He even began talking about marriage and

children with her, obtaining a promise from her that she would wait for him to return to the States.

Because of the game she and Ruby were running on him, he was totally taken.

"Girl," Ruby said with a laugh, "that man can't eat, breathe, or take a dump without thinking about you."

Before long Bambi knew she had Douglas eating out of the palm of her hand while at the same time her other hand was deep into his pockets, getting a monthly allowance and all tailor-made clothes and other items that could only be found in Korea.

Doug sent a picture of some wedding rings in a magazine to Bambi, talking marriage and suggesting this was the ring he wanted her to have. Bambi surprised him by purchasing a set of rings. She sent one to him with a note that said yes, as if he'd formally proposed. The plan was that they would marry shortly after he returned to the States.

Shortly after sending him the ring, Bambi sent Doug a picture of a beautiful white house. Along with this she sent a hand-drawn picture of a stick family to symbolize their future family.

The next time Douglas called, Bambi cried over the phone about how the bank had turned down the loan to finance their dream house. A house she wanted him to believe she just had to have. He responded, "Do you think my info will help?"

"I'm not sure if that would help, especially with you overseas. How would you even be able to sign the papers from there?"

"Well, I'm sure with the help of my commanding officer, something can be worked out," he suggested.

"I don't know . . . Maybe we should just wait till you return home."

"No, I won't be home for another two years, and I want you to have everything in order when I get there. I'll figure something out. When I call you, I'll have a better idea of what we can do. Remember now that I won't be able to call you for another two to three weeks because of my training schedule, okay?"

"I know."

Doug had once told Bambi that he expected to have the finer things in life and to have the Joneses strive to keep up with him. He was eager to start their new life together, and he bought right into Bambi's story about her having trouble getting the house financed. Already he had sold some of the land his mother had left him to give Bambi money for the down payment on their dream house. He had also located some of the most exquisite furniture that money could buy. Her favorite piece among the things he'd shipped back stateside was a unique coffee table. To the naked eye the oversized coffee table was big and round, but once the right button was pushed and a combination was punched in, it opened and could be used as a chest for storage. Bambi used it as a hope chest and stored her precious photo albums and other personal and valuable items in it.

Once Bambi had everything in her name and all the documents were final, the excuses started rolling in.

"I've been so busy, fixing this and that on the house. They sold me a handyman's special and didn't even tell me."

She whined to him about how nothing was going right and how she needed money for this or that to get things fixed up. Doug was caught in her web and powerless. He didn't know what to do or what direction to take things. Shoot, he was half a world away from her. And Bambi knew there was nothing he could do. So she continued taking advantage of him while bouncing back and forth between Richmond and Dallas. Her business was thriving, and with the extra money from Doug, Bambi and Egypt went on a trip to Vegas for a week and another trip to Vail that winter to go skiing. Bambi also bought her mother a complete set of furniture and told her it was "compliments of an old friend."

Bambi knew she had to continue to string Doug along, and she did with finesse. She wrote him letters and sent him cards all the way up to one month before he was due to return home on leave for a few weeks before going back.

When he tried to call her, her number was disconnected. All the letters he sent her were returned to him. When he returned to Houston on leave, he discovered the address he'd been writing to, which was supposed to be his six-bedroom, six-bathroom home, was actually a two-bedroom corporate suite Bambi had rented while doing business in Houston. The white upper-middle-class woman who answered the door told him that she had been living there for the past month and that she had no idea who or where the former tenant had gone.

Doug stopped at the rental office to inquire about Bambi. The rental clerk asked, "What's your name?"

He told her. The clerk said to him, "Ahhh, yes, she said you'd be by. Wait one minute. I have something for you." She handed him a metallic red envelope that had a beautiful red-and-white bow on it. He smiled at how it was perfectly wrapped. He was sure this was the good news he was waiting for.

He opened it.

I guess now you understand that all those sayings are true—that you do reap what you sow and that what goes around, comes around, and especially that every dog has its day.

It really didn't have to go down like this! You had nine

*months to make things right. All you had to do was apologize
for tormenting me in school, but you never did! How dare you
think that we could ever be anything together after you did
every mean, hateful thing that you could think of to hurt my
feelings just so you could impress your little prep-school so-called
friends who never liked your half-breed ass anyway. Well, I told
you a long time ago, I think when we were in the fourth grade,
that I was going to get the last laugh. Well, guess what, motherfucker???? I am laughing all the way to the bank with YOUR
MONEY!!!!!*

*And guess what, there ain't a damn thing you can do
about it!*

XOXO!!

Then Doug saw that Bambi had put her red lipstick on and
kissed the envelope. At that moment all he could do was break
down and cry. There had been so many times that he had
thought about apologizing to her, but since she'd never men-
tioned it, he hadn't seen the sense in bringing it up. Now he
stood there broken. He wanted to end his life right then and
there, he was so in love with her.

In the meantime, back in the outskirts of Richmond, Bambi
sat in her brand-new half-a-million-dollar home, built from
the ground up according to her specifications. The rental agent
in Houston called to confirm that Doug had received Bambi's
letter and described for her blow by blow how he had reacted,
crying as if he had just lost his best friend. Bambi had tipped
the agent handsomely to perform this duty on her behalf. With
Doug still in the service, there wasn't anything he could do.

He'd have to go back to Korea. Would he come after her when he got out? Bambi didn't know and didn't care.

Bambi toasted herself. "To the sucker born every day. . . ."

"Hold on, let me propose a toast," Egypt interrupted. "To my homegirl, my li'l sister Bambi, who has taken the game to the ultimate level, who didn't even have to get off of her poonannie; what you did was sell some words and some dreams, breaking a dude down and draining his pockets."

"Shit, I'd drink to that," Ruby said.

"Nooo, noo, let me get my two cents' worth 'cause truly it's true, there's a sucker born every day," Bambi said as she raised her glass to toast, but deep down inside she didn't feel the sweet satisfaction she thought she would.

CHAPTER 22

Birds of a Feather

Bambi set up an office in Dallas, Texas, and it was bringing in big bucks. She rented a charming three-bedroom house in Dallas for Ruby, who would coordinate things there. Ruby decided that Texas would be her chance at a new beginning. No one knew anything about her in Texas, so she could build her life and not have to deal with any of the issues from her past. However, some things Ruby couldn't escape—including the impact that prison life continued to have on her even though she was free.

Bambi and Egypt banged on Ruby's door. Bambi paced back and forth; she had to go to the bathroom really bad. When Ruby opened the door, Bambi ran past her and headed straight to the bathroom. She entered and saw that Ruby must have been in the process of getting ready to go herself, because the toilet seat was lined with toilet paper. Bambi used the bathroom, but seeing the toilet paper on the seat deeply hurt her because she felt that Ruby still was not free from her prison experience—not even in her own home.

Bambi decided to sit Ruby down in the living room for a heart-to-heart talk with her as Egypt sat in the kitchen reading the newspaper.

"Rue, you know I love you, right?"

"Yeah."

"And you know we keep it real with each other, right?"

"Yeah." Ruby nodded and then asked, "What's up?"

"Ruby, this is your place. You don't have to line the toilet of your own bathroom. You can't catch nothing from yourself. Ruby, this is yours. If it breaks, fix it. If you don't like it, get rid of it. I went through your bedroom, and you got food stored up all under your bed: can sodas, chips, and all kinds of snacks. Ruby, you have a kitchen with plenty of cabinet space and a refrigerator. Ruby, I love you and the whole nine, but come on now. You got money saved in a stash here, plus you got a bank account. You're not starving and can afford whatever you need or want. Now please tell me why you have sheets hung on your windows?"

Ruby studied the sheets on the windows as if she'd never noticed them before. But before she could answer Bambi, Egypt ran into the living room. "Girl, we need to go find us some funeral outfits."

"What?"

"Yes, hurry up. We got to go to the mall."

"What?" Bambi said, looking at Egypt like she was crazy.

"Yes, I need to get me a superchic black dress," she said, grabbed her pocketbook, and waited by the door.

"Who died?" Ruby asked, looking dumbfounded. "You say

a funeral, well, why you got smiles like you going to a party, then?"

"What other place to find a baller or shot caller than at another baller's funeral? And they call him Black Money, too. Then to top it off, he was out on a one-million-dollar bond. Shit, if a nigga can post a mill bond, he's worth some paper, and I know birds of a feather flock together. So I am going to be at that funeral front and center, honey."

"We don't know him, though," Bambi interjected.

"Shit, you think the family going to tell us to leave?" Egypt asked. "No, they don't know who he knows."

"B, I think she's right—there is going to be all kinds of money rolling in there to show their respect, not just hustlers but his other associates, too," Ruby added, seeming to be getting hyped, too.

"Y'all are crazy. How could you be happy about a funeral?" Bambi said, shaking her head at the both of them.

"Here, just read the write-up in the paper," Egypt said, handing Bambi *The Dallas Morning News.*

As Bambi read the front-page article out loud, Ruby stood over her, and Egypt smiled as if she'd just hit the Texas lottery.

"'Police have identified the body found by a housekeeper in the basement of a house yesterday as Michael 'Black Money' Stommer. The cause of death was a single gunshot to the head. There have been no arrests and are no suspects at this time. According to court records, Stommer was awaiting trial for crimes ranging from money laundering to the Continuing Criminal Enterprise Act.'"

Bambi put the paper down and looked at the other two with wide eyes.

"Girl, listen to this part right here," Egypt stated, excited as she picked up the paper and continued to read. "'He was facing life in a federal penitentiary and was out on a one-million-dollar secured bond.' Did you hear that, a one-million-dollar secured bond? Do you know what that means?"

Ruby without hesitation jumped right in and broke it down as if her girlfriends didn't know. "It means the nigga had to come up with the whole mill—not ten percent with the bondsman, not a million in property, but a million dollar for dollar in cash, baby. Not yo average dude can get out on a million-dollar bond. Now, that's some real high-post, baller-out-of-control, heavy-hitting type of shit," Ruby said.

Egypt continued to read. "'The funeral services will be held tomorrow. In spite of allegations of criminal activities, Stommer was well-known and influential in many legitimate aspects of the community, including several charitable organizations. Police officers will be on hand to control the expected crowd.'"

So they all agreed to attend the wake, the funeral, the burial, and the repass. They went by a florist, where each sent a beautiful arrangement to the funeral home. They shopped all day long. They went from the Galleria to Southbriar to all the elite boutiques in the Dallas area.

When the day of the funeral arrived, they were shocked at how star-studded it was. Not only the family but it seemed more than half of the funeral guests arrived in limos. And those who didn't have a chauffeured car showed up in the hottest, most expensive automobiles. Bambi felt out of place in her four-year-old Mercedes Benz, but then she remembered: It's not the cars, it's the stars in them. Besides, Ted's family owned that Rolls Royce dealership, and someday soon she planned to cash in on that connection.

Because attendance was more than the capacity of the large funeral home, they never got in to see the body the day of the funeral. It didn't matter, because they really had the best seats in the house. They stood outside with an excellent view, watching who went in and who came out. Most of the people were dressed to kill, but as at any event, one guy stood out in particular. The brother looked to be in his early thirties and was wearing black jeans, a T-shirt, sneakers, and a sports blazer. He was a beautiful shade of reddish brown. Standing about six feet tall, he had a slight beer belly. His hair was dark brown with ear-length dreads, which only added to his sex appeal. He was warmly embraced by the family as he offered his condolences. The way folks reacted to him, the girls wondered if he was some sort of celebrity. He didn't look familiar, not like anyone they'd seen on TV or in the movies. Still, there was an aura about him.

At the repass, which was held at a country club that the family had rented out, the people loosened up as they got liquor into their systems. Ruby met a few cats and Egypt wasn't doing too bad either, but Bambi had other plans. She had no intention of getting acquainted with anyone until she had an opportunity to meet Mr. Sports Blazer. She made eye contact with him and smiled. He smiled back, and when he did, she received a tap on her shoulder. Startled, she almost spilled her drink.

"I'm sorry, did I startle you?" Ted asked.

"Yes. Hi, Ted." She greeted him with a hug.

"What are you doing here?" he inquired.

Thinking quickly, she said, "I'm here to support my friend who knew the deceased."

"He knew people from some of everywhere. He certainly will be missed."

Just then Sports Blazer walked up. "What's up, Ted?"

"Nothing much, man. Business as usual," Ted said. "Oh, let me introduce you two."

You do that, Bambi thought, but only smiled.

"Loot'chee, this is Bambi, Ms. Party Planner Extraordinaire, from West Virginia."

Bambi was smiling so much she didn't even bother to correct him. She was used to it. Most people who never visited Virginia always seemed to get Virginia and West Virginia mixed up.

"Bambi, this is 'the Money Mogul,' 'the Black Donald Trump of Texas,' my man Loot'chee. They call him Loot'chee because that's what he does, rakes in the Loot'chee."

Loot'chee smiled as Bambi extended her hand and said, "It's nice to meet you." Bambi didn't take him too seriously. *Why would a guy deliberately brag on his money by calling himself Loot'chee as his nickname? I mean come on, get real! Well, what am I thinking? I am at the repass for a guy name Black Money, so I guess that's how dudes out here is rolling, huh?*

"Same here, baby," he said, shaking her hand. "Is this the honey that's been putting on all your lavish parties lately?"

"Yup, right here in the flesh," Ted boasted.

"Well, maybe I can hire you to plan us a private party, just me and you," Loot'chee said with a sexy grin.

"I'm going to leave you two alone on that note. Bambi, we'll touch base tomorrow," Ted said as he walked away.

Time flew as they sat at the repass getting acquainted. There was no doubt about it: There was definitely chemistry between the two of them. He went to get her a drink and brought it back. When he passed the drink into her hand, their fingers touched and stayed there for a few long seconds. Both of them wore big Kool-Aid smiles as they continued to talk.

CHAPTER 23

Daddy Warbucks

Right away fireworks flew between Loot'chee and Bambi. It could never be said that Loot'chee didn't have class. He wined and dined Bambi at only the best of the best restaurants in Dallas and flew her to nearby Louisiana, Oklahoma, and Arizona for fun-filled evenings riding ATVs. It was just what the love doctor had ordered for Bambi. Not only was he refined, with a unique style and flair, he also had a manner of advising and counseling her that always showed he had her best interests at heart. Of everyone that had ever influenced her life, his cheers for her to win were the loudest.

Bambi liked the fact that he was "all man," he was very independent, had his own money, and didn't expect anything from her. He didn't need her to put any cars in her name because he didn't have a license or anything of that nature. And what made it all the sweeter was the fact that he had his own place that *he* owned. He wasn't shacking up with his baby's momma or any woman for that matter. Although not all his income came from legitimate businesses, Bambi saw that he knew how to live and he had dreams and goals. He might have a hand in the drug trade, but she didn't think he'd stay there forever, especially if she had anything to do with it. For the first time since Lynx, she felt that she had finally met someone truly worthy of her attention.

Dag, they say God always comes right on time. I truly like Loot'chee. He is the perfect dude, and I damn sure can take him home to Momma knowing he'll pass her scrutiny with flying colors. The only thing that he is lacking is a big dick, but then his tongue game, now that's a different story. Between his money, the way he treats me, and the tricks he can do with that tongue of his, I can work with that li'l dick any day!

After they had been dating for six weeks, Loot'chee decided to get a guesthouse and game room added to his house; so he suggested to Bambi on the down low to get a luxury apartment for them to stay in together in Dallas since Egypt lived with her in her house in Dallas. She was able to rent an expensive, upscale apartment for the two of them in the suburbs of Dallas. Together they decorated it, picking out expensive furniture that he paid for without hesitation. At first it was awkward living with a man, but then because they were both constantly on the move traveling, living together in that apartment was not an actual burden. After a while, Bambi felt the apartment was a waste of money since they seldom actually stayed there. Still, she never complained since the rent was always paid. More often, Loot'chee would just show up at the house Bambi shared with Egypt in the middle of the night and slide into the bed with Bambi.

Loot'chee called Bambi from Las Vegas, where he was taking care of some business. Bambi was in her headquarters in Richmond.

"Hey, B, what's up, baby?" His sexy voice sent chills up her spine.

"Just sitting here thinking of you," she said freely.

"I was laying here thinking of you, too. Look, I want to see you."

"And you know that's likewise. I wish we could see each other," Bambi said to him in her sexy, seductive voice.

"Look, baby, call the travel agent on three-way and see what time the next flight leaves."

She got the travel agent on the line, who told them that the last flight scheduled to Las Vegas would leave in two hours. Bambi said, "That's not enough time, because I won't have any time to get packed."

"Don't worrying about packing," Lootchee said. "I'll take you shopping once you get here."

"That's what I am talking about! I sure wish I had a man like yours, Bambi," the travel agent cut in.

Lootchee gave the agent the info to pay for the ticket. And just like always, Loot'chee always seemed to fulfill her every wish and need.

The next day they had dinner at the restaurant atop the Stratosphere Tower, with a breathtaking view of the entire Las Vegas Strip. Loot'chee tried to make small talk, though Bambi seemed distracted. When he realized he didn't have her undivided attention, he commented, "Baby, I see your beautiful body is here with me, but where is your mind? What's running through your mind? What are you thinking?"

She smiled, pleased at how attentive he was to her, and said, "Nothing much."

"It's something! You'd be lying if you tell me nothing again. Baby, you know you can tell me anything," he said as he looked into her eyes and tried to reassure her.

Bambi was reluctant to pour her heart out to him as she had done over two years ago to Lynx. So she decided to lie. "I'm just enjoying the moment. And brainstorming about ways I can make my business even more lucrative than it already is. Then I'll be able to always live this life, with or without you."

"Well, baby, just keep on making me happy and being you. If you never change, then I'll never change and we'll always be happy. I'll make sure we live a life of luxury."

"Sounds good, but baby, you've got to understand, slinging cocaine doesn't guarantee a long life of luxury," she said, letting on that she knew that he had been doing something illegal as much as he tried to hide it from her.

"Baby, I want to share something with you, though I know you probably won't believe it. . . ."

"What?"

"I've been out of the drug trade since shortly after we met."

"Really?" she asked, surprised and happy at this new development.

"Yup, I've always known how to make money, a lot of money at that, in many different ways. I only flipped keys of coke because it was plentiful and at my disposal. Before I met you, I'd always thought about quitting while I was ahead, but I never did because nothing really motivated me in that direction." He grabbed her hand. "But then I met you and I knew you were the one for me. You gave me the desire and initiative to back up off of the life, and now I'm using what I have to go in a positive direction."

Bambi was speechless. Loot'chee pulled a small velvet box from his suit jacket. Bambi froze, unsure of what was coming next. Loot'chee opened the box, revealing a sparkling six-carat certified natural Colombian emerald. *"Oh my God!"* she exclaimed.

She started fanning herself; she couldn't believe her eyes.

"Emeralds are my birthstone," she said when she caught her breath.

"Baby, this ain't just any emerald. I had to order it from Fred Leighton over in the Bellagio."

When he said Fred Leighton, she knew that meant money—*big* money!

Damn this nigga must really dig me. I remember looking at one of those certified Colombian diamonds, but they were worth more than my car, cashing in at close to eighty G's. I know I got a winner on my hand any time he'd pay for a ring like this.

She admired the ring on her finger.

"Baby, there's one thing you need to know," he said.

"What?" she asked, never looking up from the bling-bling of the ring.

"This ring is not your engagement ring."

She never spoke but thought, *Damn if this ain't the engagement ring, then if it ever comes to that, I wonder what it'll look like?*

"This is a promise to you from me. I promise one day we'll get married. I'm just not ready for that yet, but I want you to know that I do truly adore you."

"Just remember, a promise is a promise," she said.

"I agree! All I want to do is bring safety, security, and happiness to your life. And the day I can't do that is the day that I want you to roll out."

"Just like that?" she asked.

"Just like that."

Later that night as they were lying in the bed, making pillow talk, he said to her, "Baby, I was just thinking over what you told me today about your business. I know a way you can make some major money with your parties."

"How?" She wanted to hear what he had to say.

"I know that in moving to Texas, you feel you took your business to its next level. Well, I have a foolproof way that you can make a lot more money. I'm talking about six-figure money. You know how entertainers and personalities do those cruises to the Caribbean?"

"Yup," she answered, wondering why she had never thought of the idea she anticipated he was about to present her.

"Well, you should put together a big party in Jamaica, get some entertainers to come through, have shows and specialty parties every night—sort of how they do on cruises. As a matter of fact, don't do Jamaica; do the Cayman Islands or something. Someplace people are just discovering. Our people are so caught up in running to Jamaica or the Bahamas, all they need is to be provided with an alternative."

"Don't forget Cancún," she added.

They both laughed.

"Ohh, that's such a good idea. Like one night I could have a bonfire on the beach, then like a singles' party, a pajama party, and so on."

"Yup, and you should have shows with big names attached to the ticket and everything. Book rappers, and include everything in the price of their tickets or at least the majority of everything in the tickets. Make it all-inclusive so they can really feel like they get a lot for their money. I'll help you promote it. Since I know folks all over the country, it'll be a cross-segment of the entire black population."

"I'm on it. I love the idea," Bambi said, sitting up.

"I gave you the idea. Now all you got to do is make it happen."

"And that I can do. The only thing is, it will require a bunch of out-of-pocket money." She sighed. "Putting down deposits and everything. There'll be contracting rappers to do the shows, ensuring hotels and airline accessibility, reservations—all this if we're going to do it really big."

Bambi's business was good, but she had an expensive lifestyle and took care of her momma; and she had Ruby, Zonna, and Egypt on her payroll. The money she had scammed off Douglas was long gone. She didn't have the kind of money available to fund this new venture.

"And if it ain't *big,* it ain't us. We've got to find the hottest hotel and reserve all the rooms and suites; put the whole hotel on lock. And baby, don't worry. I'll take care of whatever you need as far as finances. I just want to make you happy, and I know having successful parties is one thing that makes you happy."

On that note she jumped out of the bed, grabbed her notebook and pen, and started jotting all her ideas down.

CHAPTER 24

Party Time . . . Oooh,
It's Party Time

On the flight back to Richmond, Bambi put together an airtight marketing plan that made the 2,500-room hotel a *major* sellout event. She could have easily filled up another hotel, but she didn't want to bite off more than she could chew. She had to concentrate on the Who's Who she had already booked. She was well aware if she kept everything intact, this would be the beginning of something that could generate her millions. After all, it wasn't the quantity of people that she raked in, it was the quality of service she provided.

This was to be the biggest, most lucrative event she had ever pulled off—earning her money from the airlines, the hotels, and the transportation companies in Grand Cayman. Also, she would generate income from each state her people would be flying in from. Using her business savvy, she had added an additional hundred-dollar charge to each participant's ticket price so that she was able to supply a few tickets as giveaways to radio stations for contests to get publicity. Also she provided the promoter in each city with high-ticket sales with free tickets and complimentary luxurious suites to show her appreciation.

It only took three months to make the arrangements and make it happen. To her surprise she had a lot of rappers, ball players, shot callers, and heavy hitters who supported her event. With that being the case, the hoochies, sac chasers, gold diggers, and high-priced hookers all made sure that their tickets paid for themselves once they got there. She was very proud of herself for pulling off an event that could be compared to the Essence Music Festival. Most of all, she felt fulfilled to have a man like Loot'chee backing her efforts to the fullest.

After all of Bambi's guests were checked in, she decided to take a short break and admire her work. Sipping on a piña colada, she leaned over the balcony of her suite.

"Baby, you did it!" Loot'chee said as he came up behind her, gave her a kiss on her neck, and hugged her. They looked at the breathtaking beachfront view. "You really pulled this shit off. And you pulled this off in a matter of months! Damn, baby, you something else. You my superwoman, for real."

"I could never have done it without your support," she said, thanking him with a long, wet, juicy, passionate kiss.

"Oh, that reminds me," he said, letting her go. He entered the closet and pulled out his suitcase. She looked on as he opened the lining of the suitcase, which was crammed full of money. "Look, I need you to open up an account here and deposit this money in it. I don't want us to keep this money just laying around."

She was shocked at how much cash he had, but didn't let it show. *Damn, that's a lot of money, but why am I surprised? I know the caliber dude I am dealing with. He doesn't cut any corners, none whatsoever!*

She wasn't going to ask him for an explanation, but he gave

her one. "I wanted to make sure we had enough emergency money to cover us in case anything came up. Almost anything could come up. You know them foreign ma'fuckers don't really like Americans. Shit, I didn't want nobody to get locked up and we can't pay what we need in bribes and whatnot. I didn't want to be caught sleeping in a foreign country unless I knew I had our back covered. Plus I wanted to be certain we had enough money to cover the fees, deposits, and everything." Then he handed her a brochure which detailed all the duty-free shopping that the Caymans offered and added, "Not to mention, I know you're going to want to shop, shop, shop."

The next morning, Loot'chee purchased a briefcase to put the money in and Bambi went to the bank and opened up an account with no problem.

This first event was such a big success that on her last night there Bambi decided this would not be the last one.

"Loot'chee, I was thinking," she said as she got into the Jacuzzi in their lavish honeymoon suite.

"Aren't you always?" he said, joining her in the Jacuzzi and giving her a peck on her lips.

"I'd like to put together these events at least six times a year. Every other month. What do you think?"

"Damn, baby. Get yo money! I think that's all good, but at the same time, you don't want to burn out your people. Then it'll get all watered down."

"I know, but I am not talking about the same group of people. I am talking about different groups of folks. Like I'll put together one that only caters to the gay and lesbian community, then one for church folks and invite Shirley Caesar and other top gospel groups and singers. I can put together one for the forty-plus crowd with the Temptations and other old-school entertainers on the ticket. Do you feel me?"

He took her in his arms and said, "Baby, you know I feel you. That's one of the reasons I fucks with you so hard, because you always thinking ahead. You got dreams and want to go somewhere in life. Yo, I loves the shit outta you for that."

She smiled and thanked him with some good Cayman Island sex, even though she was tired from having to get all her guests checked out and safely to the airport. This was the only night that she was able to give Loot'chee her undivided attention. She was glad she had agreed to stay an extra day.

The next morning she was up at the crack of dawn.

"Why are you up so early?" Loot'chee asked.

"Baby, I've got a lot to do before we leave today. I've got to go to the bank and get the rest of your money out," she told him as she put on her lip gloss.

"No, baby, all you have to do is just wire half of the money to yo account in the States. Once we get back to the States you can just write me a check. It's no sweat. Keep the other money in the account here since this is something that you will be doing on the regular. Having an account here would definitely be a good thing," he assured her. "Plus, I wouldn't dare try to take that much cash back with me. Bringing it down here was risky enough."

This sounded all on the up-and-up to Bambi. Loot'chee patted the bed.

"How about giving me some breakfast in bed?" he asked. But Bambi just shook her head.

"As long as I'm already up, I'm going shopping." She kissed him and then took a purse full of money with her and walked out the door.

CHAPTER 25

Old Feelings Never Die

Home Sweet Home! Bambi plopped down on the bed, almost smashing Snowball, who was so happy to see her he couldn't stop purring. She was back in Richmond and tried to gather her thoughts. *I have so much to do. Coordinating these trips and traveling so much always takes such a toll on my body. I don't know how Loot'chee does it. Damn, I got to go to the bank to get Loot'chee a check from this last Cayman trip.*

Her thoughts were interrupted by the telephone. She looked at the caller ID; it was Egypt.

"Hey, girl," Bambi said, answering the phone.

"Hey, mamasita, what you doing?"

"Girl, tired as I don't know what," she said as she yawned and stretched.

"Look, I just got a quick question to ask."

"What?"

"When is your gay and lesbian event in the Caymans?"

"Ummm, on the twenty-sixth," she said with a yawn.

"Good, because I am going to need you to go somewhere with me. It's real important."

"Okay, no problem."

"But I need to drop by this form for you to fill out so you can go."

"Okay, but what kind of form?"

"It's just like a background form that you have to fill out so you can get in."

"E, where we going? To Fort Knox?" Bambi sat up in the bed to try to get this straight.

"No, but close," Egypt said, getting a little tongue-tied. "Ummmm, we're going to Atlanta."

"That's good. I can hit up the malls and the shops down there, but please tell me what you got up your sleeve. Why do I need to fill out a background check?"

"Because we going to see my Boo, my Big Daddy, my friend in the can in Atlanta."

"What?" Bambi asked in alarm.

Egypt quickly cut her off. "Look, he gonna pay for both of us to come—airfare and hotel plus give us some spending money and everything. He just doesn't want me to come down there by myself, that's all. And plus, I don't really want to go by myself anyway."

"And what am I supposed to do while you're visiting with the love of your life?"

"You can either sit and talk with us—you know I don't have nothing to hide from you—or I can tell him to put your name on one of his homey's lists. You can call him out, and he can keep you company," Egypt explained.

"Oh, hell nah! I am perfectly fine cock-blocking at the table with you," she joked. "Do you think I am about to go on a blind prison date? No ma'am, you got me all fucked up." She laughed as she played out the episode in her head. "You think I want be in there for at least five hours talking to a nigga I don't even like? *Oh, hell nah!*"

The day finally rolled around when she and Egypt headed to Hotlanta for the visit. Egypt was decked out to the fullest, Gucci down: Gucci pants with a plain white Gucci shirt, Gucci loafers and topped off with a full-length Russian mink coat. Her hair lay in the perfect bob, while her nails sported a French manicure.

On the other hand, Bambi was dressed down. She wore a Bebe sport fleece sweat suit and some Bebe sneakers to match. She threw on her big, puffy Bebe coat and was ready to visit the penitentiary. "Shoot, I ain't looking for no man. I'm not going to put on anything to work these niggas, or get their dicks hard. I'm going to be comfortable," Bambi told her friend.

When they got there, they entered a white building that housed a small waiting area and a metal detector. They were one of the first ones there, and the officer informed Bambi that she wasn't on Egypt's boyfriend's visiting list. At first, Bambi was going to leave; then a woman who had arrived right after they did instructed them, "Call the duty officer or the lieutenant. I have been coming to the system to see my husband for over thirteen years, and every now and again, they come up with a reason why my name is not on the list."

They did. The two guards were a little pissed when they asked to see someone in charge. It took another hour for them to get the situation straight, and then they got the word that Bambi's name had indeed been added to the list and she could go in. They were then told to remove their shoes and put them up on the security belt for inspection. After that they went through a metal detector, which meant if they had underwire in their bras or bobby pins in their hair, they would not be able to get in. It was at this point that they felt like they had better luck hitting the Lotto than getting in.

After that they were told that they had been randomly selected for a drug test. Both Bambi and Egypt had to rub a piece of paper that looked like a dry Stridex pad all over their clothes and then put it in their pockets. Then they had to give it to the guard to perform a drug test. The guard inserted the piece of paper into the machine, which emitted a long beep, indicating the test was positive for drugs. The officer shook his head, and said, "You can't come back for forty-eight hours."

"Oh, hell nah! Neither one of us do drugs, never have, never will."

"Well, maybe you were around someone who did?" the officer informed Bambi.

"No, we don't hang out with junkies."

"Well, the bottom line is you can't go in."

As soon as they were about to exit the door, they heard another long beep and then came a loud voice, "*Fuuuuck* no. Yo machine is on crack. Talking 'bout I done used crack cocaine. I am a nurse, and I don't use no drugs," one woman went on and on.

"Sir, I am not trying to give you a hard time, but if all three of us tested positive, we need to see the lieutenant," Bambi said.

They waited for the duty officer to come, and as they waited, every single person in that room tested positive for drugs.

"Now that right there don't make no sense," Egypt said. "You mean to tell me you seriously believe that that woman right there is using drugs? She's got to be seventy or eighty years old."

"It doesn't matter what I think; it's what the machine thinks," the officer said.

"Can't you use your common sense and figure out that all of us wasn't congregated in the parking lot smoking coke and weed before we came in?" Bambi asked the officer.

When the lieutenant finally arrived, he was surprised to see that Bambi and Egypt had not gone back yet. Together they acted as union foremen for the family and friends of federal inmates. Egypt started right in on the man.

"All these folks here have tested positive. This woman right here is eighty-five years old, walking with a cane. I am willing to bet you money she hasn't been using any drugs. Something is wrong with your machine."

"Well, I'll tell you, there's nothing I can do since we already logged the tests into the book. The rules are the rules. The bottom line is we paid a whole lot of money for this technology and—"

Bambi interrupted. "You mean we," she said as she pointed to all the folks who had surrounded the lieutenant. "We as federal taxpayers have paid a lot of money for this machine that is either broken or hasn't been serviced."

"That's right," the visitors said, getting a little hyped.

"Ma'am, understand I have a job to do here." The lieutenant was starting to get nervous. "What is it that I can do to make you understand it from my point of view? I don't want to have you leaving here in an uproar, but understand that we have rules."

"Well, listen, I only see one way of solving this, and I am sure we will all agree." It got so quiet that Bambi could hear a pin drop as everyone listened attentively. "Look, you say nothing is wrong with the machine, right?"

He nodded.

"Well, if you truly believe that, then why don't you take the drug test? If it comes back positive, then it's clear that something is wrong with the machine. However, if it comes back negative, then we will all leave in total silence."

He agreed and took the test. The long beep occurred again. Embarrassed, he was finally convinced that the machine was indeed broken. The visitors were all let in without any more harassment. One of the ladies asked Bambi, "Are you a psychologist?"

"No, I am a party planner. I have a business called Events R Us. If any of y'all ever need a party, let me know. I have some cards in the car. I'll give them to you when we leave."

"We think you are in the wrong business, considering how you manipulated his mind," another lady said, and the woman murmured in agreement, boosting up Bambi's ego.

Once they were finally in the visiting room, Bambi felt like a kid in a candy shop as she looked around.

"*Dammmn . . .* it's some fine-ass niggas up in this place here toooooday," she said as they sat down in the plastic brown chairs to wait for Shawn, Egypt's friend, to come out.

"They talk about it ain't no men—shit, that's because they all locked up. I tried to tell you there was some quality dudes here, but you don't listen to me." Egypt rubbed it in her friend's face.

"Maybe I need to organize 'love on lockdown' matchmaking systems. I know a bunch of chicks that must not be hip to all the fine-ass male specimens in this place. The niggas on the street ain't got nothing on these men! I don't see a ugly one in sight." Bambi looked around the room, inspecting every guy at every table. "Well, the one over there, but he is so clean-cut that I could work wit him," she told Egypt as she continued turning around in her chair, not caring what females were thinking of her as she stared in every man's face there. *Egypt ain't crazy, after all. Shoot, if I didn't have Loot'chee I'd hook up with a pen pal or two myself.*

"I feel like writing to the president asking him just exactly what the hell is he thinking, keeping all these fine-ass dicks—I mean men, and black men at that—behind bars in a cage," she told Egypt.

The next day Bambi dressed up more stylishly for the visit than she had the day before. She pranced around the visiting room, going to the snack machine and cooking a chicken sandwich in the microwave for Egypt and her man. About two hours into the visit, she went up to make some popcorn when she heard a deep, soft voice say, "Bambi." The sound was so sweet it made her underwear wet. She turned around and felt a shock wave when she saw who it was.

"Don't speak to me!" she snapped, trying to put up her guard.

"What? What the fuck you mean, don't speak to you?"

"That's what the fuck I said," Bambi said, as sassy as she knew how.

"Whoaaa, whoaa, watch yo mouth. I think you got it all wrong," Lynx tried to explain to her.

"I got it all wrong? Let me remind you, you were supposed to be the man of my dreams, to protect me—"

He interrupted her. "I still intend to be."

"You asked for one chance. I gave it to you, and you blew it. You decided to disappear."

"I can explain if you just listen."

"Look, I took you to meet my mother! I believed in you! And you played me just like the rest who you talked shit about and claimed to be so much better than."

"Listen," he said as he threw up his hands and looked into her eyes. "That day I left you, the feds picked me up. I was down at the jail and couldn't call your cell phone collect, and that's the only number I had for you. You were so busy with your guard up when we first met, all I ever had was a cell phone number for you. And when I got on a three-way to try to call your cell, you never picked up."

She knew he might possibly be telling the truth because she never answered numbers that didn't look familiar to her. So she listened as he continued to explain himself. The smell of his prison-bought Fahrenheit oil was practically winning her over just as quickly as the explanations he was running down to her. "Cook'em-up got locked up too, but he beat his case. When he got out, I told him to go by your business and let you know what was up, but he said they kept telling him you were out of town. I thought about you every day, and I still intend to do everything we planned."

She wanted to break down and cry, especially when she realized they could have had a two-year-old son or a daughter together. Tears formed in her eyes as she hugged Lynx. When they embraced each other, the white prison guard, who was a hard-looking woman, frowned in disapproval. The woman had extremely short hair and walked like a man. She came over and told them there was to be no physical contact and that they must return to their visiting table.

They both acted as if she hadn't said anything. "Who's up here visiting you?" Bambi asked Lynx.

"This shorty, but nothing for you to worry about."

"You mean to tell me you got a bitch up here visiting while you over here confessing your love to me?"

"I had to get someone to roll with me since you wasn't around. You trying to come hold me down? You trying to come through on a regular to see me? What's up?" He looked in her face and smiled.

"Go tell that bitch to leave *right now*! Tell her thanks, but her services are no longer needed now—that wifey Boo is here now. We appreciate her, and I'll gladly pay her if she need to be paid for any stamps, cards, photos, or gas money that she might have dished out. Then get her funky-ass name off your list, and when you send me the institution confirmation forms that her name is off, I'll do whatever I need to do to help make the time pass by until you come home."

He shook his head in disbelief, but before he could respond to her foul mouth, the female guard told them again, "Look, you two need to go over to your table, or I'll have your visit terminated."

Bambi stared at the woman for a minute and rolled her eyes, but she knew she had to bite her tongue or be put out, so she chilled.

"Look, I am going to take care of that, but make sure you got me," Lynx said.

"I got you! I promise!"

She studied Lynx's body language as he went back over to the table and told his visitor that she had to go. The girl looked over at Bambi and gave her a deadly look. Bambi looked right back at her and then waved to her and mouthed, "Bye-bye, beeatch!" along with a big Miss America smile. The girl read her lips and rolled her eyes. Bambi could see the smoke coming from her head. Bambi just smiled.

"What's going on?" Egypt asked.

Bambi happily explained and then said, "Oh, I need to make sure of his government name, so I can write him and get him my address." Bambi hopped up and went over to where Lynx was sitting and asked him his mailing name.

As Lynx's former visitor left, a new batch of folks came into the visiting room. Bambi played it off and sat down at Lynx's table. The female guard had left the visiting room right before Lynx's visitor had made her exit, and the other guards didn't even catch on to what was going on. Before they sat down, they went to take pictures. Then they sat and began to catch up. She could feel the other visitors' and inmates' eyes on them, wondering what was going on. She could not care less. She was with the man she'd always felt she was destined to be with.

The next two hours flew by, when a male guard yelled out, "Ten more minutes."

"Damn, time flies when you're having fun," she said to him, mad that time was up already.

"Look." He grabbed her hands and said, "You never asked when I was coming home or how much time I got."

"Because, Lynx, I don't really care. If you got twenty years, then I'll be coming here for twenty years."

He laughed. "That's sweet, and I'm glad I know where yo heart at, but I'll be leaving here for a halfway house in three months."

"For real?" She smiled. "I'll pick you up."

"Thanks, that'll be real good! You know if you pick me up, I am going to want to stop at a hotel to get some of that good stuff I've been missing."

She smiled and said, "I wouldn't have it no other way. I better be the last one you was with and the first one you going to be with."

"No doubt. Hope you can handle a nigga like me. All backed up. You know I am going to tear you up, right?"

"I hear you talking. All you going to do is come real quick as soon as you get a sniff of this."

"We'll see."

"Lynx, what you going to do when you come home?"

He sighed. "Look, I'm going to be real honest wit you. When

they picked me up the police took a lot of money from me. Some they reported and some is paying for their kids' college tuitions. I tricked up a lot of money rumbling with my case. I spent a couple hundred thousand dollars on lawyers, which I couldn't avoid because I had some real serious shit looking at me. I wasn't cutting no deals, and you know that snitching, that shit, was dead. But my lawyers beat the drug charges. This bitch-ass detective Columbo was on my back. This ma'fucka has been after me for years, since I was young. I'm talking thirteen years old. His whole existence revolves around trying to catch me. He thought he had me cornered, and honestly he basically railroaded me. He was at court every day doing all this extra shit to make sure I got sent up the river forever and a damn day, and I guess the judge felt like he had to give Columbo something just for his effort—which was to slap me with an illegal weapons charge. And so that's what I'm doing here."

"I think I remember you mentioning him."

"Dude was mad as hell that the feds picked up my case. They used his ass, made him do all the work, and then they stepped in. That's what that dick-breath ma'fucka gets." He changed the subject. "Then I had to pay for Cook'em-up's lawyer." He shook his head and took a deep breath. "And this nigga who used to be my man—I don't think you ever met Ronnie."

She shook her head no but said, "I heard you talk about him, but I never met him."

"Well, he crossed me."

"For real? As close as y'all used to be?"

"Yup." He shook his head. "He stole a few hundred thousand from me. With this bid, I been taking loss on top of loss. So basically I am broke. I still got my Benz, but my Navigator, my mom's sold that shit. And you know her larceny ass only gave me part of the money. Not to mention, you know she had her hand deep, way down in the cookie jar."

"Damn, baby, I wish I would have known."

"Me too! I'm not tripping off being broke, though. If I don't know nothing else, I know how to get money. So me being broke—that shit is only temporary! Once I get out there I'll be okay," he assured her.

But Bambi didn't care about him having any money. She would accept Lynx barefoot and broke. She loved him, plain and simple, like she had never loved anyone, and she knew he was telling her the truth.

"Baby, don't worry about money! I got a real lucrative business going now. I got money and good credit. And whatever you need, I'll make sure you get it."

"That is a helluva gesture, baby, but you know how I do. I have to have my own. I need to be the provider. I already told you if I can't add to your life then you don't need me," Lynx said, looking into her eyes.

"Visiting hours are over! Try again next week," the guard said sarcastically.

Lynx escorted Bambi over to the guard.

"Yo, let me use yo pen right quick."

The guard handed Lynx a pen. Lynx handed Bambi the pen and a napkin so she could write her full address down and all her phone numbers, with the exception of the apartment where she and Loot'chee stayed from time to time. "Expect to get a letter from me this week. You should have it like Wednesday or Thursday," Lynx told her. He gave her a long tongue kiss and said, "Soon as they add yo numbers to my list, I'm going to call you."

Once Egypt and Bambi left the prison, Bambi could not stop talking about Lynx. Egypt looked at her and said, "B, I am soooo happy for you! As long as we've been friends, I have never seen you so excited about a man as you are now. I see love, love, love," she sang, "written all over your face. *But* as your best friend I have to ask you, what are you going to do about Loot'chee?"

"I don't know," Bambi answered, her smile never leaving her face. "I don't know. I really don't know. How could I feel so strongly about Lynx after not even seeing him in over three years?"

"Because, my friend, sometimes old feelings never die."

Bambi looked back at the prison gates and knew she'd be seeing those gates again and again. However long it really took Lynx to be released was however long she'd be acquainted with those bars.

CHAPTER 26

The Block Is Hot

Bambi had planned to spend some time in Richmond before going back to Dallas. She wasn't in any hurry to get back to Dallas because Loot'chee was in Reno looking into buying some hotels.

Her feelings were running wild. She didn't have the foggiest idea what her next move should be. So she went to the one place where she knew she could get an answer: Grandma Ellie's house. It never failed that Grandma Ellie could tell there was something on Bambi's mind. Ever since Bambi was a little girl, she'd always sat in the kitchen acting as if she were trying to learn recipes, while her grandma cooked. Grandma Ellie knew better. If she hadn't picked up the recipes after all these years of hanging around the kitchen, then she wasn't going to.

"Chil', what's wrong with you?" her grandmother asked.

"Nothing, Gram. I just wanted to spend some time with my favorite gram, that's all," she said as she licked some leftover cake batter.

"Girl, you knows I know better. I may be old, a little slow and a little deaf, but the ol' girl don't miss a beat. Now I know good and well that something ain't right with you," she told Bambi as she peeped in the oven to check on her pound cake.

"So when did you get that new wig?" Bambi asked. Grandma had on a bob wig that could have come from Diana Ross or the Supremes' closet. Her grandmother was the queen of wigs. She had all styles, colors, long ones, short ones. She had a room that was like a shrine for all her wigs, and everybody in the family knew not to enter.

"This old thing?" she said, and sucked her teeth. "Chil', I done had this thing since Carter was president."

Bambi laughed. "Gram, you need to throw that thing out."

"This is human hair, and it has a lifetime warranty. I'm not throwing this bad boy out. I just cleaned out the attic and found it in there."

Her grandma looked out the window as the food cooked. "You know that Martha's son, uhhh, Johnny Boy? You know they came in Martha's house and locked that boy up?"

"For real?" Bambi asked.

"Yeah, he was stealing people's checks at the nursing home."

"How you know? I thought you stopped talking to Martha since she called the city and told them you were burning trash."

"I don't, but Hilda told me. Say the detectives is looking for his girlfriend, too. I see her creeping up Hilda's house on the late night," Grandma Ellie said as she pulled back the blind in such a way so she could not be seen. "That chil' used to be so pretty. Now she chasing behind the dope boys trying to get a hit."

"How you know that one, Gram?"

"Because I don't miss a beat. I keep telling you."

After Gram gave Bambi more neighborhood gossip, Bambi

asked, "Gram, how do you know when to gamble and when to hold tight?"

"Well, it all depends on what it is." Grandma tried hard not to pry, but it was almost impossible. Her eyes said it all. She wanted to know exactly what Bambi was confused about.

"It's too complicated to get into."

"Well, if I don't know, I can't give you advice."

"I have to make a life-changing decision, and I don't know what to do. Do I listen to my mind, or do I follow my heart?"

"I hope you ain't fixing to mess back with that Reggie. You know all that mess he done to yo momma, and on top of that, you know that boy ain't right. If I was you, I wouldn't even think of messing with that boy."

"Gram, you know good and well that boy got killed in jail."

"Chil', shut yo mouth. How did that one get by me?"

"I don't know how you missed that one. But even if he weren't dead, I'm not crazy or desperate!" Bambi assured her grandmother. She got up and put her arm around her grandmother. "Gram, I would never in a million years ever mess with Reggie. So that's one you don't have to worry about. I promise you that."

"You betta not, because I'll skin you alive." Grandma got up from the table and went over to get the cake out of the oven.

Bambi giggled a little as she followed closely behind her grandmother as she had done when she was a little girl.

"Well, let's see. It's still hard to say, because sometimes your heart can get you in trouble. And if you listen to your mind, your heart may be broke for a long time. Baby, it's not a matter of listening to either. It's a matter of which is right for you. Honey, you just have to put it in God's hands, and when you do he'll guide you."

"Gram, I ain't trying to be funny, but sometimes God takes forever."

"Honey, let me tell you something. He may not come when you want him, but he is always on time. Listen to yo grandma now. You know I ain't going to tell you nothing wrong."

She hung out with her grandma for the rest of the day, and before she left, her grandmother prayed with her. At the end of the prayer, Bambi asked, "God bring to pass what I have confessed. Please come quickly and speedily, Lord, in Jesus' name I pray."

"Now when you leave here you have to believe that God is going to give you the answer you are looking for. If you believe that, then it shall be done," her grandmother reminded her before she went out the door. "Be safe and call me when you get back to Texas."

Bambi's flight to Texas was rough. She missed the first flight, which caused her to be booked on another flight with a different route that added three more hours to her travel time. By the time she reached Texas, she only wanted to crawl into the bed and go to sleep. Her and Loot'chee's apartment was closer to the airport, so she told Ruby to take her there. They picked up some Popeyes on the way, and Ruby came up to eat with her. Once they had entered into the apartment, she was surprised to see a bunch of brown boxes stacked almost to the ceiling, and all the boxes were addressed to her in her full name, Bambi Ferguson.

"What the fuck?" she said, staring at the boxes. For a minute she thought they were some kind of gifts for her. *But an apartment full of gifts? I don't think so.*

"I know this motherfucker is full the fuck up with money and power, but for some reason I smell a rat—a big fat rat!" she said to Ruby as she looked closer and read the warning on all the large boxes that read KEEP AWAY FROM HEAT—HIGHLY FLAMMABLE. Without hesitation, she ripped opened the first box.

"What the hell is this?"

"It looks like a big steel drum?" Ruby said.

Bambi opened up the next one and the next one. All the large boxes contained huge steel drums. Then she got to the smaller boxes that were marked FRAGILE, DO NOT DROP, Bambi pulled out bottles of vanilla extract and Karo Syrup. And when she did, it all started making sense to Ruby.

"Oh, hells no! Girrrlll, this motherfucka ain't shit! I know what da fuck is going on now. He ain't slick! Oh, I just can't believe him." She pointed her finger. "I know his kind all too well," Ruby said, raising her voice as she started pacing the floor.

Bambi looked confused, but she knew whatever Ruby was talking about, it was something foul. Ruby rarely got upset.

Bambi stopped opening the boxes and said, "Tell me what's going down. I know it's something, because you never get this way unless it's some low-down, dirty, funky, doo-doo going down."

"Please don't get mad or think I'm hating or anything like that when I give you this piece. You know I love you like the sister I never had, so I got to give it to you raw."

"I would never think that. Now tell me!"

"This nigga . . . Girl . . . I am so mad right now." Ruby took a deep breath. "And how about this nigga is pushing fucking love boat? And got the nerve to have it stored here."

"What's that?" Bambi asked, frowning her face up.

"Love boat is embalming fluid," she said, and looked dead in Bambi's face.

"Okay, why would he have embalming fluid in here?"

"You know that CD by Master P that you listen to sometimes, 'Bout it Bout it.' And he talking about the boys in the park selling water?"

"Yeah." Bambi nodded.

"Yeah, well they talking about embalming fluid. They call it wet, water, love boat. It's just a lot of different names for it. It all depends on what part of the country you in."

Ruby shook her head and continued. "Girl, and this shit here is a whole bunch of shit. As a matter fact, we need to get the fuck up out of Dodge. This shit here can land both our asses up under the fucking jail. All this shit in here can get us a kingpin charge. And the vanilla extract jars, and the Karo Syrup jars. He was going to empty that stuff right down the drain and then distribute it in those. See, you got to sell it in glass, and he has different sizes. See, this is just an ounce and he probably using these as samples," Ruby said, holding up the small vanilla extract jars. "And this is four ounces." Then she held up the bigger size. "But, look, you see the majority of the bottles are the Karo Syrup bottles—that's sixteen ounces. That nigga is 'bout to get paid." Ruby put the bottle back down in the box and paced the floor.

"You know what, Ruby? I honestly ain't got no problem with him getting his money. But for real, it's personal now because every single one of these boxes is addressed to me, and this apartment is in my name. He didn't even have enough courtesy to put it in an alias name. Nothing here but a few clothes even links him to this place." Anger took over her whole body as she raised her voice a little. She stood up and pointed her finger. "And to top it off, now that I think about it, the whole time this dude was acting like he really cared and wanted the best for me. How about the whole time he was using not only me but my business, too. He even had me fucking laundering money."

"What?" Ruby said.

"All those times I did trips over in the Caymans, he was getting me to add money to the account and then write him a check for half of the money."

"And you know to clean money, they pay forty to fifty percent," Ruby chimed in. "So technically he paid you to do it without even saying. He knew what he was doing."

"Well, he can count on his money gettin' straight bucked on, 'cause he ain't getting none of it back."

"I don't blame you. Girl, don't be no fool. Well, I know I don't have to say that."

"Girl, the feds could come and get me any day, and how about I'll be guilty as fuck!" she said, breaking one of the bottles in rage.

Ruby just nodded her head and said, "You so right."

Bambi broke down and started crying.

"How could he do this to me? This dude played me like a piano," she screamed.

Ruby didn't answer, because tears formed in her eyes as she flashbacked to her own past. "B, please don't cry, because you are going to make me cry. I know exactly how you feel. I've been there, done that, for real. You know I have. I've got the T-shirt and ten years to show for it."

Bambi hugged Ruby, and Ruby told her, "Come on. Let's just go."

"Wait a minute. Just for kicks I gotta see what is in these other boxes and what else he might have in here."

She ransacked the apartment with Ruby's help. This time they were more prepared for what they found: cocaine and more than three hundred thousand dollars in cash.

Bambi cried, dropping to her knees. Once again, love had not loved her back. Once the initial shock was over, she had to get her mind right and think quick.

What can I do to let him know he done fucked with the wrong bitch? He used me, and no telling how many other chicks he's using or has used. I can't rob him and get away with it, although I am sure that the stuff at the apartment isn't going to make him or break him. He'd come looking for me. Now, let me think. How can I make a clean getaway from him? He told me that I could just walk away if I wasn't happy or didn't feel he was treating me right. But how will I ever be able to sleep at night knowing this man put my freedom in jeopardy and everything that I worked and struggled for? How can I walk away? I need the last laugh. At the same time, how do I get back at a multimillionaire nigga that can have any woman he wants? How do I hurt this nigga and make him feel sooooo fucked up?

For one minute she stopped and thought about something that her grandma had told her: "Baby, bumps come in the road. Some of them you just slow down and roll over; others you have to cautiously go around. And some of the time you have to analyze and use your common sense. Realize this though, sometimes you have to get yourself something bigger. Then you put the pedal to the metal and roll right through it!"

That's what I need to do. I need to be like a Hummer and roll over this nigga. Now how do I do that? It's only one way: to take his livelihood from him! How do I take his way of living? He's a millionaire with money, power, respect, and more money. It ain't but one way to strip him down and that's . . . the feds! Believe me, niggas is afraid of the feds. When they hear feds, they run!

Bambi was up at the crack of dawn, mapping out her plan. She first went over to her office and gathered all her files and computers. Luckily, everything was able to fit in her and Ruby's cars.

At 8 a.m., she called almost every moving company in the Yellow Pages until she came across the one with the smallest ad.

"Adkins Moving Company," a man with a deep voice answered after the third ring.

"Yes, who am I speaking with?" Bambi asked.

"Who you want to speak to?" the man inquired.

"The person in charge."

"You selling anything?"

"No, just trying to see about getting my stuff moved," Bambi explained.

"Well, lady, you calling the right place and the right person is on the phone."

"Who is this?"

"Rocky," he said with such pride.

"Rocky, how soon can you move my stuff out?"

"Where's it going, ma'am?"

"Cross-country," she responded, the words like music to her ears.

"You know that's gonna cost you a pretty penny."

"Okay, but how soon can you move my stuff?"

"As soon as you're able to pack the stuff up."

"It's already packed and pretty much ready to go."

"Well, I can be there at about eleven a.m.," he said. "For long moves like this, I prefer to be paid in cash," he added.

"That's no problem. I don't want no mess from you, Rocky. I've seen *20/20,* and I know what type of shit movers put in the game."

"Look, I am just trying to make me some money. Where do I have to take your stuff?"

"Virginia."

"Okay. I'm gonna need about a week and a half to get it there."

"How about a week?"

"Okay, a week it is. I require half of my money up front and the other half when I get there."

"That's fine," she said, cutting him off, wanting him to hurry over to get her belongings out of the apartment.

Damn, good times always have to come to an end. Texas showed me a lot of love, but me and Events R Us got to get the hell up out of Dodge, she thought to herself, disappointed that she would have to close her business down so abruptly.

On the way to meet the movers, they stopped by FedEx to send the office boxes off to Virginia, only to find out that she had two accounts under her business name: one that she had been using for her business and another that Loot'chee had set up. This only got her blood boiling even more at his betrayal.

When she first saw Rocky, her initial thoughts were to send him on his way. He looked like Uncle Jesse from the *Dukes of Hazzard.* He had a beard, pot belly, and faded light blue jean bib overalls. His truck even had Confederate flag seats.

"I don't know about this," Ruby said.

"Girl, I'm desperate, the block is hot, and me and my shit needs to get out of Texas!" she whispered under her breath to Ruby.

Although Rocky didn't look too promising, after talking to him face-to-face, Bambi had a better vibe about him. Rocky and his crew got all the boxes and the furniture out of the apartment. It took them more than four hours to load up the truck. While Rocky was loading up the truck at the apartment, she had other movers over at her and Egypt's house packing up the stuff there. She was through with Dallas. If she wanted to expand her business, she could always go to Atlanta or Miami. Once Rocky was finished, she instructed him to go and pick up the other stuff, which he did.

Before the end of the day, Bambi and Ruby were headed to the airport. She had to make one stop; she randomly chose and stopped at an attorney's office.

"Hello, how are you today?" the receptionist asked, greeting Bambi.

"Hi, my name is Bambi Ferguson, and my car broke down. My cell phone battery is dead. Is there a way I could possibly use your phone to page my boyfriend to tell him what's happened to me?"

The receptionist looked her over and could tell Bambi must have some money. "Sure, Ms. Ferguson. What's the number you need to dial?"

Bambi recited Loot'chee's sky page number to the receptionist. "Please call Bambi—it's an emergency—at . . . ," she said, and gave the Skytel operator the number that the receptionist had given her.

In a matter of minutes, the receptionist answered the phone and put the caller on hold. "Mrs. Ferguson, I am going to put you in the conference room so you can have some privacy," she said.

Bambi followed her into the conference room and waited for her to leave before she picked up the phone to talk to Loot'chee.

"Hey, baby. What's such an emergency?" he asked.

"When I got back yesterday, the police came into the apartment and locked me up. I'm at my lawyer's office and just got out on bond."

"Who was it, the local or the feds?"

"The feds," she responded, and as soon as she did, the phone went dead. He had hung up. She paged him again, but he never called back. Within two hours his number had been changed, and in a matter of days he had gone underground, disappeared, vanished, gone, and was never to be heard from again. She was free of him. No more Mr. Flamboyant, no more balling out of control, driving fast, expensive cars, or spending major paper. His name was now Mr. Incognito, and U.S. soil was not a place that he'd be stepping foot on any time soon. He would be sure that she had rolled over on him and was probably expecting at any given time that he'd see his face plastered on *America's Most Wanted.* So distance is what he put between him and anyone he knew. She had succeeded in stripping him of his livelihood.

She had heard people talk about how ballers were not afraid of anything, no ghost, gunshots, dogs, snakes, tornados, hurricanes, or earthquakes. Now she knew firsthand exactly how much they feared the DEA, ATF, and the FBI—the feds!

Those four little letters . . . Feds pack a lot of power! she thought to herself.

CHAPTER 27

Back on da Bricks

Once Rocky and his moving crew arrived in Richmond and stacked all her belongings in the self-storage, Bambi's prime focus became Lynx. He was able to get her name on his visiting list in a matter of days, and every other weekend she was at the FCI-Atlanta visiting him.

Having Lynx back in her life filled a void. Even though he was broke and in prison, there was something about him that confirmed for her that he was "the man" for her. She felt secure in her relationship with him. Their major complaint was the limited amount of communication they were able to have on the telephone. The feds only allowed him three hundred minutes a month in fifteen-minute intervals. The first month they went through those minutes in just ten days talking only twice a day. It frustrated Bambi to have to go without talking to her man by phone for the rest of the month. She wrote letters every day to inform him of all the things going on in her life. She had to figure out a way to expand their phone communications.

It came to her one day as she sat in the beauty parlor under a hair dryer, reading *Vibe* magazine. She saw a sky pager being advertised—and it wasn't just the pager but a watch that had pager features. As soon as she left the shop, she ordered the watch and had the service activated.

The following weekend she wore it in the visiting room and switched watches with Lynx. She paged him every day, just to tell him "I love you," or to let him know she had made it home safe from a visit, or just to tell him she was thinking of him.

Lynx stood outside the prison, holding a paper bag containing mail, the majority of which was the cards, letters, and pictures that Bambi had sent him. He had received mail from other chicks while he was inside, but he threw them away before he even hit the bricks. All the personal belongings that he'd acquired while doing time, he gave to a few of the brothers. He'd figured that they needed it more than he did. Bambi pulled up to the prison in her Jaguar, jumped out of the car, and ran over to him. When she hugged him, her feet totally left the ground. Their passionate kiss nearly drove him insane. He couldn't wait to get to the hotel so he could make love to her.

She drove him to Norfolk, Virginia, where the halfway house was located. He wasn't due for another three hours, so she got them a room at the Radisson Hotel, a few blocks away.

They took a shower together, and then they stretched out on the bed. She lay facing him, silent and unmoving. For a minute or so he watched patterns of her silhouette on the ceiling, absorbing the sensation of her presence in the bed next to him. He could feel her exhalations, feathery on his shoulder.

He took a slow breath, let it out gradually. She watched him, her eyes warm but also nervous. He closed his eyes and reached for her. Her chocolate skin felt impossibly smooth and soft to the touch, and she smelled fresh and lush like a tropical forest of exotic flowers and rich soil. He buried his face in her neck, in her skin, in her hair, tasting sweetness. He felt her arms and legs wrap around him and the warmth of her body all along his. He breathed her scent and stroked the skin of her shoulders and back as she rocked him and pressed herself tighter against him.

He felt his own urgency but was determined to take his time and make this, their first time back together, intense and passionate. He kissed her longingly and with intensity, immersing himself in the sensations of her mouth on his, the strength of her body. He nuzzled her neck and cheek and told her how much he needed her, loved her, and wanted her.

Bambi kissed his ear, then drew back, keeping her legs twined around him as she grabbed his manhood and positioned him to enter her. His size once again astounded her. He paused for a moment, unable to move. Once it was all the way in, she started working the middle. They both wanted to enjoy the moment and draw out their mutual pleasure and express their need for one another. They were anxious, and it seemed to take only minutes before they reached ecstasy together.

In the aftermath of their lovemaking, they lay exhausted in one another's arms, talking sweet nothings. Bambi told him, "I love you so much."

"I love you, too," he assured her.

"I love you more than you could ever know."

"How much?"

"I can't even tell you, it's so much. More than I've ever loved anyone before. There ain't nothing for your love I wouldn't do."

"Would you kill for me?" he asked.

"Would I kill for you?" she asked, totally caught off guard by the question he'd sprung upon her.

"Yes, would you?" he asked again.

"I mean if someone was after us and your life depended on that action on my part, yes. Would you kill for me?"

"No doubt. I have before."

She was speechless. She searched her mind for an explanantion, piecing the parts of the puzzle together that she had no idea were even connected. It was Lynx who'd had Reggie shanked while he was at the city jail.

They lay in each other's arms meditating on how deep their love for each other went, drifting off into a short but deep blissful sleep until the alarm in Lynx's watch went off, alerting him that he had thirty minutes before he was due at the halfway house. For a minute he thought about calling the halfway house and telling them he was running late because of traffic, but he decided against that. There was no sense in trying them—not yet anyway. He had to get in there and feel them out.

The next few days Bambi and Lynx spent as much time as possible talking to one another over the phone. After two weeks the halfway house finally let him out to look for work. Bambi gave him a job at her company. The job was only a front, but it served the purpose. This allowed them to spend every day together, and for the first week of his "job" she stayed in the Hampton Inn so she could pick him up each morning. He got a cell phone and snuck it into the halfway house so they could talk each night.

"Baby, you know if I hang up on you, it's only because someone walked in the room," he told her.

"I know, baby," she would say.

After a month at the halfway house, Lynx told Bambi, "Look, baby, I need you to take me to get my license, and then after that I need you to put my car in your name, so I can get some tags."

She did as he asked her to do, but was a little jealous. She wondered for a minute, *Since he doesn't need me for a ride anymore, is our relationship still going to be as strong? I know he has things he has to get in order, but at the same time will he forget about me? I know I shouldn't think like this, but how else am I supposed to feel? Once he hooks up with Cook'em-up, where do I stand? After all, Cook'em-up hates me. Cook'em-up, he could have so easily found me and put us in touch. The dude came to a few of my parties, and the times I was making my way over to see him, he would go the other way. I never pressed him, but I should have tracked that nigga down like wild game. I am sure Cook'em-up got bitches lined up for Lynx to holla at.*

She was also concerned about him parking his Benz around the corner from the halfway house, even though a lot of the residents did. She didn't want anything big or small to jeopardize his freedom. She always asked, "Do you know what you are doing?"

"If I didn't then I wouldn't be doing it."

Although she wanted him every second of the day, Bambi knew she had to give him his space.

After four months he was discharged from the halfway house. Bambi gave him a small coming-home party. When it was over, she handed him an envelope filled with hundred dollar bills, which he wouldn't accept.

"Look, baby, use this to get on your feet," she pleaded.

"No, I can't take money from you."

"Yes, you can. This is our money, not just mine. We are going to be together until death do us part. What's mine is yours and what's yours is mine."

"Well, I gotta get mine first."

Every time she tried to offer him money, they'd end up having a small argument.

She could tell that Lynx was frustrated because the game seemed to have changed so much in the time he was away. Even dudes whom he'd had to put on their feet were acting jealous-hearted. Cook'em-up was the only dude looking out for Lynx, but Cook'em-up had never been a real hustler. He needed Lynx to lead him.

As much as it hurt her, Bambi could only watch as Lynx tried to come back in the game. She struggled with whether or not to give him Loot'chee's shipment of narcotics that she had tucked away in storage. At first, when she'd taken it, she'd been all for him having it. But now, because he was such an important part of her life, she didn't think she could handle the pain and anguish of him being locked up again. At the same time, she knew that Lynx wasn't happy and felt his frustration. The straw that broke the camel's back was when a so-called friend of his who had been promising to give him three kilos to get on his feet reneged on him. Three days went by with the dude ducking his calls. Lynx's attitude was heavy with defeat and frustration.

Lynx tried not to take it out on Bambi, but when a man's money ain't right, it's usually the one closest to him who suffers. Even if it was wrong, she knew she had to help him get back in the game. Once he got some money, then he could go legit. But if it stayed like this, she didn't think the relationship could survive.

Bambi took a deep breath, finally deciding to break down and tell him. "Later tonight, I need you to go with me to pick up some boxes I have in storage, okay?"

"A'ight, baby," he said, never looking up from the television.

That night he rode with her to the storage bin, and she tried to make small talk; but she could feel that he was distracted. When they pulled into the storage place, she said, "Look, I've got to share something with you."

He turned to her, giving her his undivided attention. "Remember when you were in jail and I told you that I figured out that Loot'chee was using me to launder his money? I never told you the whole story. No one else knows it besides Ruby, not even Egypt. That's how deep it is. But since we are going to be together, I have to tell you."

She filled him in on everything. She told him how she had found the boxes in the apartment, how she'd had the movers put the stuff on the moving truck for shipping to Richmond with the rest of her belongings, running everything down on how she'd played Loot'chee.

"Damn, baby, you gangsta for real," he said, impressed.

She gave him the keys to the storage bin and pointed out the boxes that were loaded with cocaine and love boat. The next day he met up with Cook'em-up and told him what was going on. They went to DC and opened up shop. He had never known too much about slinging embalming fluid, but he had heard the DC cats in Atlanta talk about the dippers. They would dip their cigarettes in the embalming fluid and get wasted.

Now the benjamins were rolling in again, and they were rolling in fast.

With the benjamins rolling in so plentiful, all the beggars showed up. First there was his momma, Lolly, up to her same old tricks, and since he was on probation, legally Lynx lived with her—giving her the excuse to keep her hands deep in his pocket.

Bambi couldn't keep track of the times Lynx had visited his mother's place to find an eviction notice on the door. Lynx would go into the house and ask his mother as she was cooking chicken and getting ready for a card game, "Ma, didn't I give you the money to pay the rent the past three months?"

"Uuum, I ain't wanna tell you, but somebody stole it out my housecoat," she'd lie. Or, "I did pay it, but they making me pay a large deposit since I had to add you to the lease. I didn't want to say nothing to yo tight ass because I didn't feel like hearing yo mouth."

Lynx knew his mother probably had gambled or show-boated with the money, so as always he bailed her out from her troubles. Bambi would never understand why Lynx always allowed his mother to play him like that. What hold did she have over him? But she knew better than to ask or interfere with the relationship between son and mother in any way. There was no way to win in that phase of the game called life.

Then there was the girl Lisa from the visiting room, who'd done part of his bid with him. Now that Lynx was out, she felt like Lynx owed her something since she'd run up and down the road to see him. She would chase behind Lynx begging for some dick, knowing good and well Lynx wasn't thinking about her. He knew that was one coochie he could not get anywhere close to. She was too emotional, and with those feelings, at any moment she could step out of line. He would give her money from time to time if she was in a bind, feeling it was the least he could do whenever she rolled up on him, standing with one hand on her hip and the other hand out.

To keep the commotion down, Lynx told Bambi about her.

"You don't mind if I give Lisa a few pennies from time to time, do you?"

"Who is Lisa?"

Lynx looked at Bambi like she was being funny. "Stop tripping. You know the broad that was coming to see me when I was locked up."

"She don't have a job? I mean, why you gotta give her money?"

"I don't have to, but she did invest a lot of time with me, when I was on lock. She could never understand why I chose to dismiss her after the day fate put us back together."

Bambi heard every word Lynx said and knew he made sense, but she said, "Fuck that bitch Lisa! Let her find her own man or get a J-O-B!"

"I know, but I feel kinda guilty how I rolled out and shorty cool."

She knew that Lynx's mind was made up, so all she could say was, "Okay, but make sure that bitch know your wife is crazy and I don't want to have to kill her and you."

Lynx smiled and agreed.

CHAPTER 28

New Year's Eve

As the year came to an end, Lynx promised Bambi that his dealing and street life would end with the old year. In the new year, they planned to settle down and live like an ordinary couple with a house with a picket fence and travel and enjoy life together.

While there were a number of places Lynx and Bambi preferred to be on New Year's Eve rather than Richmond, Bambi had no choice; her company had secured a city contract to organize over ten major parties. A few were gala events, while others were more casual. She decided to attend the party where Lynx and his boys felt the most comfortable. This party marked Lynx's return to major party life since coming home more than nine months ago. There were so many folks trying to hug, speak, and politic with Lynx. One person in particular he made eye contact with was his old friend Ronnie. Ronnie was the person he had entrusted with his money when he and Cook'em-up were locked up. Ronnie had played his position for many years to gain Lynx's trust. It was true that over the years he had stolen from Lynx, but it had never really been enough to draw Lynx's attention. When Lynx took his fall, he had put over half a million dollars in Ronnie's hands. And Ronnie had robbed Lynx of every cent. When the two locked eyes, murder was written all over Lynx's face, while fear ruled Ronnie's glassy eyes. Even though Ronnie was as high as any dope fiend could be on New Year's Eve, the look he'd gotten from Lynx told him there was a good probability he would be the first murder victim in Richmond in the new millennium.

The party was jumping, and the liquor was pouring. Egypt and Ruby were having a ball mingling with the crowd. Everywhere Bambi turned she seemed to run into some of everybody she knew. When she was coming out of the restroom, she came face-to-face with Smooth. This was the first time she had seen him since she left him in the hotel parking lot buck, bald naked.

"What's up, baby? Can I holla at you for a minute?" he asked, licking his lips.

"Why the fuck you did that shit to my momma?"

"Because the drunk bitch deserved it. I couldn't get to you, so why not get to you through the one you love?"

She spit on him. He laughed. Then he wiped it off, put her spit in his mouth, and licked his fingers.

"Bitch, if you ever spit on me again, I'll beat the shit out of you," he said, pointing his finger in her face.

"You would try to fight me, wouldn't you? Why can't you pick on someone your size?"

He looked her up and down and said, "As a matter fact,

bitch, give me my boots back now!" She had forgotten that she was wearing the boots that Smooth had bought her years ago and although they were ugly to her years ago they surely set off her outfit this night. "Give me my fucking boots now."

"Wait on it, motherfucka," she said, turning to walk off.

He pushed her to the ground from behind and tried to physically take the boots off her feet. Two guys in the crowd intervened, and he hit one of them. With no hesitation they started to beat him down, and before anyone knew what was happening, security was on the scene.

Lynx didn't get a whiff of what was going on across the club until everything was over and Smooth and the guys who had defended Bambi had been thrown out of the club.

Later that night, after Lynx tucked Bambi in and she was fast asleep, he and Cook'em-up talked. "Man, this clown Smooth got to go."

"Man, I feel you. That stunt he pulled tonight was way out of order."

"I need to get some info on him, because I am going to put his dick in the dirt, sho nuff," Lynx said.

"Man, I can't let you do that shit. You on papers, and the last thing I need is for you to get bagged again. I need you out here. It's better that I take a fall than you. If you're out here, then I know I'll eat. So just chill and I'll take care of things," Cook'em-up said.

"Thanks, man." They gave each other dap.

As Cook'em-up headed to the door, he turned to tell Lynx, "Never think I'm doing this for her. It's strictly for you. I still don't trust her. I'll kill for you because I know you would kill for her. But with all my heart, I don't believe she can be trusted; she just ain't from the streets. She don't know about the struggle."

"Man, a broad ain't got to be from the streets to understand struggle."

Cook'em-up could feel his friend's anger, so he let it go and said, "Okay, I'm going to get on top of things . . . for you."

"'Preciate it, man."

"It ain't nothing, and if Ronnie crosses my path, I got him, too."

"He ain't nothing, man. He's a dope fiend. He'll eventually kill himself, one way or the other. All the drugs that clown shoot, his kidney and liver will eventually give out on 'im any day now." Then Lynx smiled. "If he don't run across a hot shot. He knows he fucked up, knows death is just around the corner for him anyway. Save yo bullets for Smooth."

"A'ight," Cook'em-up agreed.

Date with Lucifer

On January third, Smooth stood in the John Marshall Courthouse to see if the judge would give him a continuance for the many sexual battery charges he faced. He had been going to court for over a year, putting off the case time and time again. His lawyer had warned him that the judge might revoke his bond if a continuance was requested. Either way he knew he could land in jail if convicted. Therefore, he was willing to risk asking for a continuance. Again the judge granted him another court date. "This case will be tried on January twenty-fifth, and if you are not ready to proceed, counselor, your client will sit in jail until you are," the judge said.

"Thank you, Your Honor," Smooth's attorney said respectfully.

Smooth pimped out of the courtroom with triumph in his eyes, but Cook'em-up was singing a whole 'nother tune. Cook'em-up was glad he didn't have to catch a petty charge to go to jail just so he could shank Smooth; with the continuance, his work was going to be easier than he had imagined.

Smooth walked down the stairs of the court building and hopped in the car of the junkie he'd paid to drive him. There'd been no need to drive his own whip since there had been a chance he might get locked up.

"Take me to PJs," he demanded before he had even closed the car door.

On his arrival he offered up some dap and rapped with the neighborhood hustlers. After he collected his debts, he bent the corner. Just as planned, Smooth and Cook'em-up bumped into each other.

"My bad, man," Cook'em-up apologized.

"Nah, you good, shorty."

Cook'em-up hadn't had a haircut and was dressed in some old army fatigues with scuffed-up Timberland boots.

"Brotha man, you know someone who trying to buy a spanking-new nine millimeter? It's brand-new, no bodies or nothing on this jank," he said to Smooth, rubbing his nose and scratching, trying to put on his best dope fiend impersonation.

"You got dat?"

"Yup," he told Smooth.

"What you want for it?"

"Two hundred," Cook'em-up said, sniffling like a dope fiend.

"A'ight, where it at?"

Cook'em-up couldn't believe he was selling Smooth his own death. *Damn fool.* He laughed to himself. Smooth wasn't even strapped.

"Right here." He put the clip in it and handed it to him.

Smooth gave him $125.

"Motherfucka, I don't give no dope fiends fucking full price for shit, as a matter of fact," he said, and pointed the gun at Cook'em-up. "Give me my ma'fucking money back."

Before Smooth realized that the clip was empty, Cook'em-up was two steps ahead of him. Cook'em-up pulled his .40-caliber and shot Smooth in the head, *bloom,* and then two to the heart: *bloom, bloom!*

The .40-caliber echoed between the apartments. Cook'em-up threw down some dope and a few dollars beside Smooth and walked away.

Later that night while Bambi and Lynx lay in the bed watching the eleven o'clock news, the reporter said: "On the city's Church Hill, the second murder of the New Year. In what seems to have been a drug deal gone bad, one man was left dead. There are no suspects or known witnesses. If you have any information on this or any other crime call Crime Stoppers at 1-800-STOP CRIME."

"Baby, that's one for you and your mom!"

"How? You were with me all day."

"Just because I am not there, don't mean I can't make shit happen."

At that moment the phone rang, and it was Egypt calling to deliver the news of Smooth's death. Bambi played dumb and chatted with Egypt for a while. When she got off the phone, Lynx was asleep.

CHAPTER 30

Till Death Do Us Part

Two days later, Bambi sat in the car waiting as Lynx ran into the drugstore. He had been in there more than ten minutes when she called him on his cell phone. He answered, saying, "I'm paying for my stuff right now. Just hold tight, baby."

"You know we're going to be late to the movies."

"I know. Boo, for real, I don't even feel like messing with the movies. As a matter of fact, I need to talk to you about something."

"Okay," she said. As he walked out of the store she was struck by how good he looked. Something about the John Smedley sweater he wore made her even more attracted to him. Loving how he wore the sweater, she didn't even notice him carrying the small white, flat bag in his hand.

He got into the car and handed her the bag, which had a card. She smiled as she read it. It was a Mahogany card, the type she used to send him when he was in prison, and it told her how much she meant to him. As she read it, tears started forming in her eyes. He'd signed it with the question, "Will you marry me?"

She sat speechless in the front seat of his new Porsche. When she finally looked up, he was holding a ring that had so much bling she was nearly blinded. Because she was silent, Lynx felt something was wrong. "If you don't like the ring, that's cool. We can always take it back, and you can pick out what you want. I got it from that place that you like in Vegas, Fred Leighton. I wanted you to have something special, and I know they sell rare collectible jewels. And this is an Asscher-cut diamond. The lady who sold it to me told me that the largest cut diamonds in the world were cut by the Asscher family."

"No, it's not that. I don't care about no ring. As long as it from you, I'll accept anything."

"Then what's wrong?" He took her into his arms as she began to sob.

"I can't marry you."

"What? What you mean you can't marry me?"

"I just, I just . . . can't."

"I don't understand. I love you like I never loved no other, and you tell me every day you feel the same. You held me down while I was locked up and been there for me every day since. Do you not love me? Is it some other nigga you love? What?" He raised his voice, confused.

"No, I love you and I want to be with you but . . ."

"But what?" he demanded.

"But I can't have any kids, and I know no man wants a woman who can't give them a child," she blurted out.

He was silent for a split second. "So? I don't care about no kids. I love you. And plus, how you know you can't have children? It's doctors that we can go to that can get you pregnant."

"No, I already been through all that. I know for a fact I can't have no kids." She continued to sob. "I can't marry you. I just can't. I know you say it ain't about kids now, but what about later? It'll really break me down if you cheat on me with someone else and she gets pregnant."

"You talking crazy now. I don't fuck around, and if I did do you really think I would go up in a chick raw dog?"

"I'm just saying mistakes happen. And just my luck, she'll turn up pregnant. If she does, would it even be fair for me to expect you to kill the only possibility of you having a child?"

"Look, baby, I am not tripping on no kids. I love you, and if you can't give me one, then I'll sacrifice and not have any! I mean that! Look, I love you and I want to spend the rest of my life with you. Now what's up?"

"Lynx, I am sorry, I just can't marry you. We can still spend the rest of our lives together, but I can't marry you. At least if you have a baby by another girl I won't feel too much like a fool if I am not your wife. "

Lynx was getting frustrated with the whole conversation. "So you mean to tell me the only reason why you won't marry me is because of a baby."

"Yup." She nodded her head.

"This is some motherfucking bullshit," he said as he started the car, pulled out of the Walgreen's parking lot, and headed in the direction of Bambi's house instead of the movies.

He was speeding, weaving in and out of traffic and driving like a bat out of hell. Neither breathed a word to each other for the next ten minutes.

"Tell me exactly how you know that you can't have any kids?"

She continued to cry uncontrollably.

"Lynx, after you were locked up and I never heard from you again, I . . ." She hesitated. "Ummm, I found out I was pregnant with your baby. I was so confused. You were missing in action. I thought you had written me off as a wham-bam-thank-you-ma'am. My mom was still hugging the bottle. I was alone and I didn't think I could go through the pregnancy by myself. It wouldn't have been fair to the baby. After the abortion I had all this internal bleeding, and I had to have surgery and they gave me a partial hysterectomy."

"You mean to tell me you killed my baby?" he asked. His face was tight with anger.

She didn't respond.

"You talk about me and my people. You ain't no fucking better. You a fucking murderer."

She continued to cry, unable to look at him. "Lynx, I am sorry."

"You know what? I can't even deal with you right now." He pulled in front of her house and didn't say a word. Before she could shut the door, he sped off.

CHAPTER 31

Can't Beat Her,
So Join Her

olly walked into her living room after a day of shopping
and saw her son stretched out on the leather sofa that she had
taken out of his house when he went to prison. She stood at the
doorway observing him flipping the televison channels. Lately
he seemed to always be showing up at her house at all hours for
no reason at all. And he was never in a mood to be messed
with. She didn't know what was wrong with him, but she knew
better than to ask.

"Hey, baby," she greeted.

"Whad up," he said sourly.

"You ate?"

"Nope, I ain't hungry," he said, never looking up.

"You know the rest of that money is due for that new
HDTV, right?"

"Yeah, Ma, I know. I ain't got nothing but a few hundred on
me. I lost a few dollars at the crap house last night."

"Damn, nigga, it seems like you been going there losing all yo li'l money the past few days."

Lynx didn't answer her. Lolly kept trying to make conversation with Lynx, but she had no luck so she walked into his brother's room and asked Cleezy, "When you gonna give me that money?"

"Did Lynx give you his part yet?"

"Don't worry 'bout Lynx. I am talking about you."

"I got you, Ma," he said, reaching for his jeans.

"What's wrong with your brother anyway, looking like he just lost his best friend?"

Cleezy went into his pocket, pulled out a knot of hundreds and fifties, and said, "I guess the deer and the cat is having problems in their jungle." He counted the money out and laid it on the bed.

When Lolly saw the bankroll, which at that moment Cleezy regretted having pulled out, she asked, "Don't you want to treat yo momma to dinner tonight?"

He shook his head and mumbled under his breath, "Got-damn, Ma, you be killing me." But he gave her a fifty-dollar bill.

"Now you know better," Lolly said as she picked the fifty-dollar bill up. "When you give them skanks money to go to dinner, don't them no-count Jezebels eat up more than fifty dollars worth of food? Well, yo momma ain't watching her weight because I don't care about being no video ho, so you know fifty dollars at a nice restaurant doesn't even include dessert for yo momma."

Cleezy cut her off, saying, "Here, Ma." And he peeled off another fifty-dollar bill, but that still wasn't enough for her.

"Now who you think going to go with me? You or your

brother sho ain't going to take me. Y'all too busy running around here acting like y'all gangstas that you don't even have time for yo momma. You know I am all you got."

"Ma, here, damn, please just find somebody to go with you to dinner. I got stuff I'm trying to do and got to get done. I'm going out of town tonight and shit hectic." He gave Lolly another hundred-dollar bill, put on his Timbs, and walked out of his room.

She walked back through the den, and Lynx was still sitting in the same place. She heard his pager go off and watched as he didn't budge. She picked up his pager and handed it to him.

"Here, your pager went off."

"Yeah, I know. I hear it, Ma."

At that point she knew something was very wrong and she had to step in and do something. This was so unlike Lynx. Lynx being lovesick was a condition she had never witnessed. If Lolly didn't know anything, she knew firsthand that pussy was power and could cause any man strong or weak to hit rock bottom; and no Bambi, Jane, or no other chick from the jungle was going to stand in the way of her and her son's fortune.

I see right now, I've got to step up to the plate. This girl is not going to make my son lose focus and get crossed up in the game. I need to find out what this girl's intentions are.

Once Lynx had one foot on the porch and the other out of the door, Lolly called Bambi.

Bambi looked at the caller ID and saw that Lynx was calling from his mother's house. Happiness shot through every bone in her body.

"Hello," Bambi answered.

"Hello, darling, it's Lolly."

"Hi, Ms. Lolly," Bambi responded, disappointed. She wondered what the hell Lolly was calling her for, but was also excited that someone connected to Lynx was on the other end of the phone.

"How you doing, darling?"

"I'm okay, and you?" she asked, hoping she would quickly get to the point.

"I'm fine, so look, the reason why I'm calling is because you've become such a big part of Lynx's life and I never get a chance to spend time with you. Y'all haven't invited me over to see y'all's place. I know it's nice. And my girlfriend Alice was supposed to go to dinner with me, but she just canceled. So I thought, let me call my daughter-in-law."

"Oh, okay." Bambi paused.

"I figure that I could get the grand tour of y'all's place when I pick you up, since I never got an invitation," Lolly said, not being able to wait to see just the style Lynx had Bambi living in over there.

"Ms. Lolly, that's cool, but just so you know you don't need an invitation. You are always welcome."

"That's sweet."

"So what time will you be here?"

"How about seven?"

"Seven it is."

Bambi hung up the phone and called Ruby. Together they began roller skating around the house, making sure it was spotless from top to bottom. Not that Bambi kept a dirty house, but she knew that Lolly was Lynx's mother and would be doing an inspection on the down low, so everything had to be in tip-top condition.

When Lolly arrived, she was very impressed with the house and a bit envious. She could tell that Lynx definitely loved Bambi. With every room she saw, the more she looked for reasons to hate Bambi. But once Lynx's puppydog sad face popped in her head, she knew there was only one way to get this situation under control for her best interests. Although Bambi and Lynx were on the outs, she knew her son and knew him well. For sure they'd get back together, and there was only one driver—and the driver of the car was Bambi. Bambi had his heart, and Bambi now had the control that Lolly had once thought would always be hers.

I can't beat this bitch, so let me join her. I'll get in good graces with this chick, but I need to let her know she better mean my son some good.

Bambi and Lolly drove to the restaurant in Bambi's car. It was a nice seafood place that Bambi liked to go to with Lynx. They sat at a table by the window and ordered dinner. After their Chardonnay arrived, Lolly leaned in toward Bambi and said in a sweet voice that dripped with insincerity, "So, look, darling. Here's the thing. I am sure just like your mother love you, I love my son, and I'm going to come to you like a woman."

Bambi knew what was coming, but she bit her tongue for a minute to hear Lolly out of respect—she was Lynx's mother.

"Look, the bottom line is, What is your agenda with my son?"

Bambi looked Lolly in the face and said, "It's plain and simple. I love your son with all my heart. I have no ulterior motives when it comes to him. We have an issue we need to iron out, but other than that, I promise you I mean him well and want nothing less than the best for him."

"You know my sons and I have always been close, and especially so since their father passed away. I truly want them to be happy, but on the other side of the coin I won't let a woman bring either of them down."

"No disrespect, Ms. Lolly—I don't know about any other woman, but I have no plans of standing in between you and your son. At the same time you have to allow your sons to be men," Bambi said as sincerely as she could, but she really wanted to tell Ms. Lolly, "A daughter is a daughter for life, but a son is a son until he gets a wife."

Satisfied with Bambi's answer, Lolly changed the subject. The rest of the dinner was filled with a lot of small talk about Lolly's favorite movie stars and Bambi's business. When it came time to pay for the meal, Lolly let Bambi pick up the check even though Cleezy had given her two hundred dollars for dinner.

"We're going to get along just fine," Lolly said as they walked out of the restaurant. But Bambi wasn't sure. For one thing she didn't know if Lynx would ever forgive her. And what good was the mother without the son?

CHAPTER 32

Bundle of Joy

Over the next week, Lynx hung out in the projects and spent time in one of the crap houses. He ran into people that he knew from back in the day and even a few he had forgotten about because he hadn't seen them in a while.

Lynx was coming out of the crap house when he ran into Shayla Love. Back in the day Shayla was one of Richmond's finest. Back then, she was a brown complexion with baby-smooth skin. Back in the day she had long, coal black hair and was built like a brick house (measurements 36-24-36). Every dude in town, from the Northside to the Southside and from the East End to the West End, wanted Shayla, and she knew it. But she would not give Richmond dudes the time of day, which only made them want her more. Funny how things change.

"Whassup, Lynx?" she asked.

He scrunched his face up and said, "Who dat?"

"It's me, Shayla," she said.

He looked her up and down. This wasn't the Shayla he knew

from back in the day. Shit had definitely changed. Standing there on the street, Lynx didn't even recognize her. She had on a baseball hat, her haircut was close on the sides, and her clothes hung loosely off her body.

"Whad up, Shayla?"

"Fucked up right now. I need a ride. I need to be gone before my grandma get home."

"How you grandma doing, anyway?"

"She's seventy-nine and still holding on. She got high blood pressure and her heart a li'l fucked up, but overall she okay," she said, looking down at the ground.

"Tell her I said hi, when you see her. How yo kids doing?"

"They doing fine. You know the three of them live up to New York with they daddy's family. I still stay up there, too."

When Shayla said that, Lynx remembered that he had heard that Shayla had three kids by some New York cat that she had married.

"Somebody tol' me he got tow off for some trafficking charge. How much time they gave him?" Lynx asked, not really caring but making conversation.

"A dime piece."

"Damn, why he have no chick riding with it? He should know better than that." Lynx shook his head. "He could've really got an asshole full of time."

"Dat's right," Shayla said, nodding. "Now I got to stay wit his people so they can keep an eye on me."

"Yeah, well, what you doing down here?"

"Long story and I need a ride," she said, looking around nervously.

"Where you going and what you looking all p'noid for?" Lynx asked, wanting to know what kind of stuff Shayla was really into.

"I'm trying to get to the mall and then gotta probably sell some pussy or something so I can get me some clothes and a ticket because I got to get back to New York."

He knew that she was hinting for him to offer to trick with her, but he didn't pay her any attention.

"Look, I am going to the Regency Mall, if you want a ride. I'll buy you some jeans and a shirt."

"Thanks, Lynx, you always used to look out. For real, my husband's people pressing me to get back. I think they know I am down here on some bullshit probably. They are my bread and butter, and I can't let them know what's going on," she said as she got in the car.

"Well, what's really going on?" Lynx asked as he started the Porsche and drove away from the crap house.

"Man, Lynx, I'm all fucked up." She twisted her hands together, and he could tell she was in deep shit.

"How?" he asked. All of a sudden he didn't feel up to playing the role of Captain Save-a-Ho but asked anyway to make general conversation.

"I met this li'l young nigga and was creeping with him. Didn't find out I was pregnant until I was about five months. So I couldn't really get no abortion. So I kept buying all my clothes in bigger sizes so my husband's family wouldn't know. When I visit with my husband, it's through a glass. Thank God, he didn't notice. They all thought that I was gaining weight. With all my kids, I never got big, so I could play it off. I just had the baby three days ago."

As he took a shortcut through Fairfield Court to hit Mechanicsville Turnpike, some nickel-and-dime drug dealers stood across the street in front of an empty building, waving folks down. Lynx glanced over at Shayla. She did look a little pudgy, and the baggy clothes didn't help.

"Damn, so how you get away with that shit to come have the baby down here?"

"Well, three months ago, my grandma was sick. So I used that as the excuse, so I could come down here to have the baby. I know if they ever find out, they'll take my kids. And he'll have me kilt. Having some other dude's baby when your man is locked up, and he's your husband at that, is the ultimate betrayal."

"I feel you. Damn, so what you do with the baby?"

She was silent for a minute. "Lynx, I don't even wanna say."

"Don't say you left it at the hospital." He turned toward her angrily.

"I was, but I couldn't," she admitted, looking downward and biting her fingernails.

"So what you do?" he asked, demanding to know.

"I left it at my grandmother's house, and that's why I am trying to get out of town," she said, unable to look him in the eye.

"I thought you said your grandmother was at the doctor."

"She is."

"Who got the baby?" Lynx asked.

"She waiting on my grandma."

"What da fuck you thinking?" Lynx snapped.

"At least my baby will have some love for the first few years of her life," she said, as if that was some kind of excuse.

"So, you just leaving yo baby? What if yo grandma call the people?"

"Then she just do. What can I do? I got to save my own ass."

"You and yo grandma talked about the baby?"

"Nope. I just had to do what was good for me."

Lynx was quiet for a minute. He wanted to stop the car and put Shayla out on the side of the road. He used to respect the way she carried herself, and now to find out that she wasn't any earthly good was disappointing to him. But she had something he wanted, something that could make his life complete.

"Look, Shayla, the bottom line is you just leaving yo baby, right? You don't have no intentions on ever coming back for yo baby, right?"

"I can't. I know it's fucked up, but what can I do?" She choked back a sob.

"Look," Lynx said, then paused. "My wife can't have kids. Let me get the baby. I'll buy it from you."

"For real?"

"Yeah," Lynx said. He knew this was exactly what he wanted to do.

"A'ight," she said, like he was asking for a piece of candy or bubblegum. Lynx shook his head at her lack of attachment to her child.

"We gonna need to get the proper papers done," he said.

"Okay, but ummm, we need to get them done quick, because I got to get back to New York," she said.

"You got keys to yo grandma house?" he asked.

"Yes."

"Well, we need to get the baby now," Lynx said, and turned the car around.

Shayla's grandma lived in a little brick house in Church Hill. They walked inside, and Shayla led Lynx into the back bedroom. There lying on the bed with pillows on either side of it was a tiny baby girl, sleeping with a bottle beside her. At least the girl had given the baby something to eat, Lynx thought. He looked down at the baby. She was brown skinned, with long eyelashes and tiny little fingers. She had a head full of coal black curly hair. He looked at her and saw that she would get darker later. He picked her up and gently put her on his shoulder. She didn't even wake up, but she nestled against him in her sleep.

"You sho you don't want her?" Lynx asked Shayla, as if she was giving away an old coat or a pair of shoes.

"Man, I already got three kids. What I need with one more?" Shayla asked, putting some diapers and a few little baby clothes into a bag for him. "I'm outta formula, so you got to buy some."

"That's okay. My baby girl can have anything she wants," Lynx said. He was already falling in love.

Lynx then called Tricia. He took the baby over to Tricia and told her what was going on and not to breathe a word to Bambi. He called Cook'em-up and told him to take Shayla shopping and to stay with her for the rest of the day. He put Shayla up in a hotel, and the next morning he took her to the lawyer's office to get all the paperwork done.

When the lawyer saw how much Lynx was willing to pay, he put everything else aside and got right to work. It took a full day of running around to this place and that, but by the end of the day, it was done. After they signed the papers, Lynx took Shayla to the airport. Before she got out of the car, he handed her an envelope.

"You got no claim on this baby, Shayla. I don't want no shit out of you when that runs out."

"Lynx you don't even have to say that. I know how you get down. Thanks for real, for digging me up out of this shit, for real," she said.

"It's thirty grand cash in there. Now go on home and try to keep your ass out of trouble," he said.

Shayla's mouth hung open as she looked inside the envelope.

"Damn," she said. "You'll be a good daddy, Lynx." Then she tucked it into her purse, waved, and got out of the car with a smile on her face. Lynx headed back over to Tricia's to see how his new baby was doing.

Later that night, as Bambi was sleeping, Lynx and the baby came in.

Bambi woke up when she heard a baby crying. *What the hell is that?* she wondered, looking around for Snowball. The cat was asleep on the pillow next to her, not making a sound. Then she saw Lynx standing in the doorway, holding something.

"You want yo momma?" he said. "There she go right there."

Lynx came up to the bed, and Bambi saw that he was holding a little chocolate bundle of joy.

"Ooh, let me see," she said, extending her hands so Lynx could give her the baby. "Who baby you got?"

"Ours," he said, sitting down next to her with a big smile on his face.

"Stop playing," she said as she took the baby into her arms. When she did, the little baby girl stopped crying like she knew exactly who was holding her.

"You told me that the only thing that was holding us up from legally being able to spend our lives together was us having a baby," Lynx said, running a finger over the baby's fat little cheek. "So I went out and bought us a baby. Got the papers in the car."

"For real? What do you mean you went out and bought us a baby?" she said as she cradled the newborn in her arm.

"Just what I said. Now, you gon' marry me or not? You know we can't have no illegitimate child, right?"

"Yes, I will marry you," she said, and kissed Lynx full on the lips, still holding the baby in her arms.

The next morning they went to the justice of the peace and got married. Egypt and Ruby came to be the witnesses, and Lolly stood next to Tricia, who held her grandbaby.

"Bambi, this don't seem right," Ruby said. "You the biggest event planner in the city, and here we are having this little tiny wedding."

"Girl, I'm not tripping on no damn wedding. I'm more concerned with the marriage. But don't worry, girl," Bambi said. "On our one-year anniversary, I'm going to have the biggest damn party Richmond has seen."

CHAPTER 33

Burying the Hatchet

The next day Bambi had to take care of a few things. If she was going to be with Lynx, she needed a clean slate. She felt there was one thing hanging over her head: Douglas. She found out his address and wrote him a letter.

Dear Douglas,

I know I am probably the last person you want to hear from. However, I have to make things right with you. I want to apologize for carrying such a powerful grudge around for so many years. I was wrong for taking you for everything, including your heart. This is not about you forgiving me, but about me living with myself and making right with the situation. I am married now with a beautiful little girl, and I am trying so hard to live from within instead of from without and take the heaviness off my heart. I have contacted a real estate agent (enclosing her business card) and instructed her to sell the house that I used some of your money to buy. Once it is sold you will get half of the money from it. I feel that half the money is more than fair due to the fact that the appreciation of the property would put your part of the money at almost a tenfold return. Just look at it as interest. As far as the furniture, now that's a different story. I thought long and hard about it, and I am enclosing a cashier's check for ten grand for the living room furniture that you had sent over. I have truly buried the hatchet, and I understand that you should have never been held responsible for the games you played as a child. The reality is you scarred me, and I hope you will teach your children not to be bullies. However, as a grown woman, I do understand that kids will be kids. I am wishing you the absolute best things that life has to offer. And as for your heart being broke, I know I can't replace the heartaches and pains you've experienced, but I can offer you one valuable piece of advice . . . to keep you from falling victim: Please don't be so gullible.

Peace and Many Blessings,
The Black Beauty

Bambi signed her name on the check and enclosed it in the envelope, taking a deep breath before sealing it. For the first time in a long time she felt good about giving something back.

CHAPTER 34

If It Ain't One Thing . . .
It's Another

Like all new parents, Bambi and Lynx never got to sleep in anymore. Finally, one night they took Baby Nya to Tricia's so they could spend a little quality time together.

When they dropped off Nya, they could see Tricia was overflowing with happiness. "Ma, what's up?"

"They just gave me a date for my plastic surgery."

"For real?"

Tricia nodded, wiping away tears of joy.

"Well, we'll give you the money," Lynx said.

"Thank you, but I only need half of it."

"What you mean 'half'?" Bambi asked. "Where you gonna get the other half from?"

"Don't worry, I got my sources," she said secretively.

"Let me find out you got your shovel back on your back, digging for gold?" Bambi asked.

"Nope. Let's just say an old friend promised it to me. And I can't talk about it because the baby is sleeping. Now, get out of here before you wake up the baby," she said as she opened up the door so they could leave.

On the way home Lynx and Bambi tried to figure out what Tricia was up to, but with Tricia there was no telling. Whatever it was, she seemed happy again.

The next morning, they lay in the bed with the rain hitting the roof of the house. Lynx had just pulled Bambi close to him for more passionate sex when there was a hard, loud banging on the door. Lynx knew the knock; it was one he had heard a few times before.

"Police! Open up! We have a warrant!" he heard Columbo's voice yell out.

"Wait a minute, I have to get my robe," Bambi screamed out, to grab a little time. For a minute she thought that maybe they were there for her and had caught up with her from all the dirt she had done. But in her gut she knew that they were there for Lynx. Lynx whispered to her that it was Columbo on the other side of the door, and her worst fears were confirmed. She took her time getting to the door so Lynx could hide.

"What is this all about? Let me see your warrant," she demanded when she finally opened the door.

Columbo smiled as he handed her the warrant. He was a middle-aged white man with a dirty blond crewcut. He was short and stocky.

"Your husband is going down for the murder of Jason 'Smooth' Carter," Columbo said as if he were singing a song. His voice was high pitched, and his mouth full of chewing tobacco.

"What?"

"I've got a witness who identified him, and he can't get out of this one, not this time."

"Now, wait a minute. Lynx was with me that night. I remember seeing it on the news," she said.

"Can you prove that?" Columbo asked. "In a court of law? I don't think so. And even if you could, we have a warrant and he's still going with us. Where is he?"

"He's not here," she said firmly. Columbo walked around like he owned the place. He had a rhino's butt and limped a little when he walked. The police officers followed close behind, tearing up the house from top to bottom. They knew he wasn't there, but they still ransacked the whole house hoping to find some drugs or guns to add to the charge.

Columbo was pissed because he didn't find a thing after being so confident that Lynx had slipped up. On his way out of the door, he said, "Tell your husband, if I catch up with him you ain't going to ever see his monkey ass again."

Once the police left, Lynx came out of the coffee table that Douglas had sent from Korea. He had to come up with a plan. "Baby, I can't turn myself in. You know that, right?"

"I know you can't, but damn, what are we going to do?" She paced the floor, upset but wanting to be strong for Lynx.

"I'm going to have to go on the run, and I need to know that you are going to hold me down while I'm gone, and that you are down for whatever," he said, taking her hands and gazing into her eyes.

"Come on, baby, you know that goes without saying—this is until death do us part," Bambi said.

Lynx peeked out the window and saw an unmarked car up the street. They both knew he couldn't leave the house—not then anyway.

"I need to find a way to get me out of here some kind of way."

"We'll come up with something," she said.

The unmarked car kept watch on their house, so Bambi and Lynx had no choice but to play the waiting game. The next day, Bambi left to go over to her mother's house to get the baby. While she was gone, Lynx was making a sandwich when he heard someone messing with the lock. He quickly hid in the coffee table before two plainclothes detectives entered the house and placed microphones and bugs throughout. Once they were done, they stood in the living room and went over a checklist of exactly where each bug was planted.

Lynx listened attentively. When Bambi came in the door, Lynx was standing in the middle of the floor, holding a big sign that said DON'T SAY A WORD. THEY CAME IN AND BUGGED THE HOUSE!

He sat down and wrote everything down to let her know what he was thinking and what was what. He told her they were going to use the bugs to their advantage.

She called Egypt. "Hey, girl, what you doing?"

"Nothing," Egypt said.

"I'm going to come and get you so I can go furniture shopping. Call Ruby and see if she wants my old stuff, since she just moved into her new place." Egypt had a feeling that something was wrong, but she played along. "Tell her that she has to come and get it tomorrow so I can get my stuff delivered right away."

"Okay. Well, can't you just pay the people extra to just drop it off at her house?"

"We'll ask the salesman when we get there."

She hung up the phone and winked at Lynx, who sat silently at the kitchen table.

The next day a furniture truck showed up, and Cook'em-up, dressed in a blue workman's suit and a moving company hat, knocked on the door. Cook'em-up and a couple of other dudes brought the old furniture out and set it on the lawn in full view of the undercover cops. They took the new furniture in the house and loaded the old furniture on the truck, including the coffee table with Lynx in it. Cook'em-up gave Bambi a clipboard to sign, and they were on their way.

Lynx didn't get out of the coffee table until they stopped in Ashland.

"Man, I feel like some fucking sardines," he said as he crawled out.

Cook'em-up looked at him nervously. "Man, I got to get you out of VA. It's hot. I told you I was going to take care of everything, and I meant that. I done some homework, and come to find out that nigga Ronnie is the one that's snitching."

"Damn, I should have been took care of that shit." Lynx jumped out the back of the truck. Cook'em-up followed him.

"It's all good. I'm going to take care of him. I just need you to be ghost like yesterday."

"Then I'm ghost like yesterday, my nigga."

Once Lynx was long gone, Bambi turned her stereo on at its top volume, practically causing the windows to vibrate. She searched and found all the hidden microphones planted by the police, carried them over to their van, and threw them in. "If it ain't one thing, it's another. Stay the *fuck* out of my house!"

The police only laughed at her. One of them leaned out the window and said, "Just tell us where your husband is; then you won't have to worry about us anymore. Maybe he's with his other woman, huh?"

"Yeah, he's with your momma!" she answered.

Three hours after she marched back across the street to her house and slammed the door, they hauled her off for questioning. She immediately called her and Lynx's lawyer, Brent Jackson, one of Richmond's toughest defense attorneys, and he had her back home before they could ask her the time.

After two more days of surveillance, the police drew the conclusion that she had no idea where Lynx was and if she did, she wasn't saying. And finally the stakeout on Bambi ended.

CHAPTER 35

A Snitch's Life

Columbo was down at the police station going crazy. He had been through every crack and crevice in Richmond, and he wanted to know how this slick cat had slipped through his fingers.

"People, tell me something! I've devoted a big part of my career to trying to corner this motherfucker, and now you people tell me you can't find him? Richmond ain't that big," he yelled, and pounded his fist on the desk.

"Boss, maybe he ain't in Richmond. Wasn't he linked to DC?" the tall skinny cop standing over in the corner asked.

"Oh, he's here somewhere. He ain't that dumb to leave town—not with a live witness against him and not this quick anyway. He didn't have any money in the house when we went there, his wife hasn't been to the bank, he hasn't been spotted with any of his homeboys—nah, he's here somewhere hiding out. I'm going to find this motherfucker, get a conviction, and put him away for life! I am not going to retire until I put this motherfucker into the jail or die trying."

He snatched up his car keys.

"Where you going, boss?" someone asked.

"To pay Ronnie Shaler a little visit."

Ronnie had just finished cleaning out his works and stashing his dope away when he heard a familiar rap on the door. Man, it could only be one motherfucker showing up at his door this time of day. He opened it up, and Columbo pushed past him.

"You're under arrest, Ronnie," Columbo said.

"Why the hell am I under arrest? I ain't killed nobody," Ronnie said, high as gas.

"No, you haven't, but you'll be dead before the week's out sitting here. Your buddy Lynx is probably somewhere out there waiting for you to slip. I've been chasing this son of a bitch for over thirteen years. He's the sneakiest, nastiest, meanest, ugliest, fastest, most dangerous murderous son of a bitch that I ever dreamt about, read about, heard talked about, or thought about. And I hear you know firsthand all about him. After all, you were his boy." Columbo got up in his face, and Ronnie could smell his tobacco breath. "You know, there's no turning back now! It's all up to you to help me put him away."

Ronnie knew all the stories about Lynx when it came to people crossing him. And more importantly he knew that the stories about Lynx were true and not folk tales. After all, they had run together. In a way Ronnie wished he had kept his mouth shut, but at the time, the ten-thousand-dollar reward for Lynx's arrest had made it seem like the sweetest way to rid himself of Lynx and ensure that Lynx would not kill him for ripping him off. He had thought that Lynx would plea the charge down and be locked away and he'd never have to take the stand against Lynx. Looking at the big picture, he realized that it was all junkie thinking. The money he'd stolen from Lynx for the most part had foolishly been spent trying to make up with Michelle and the remainder spent on getting high. With the money gone, all he had was his hundred-and-fifty-dollar-a-day undercover dope habit.

Columbo had blown his high.

"Look here, I can't go into protective custody or whatever you got in mind," Ronnie said. "With my lifestyle, police protection ain't even a option."

"Your lifestyle? You mean your dope habit." Columbo smirked. "Funny, you don't even look like a dope fiend, Ronnie."

It was true. Ronnie was handsome, brown skinned, tall and slim. There were a few blemishes on his skin, but he was still fine. He hustled and maintained himself by the skin of his teeth. He had always been a sharp dresser and kept his wardrobe up to par. Before he had fallen victim to heroin, he had been into clothes so long that the stuff he wore was always a little ahead of everyone else. So even when he fell off, he still was wearing what was in. He had plenty of women because he had the dope dick, and he could go all night long if he wanted to. It drove the women crazy. But his dope dick also kept him in the doghouse with Michelle.

"Okay. Tell you what we can do. You have any family out of state you can go stay with until we can snag this cocksucker?" Columbo asked.

"Yeah! I got family in Durham, NC."

"I'm going to send you and a couple of men on vacation down there. The state witness budget will cover it. My men won't crowd you." Columbo was trying the best he could to work it out with Ronnie. After all, Ronnie was the piece of the puzzle that held his flimsy case together.

"There are things I like to do. I likes to party and play with the bitches! I don't want yo boys around when I indulge," Ronnie explained.

"My men see what I tell them to see. Just make sure you keep them close. You are very important to my career. I am going to retire after this," Columbo then said, and spit a wad of tobacco into a cup. "You get packed up. My men will be here in an hour."

He walked out the door, and Ronnie immediately started packing.

The next day Ronnie was in North Carolina, where he had plenty of family. Ronnie planned to party until he couldn't stop. He had a couple of broads down there that were guaranteed to drop their drawers as soon as he arrived. And if they didn't, that wasn't any problem either because his brother, Dee, had all of the Durhamites and they sisters, mothers, aunts, cousins, and friends on lock. It wasn't nothing for Dee to call up one or two ladies for his brother to have a little fun with.

But he had to get these detectives to leave him alone. One usually took the day shift, while the other took the night shift. It didn't take long for them to realize that they had bitten off more than they could chew.

Ronnie set off over two dozen firecrackers in the safe house while the detectives were asleep. They hopped up and drew their guns, hit the floor, and started shooting. Ronnie thought it was the funniest thing he'd ever seen. That was the final straw for them, and at that point they said that Ronnie could do whatever he wanted as long as he checked in every day. The detectives stayed at the safe house and ordered food and pay-per-view movies.

CHAPTER 36

Putting in Work

As sweet as Columbo thought he was, he ultimately out-smarted himself. He thought that Lynx would not be stupid enough to contact Cook'em-up, and he didn't have enough manpower left after putting a couple of officers with Ronnie to put a tail on Cook'em-up anyway. But Cook'em-up talked to Lynx on a regular. The pressure was on for Cook'em-up to lo-cate Ronnie and make him see things their way. By the time Cook'em-up got to Ronnie's apartment, it was apparent that he hadn't been there in days and had left in a rush. Now there was definitely no doubt that Ronnie was the rat, for sure. Cook'em-up touched base with Lynx, who told him, "Look, find that bitch of his. She runs her mouth a lot. I know she has his beeper number or cell phone number or something. But don't push up on her with that wild-type shit. Use finesse! Play con to the broad. Give her some money and some dick, too."

"Man, I spoke to yo people, and she found out where the bitch work. She described her to me like them chicks at the beauty parlor described her. And she ain't nothing nice. A broad like her I've got to hit from the back so I ain't got to look at her. I heard she uglier than a gorilla," Cook'em-up said to Lynx.

"I know her kind, dying for some attention. Why you think she talk so much? I bet you if you put that ghetto charm on her, she'll tell you her whole life story and his, too."

"You are probably right."

"Man, I am telling you, right now, she is the link between him and us. She's his weakest but our strongest for now! So make it happen."

"You mean to tell me you want me to dick whip and romance this cave rat broad? Man, you lucky I got mad love for you, my nigga," Cook'em-up said.

Cook'em-up wasted no time to get close to the sexiest gorilla he had ever seen in his life.

Michelle worked in Food Lion in the deli section. She was one of the ugliest sisters he had ever met. She was blacker than coal, but she didn't have the shine like coal; she had an ashy look like she'd never met lotion or Vaseline before. Bambi was black, but black and beautiful. Michelle was another story. She had craters all over her skin and looked like a pit bull in the face. Her teeth were buck, and she had the gall to have eight gold teeth, four on the top and four on the bottom. But she had a body that most women could only dream of having, and her tongue was pierced. Must be what kept Ronnie's nose wide open, Cook'em-up thought.

Cook'em-up frowned when she came to take his order.

"Let me get a turkey and cheese sandwich dressed, please?"

Michelle made it and handed it to him. He gave her a twenty and told her, "Keep the change."

"Please come again," she said, flashing all her gold teeth.

"I will, trust me," he said as he strolled off, never looking back.

The very next day, he returned.

"You came back," she greeted him excitedly.

"Didn't I tell you I was?" he asked. "Look, what time you get off?"

"Six," she said eagerly.

"I'll pick you up."

"Okay." Once again, he got a look at her gold-filled mouth.

"Oh, what's yo name?" she called out as he was leaving.

"Just call me C." He smiled. He knew for a fact that the name Cook'em-up rang in Richmond. Although she may not have seen his face before, he knew she had most likely heard his name—and it wouldn't take long for her to put two and two together.

Cook'em-up was there at 5:30 and sat at the deli talking with Michelle until it was time for her to get off. Once they got outside, she asked if he could stop at Church's Chicken.

He handed her the keys to his Range Rover. "Here you go. Drive wherever you need to go."

She felt like a Big Willie pushing his Range with him leaning back in the passenger seat. When they arrived at her small one-bedroom apartment, Cook'em-up asked, "Where yo man at? Am I safe? I don't want no niggas running up in here."

"You don't have to worry about that."

He didn't try to pressure her right then and there for info. She wanted to go change and get out of her work clothes. He was glad, because the smell of peppers, pickles, and onions was all over her. She returned wearing a sexy red sheer camisole and the thong to match. She kept positioning herself so he could touch her. Before he could make his move, while they were watching TV, the next thing he knew she was on her knees between his legs putting down her massive head game. Between all that slob from her gold teeth and that tongue ring, it was apparent why Ronnie couldn't stay from Michelle for long. Once she finished, he said, "Damn, baby, you needs to be mine."

"Make me yours, then."

"How am I going to do that when I see you and that nigga right there on that picture is all loved up?"

"Fuck him," she said, crawling onto his lap.

"Why you say that?" he asked.

"He's down Durham, North Carolina, on the run for some murder shit. I ain't got time for that. The only thing he good for is his dick. He used to take care of me, but he can't even do that no more, because his habit is catching up with him."

She poured her heart out to him, giving him all the info he needed, and she had no idea that she was signing Ronnie's death certificate. He rolled her over and dog-dicked her real good. Michelle had orgasm after orgasm until she passed out. Once she was asleep, he looked at her perfect black sexy body. Her stomach muscles were developed perfectly. It was only that face that threw him off. He wondered if plastic surgery could help her. He slipped his clothes on and stole one of Ronnie's pictures. He crept out of the bedroom, leaving five one-hundred-dollar bills on the dresser and a note that read, "Thanks for everything! I do mean everything! Buy yoself something nice. I'll call you soon."

After the way she had worked her tongue, lips, and mouth, he didn't want to burn the bridge down yet. "Loyalty and business over bitches anyway," he said to himself as he locked the door behind him.

CHAPTER 37

Down A$$ Chick

The next morning Bambi stood outside on her mother's porch waiting for Cook'em-up. Tricia advised her to leave while the baby wasn't looking; otherwise Nya would be crying since Bambi had spoiled her. As Bambi sprinted to the rental car that Cook'em-up was driving, Tricia came to the door.

"When you get back, I need to talk to you about something important," she said.

"Okay, Mommy. See you soon." Bambi wondered why her mother was being so secretive, but she didn't have time to think about it now. Soon she and Cook'em-up were heading down the highway.

Although Lynx was hiding out in Canada, work had to be carried out down south. In Durham Bambi hit nightclubs two nights in a row looking for Ronnie. The third night she hit the jackpot at Neal's Lounge, a straight hole-in-the-wall where Cook'em-up pointed out Ronnie to her from afar. Bambi wore a halter top that revealed her back and cleavage and a micro-mini jean skirt that accentuated her long legs. She was the center of attention, but she only wanted to be the apple of one guy's eye this particular night.

As soon as she zeroed in on Ronnie, some off-the-wall guy asked her to dance. She didn't want to dance in this sweaty matchbox, but this was her chance to show off and grab Ronnie's attention. Once she did, she acted as if she didn't know he was looking at her. After she left the dance floor, she accidentally bumped into Ronnie and spilled her drink on him. She was glad that Lynx never brought around Ronnie, otherwise she never would have been able to pull this off.

"Oh, I am sorry. I apologize," Bambi said with a smile. "Let me buy you a drink tonight?"

"No, let me," he insisted, looking her over thoroughly. The dude was mesmerized.

"Okay, you can buy tonight, and I'll buy tomorrow night?" she said, letting her eyes drift over his body sexily. They found a couple of empty seats at the bar, and Bambi ordered a glass of Alizé.

"Where you from? I hear you got a little accent." He leaned in toward her.

"I'm from DC, but I go to Central. The dorms are so over-booked that they put us up in hotels, " she lied, knowing that North Carolina Central's campus was only blocks away.

"Oh, for real." He changed the subject. "I see all the dudes in here trying to get at you."

"I'm not feeling them. It's something about you. You look different from them."

"Probably because I'm a city nigga. I'm from Richmond, VA, baby!" he said with such pride.

"Oh, my cousin lives up there somewhere. She keep telling me to visit her, but I hear it's a crazy place."

"DC is crazy."

"I heard Richmond is getting off the chain, with that high-ass murder rate."

"Yup, we do be putting niggas' dicks in the dirt," he said, like he was a real gangsta.

"I like your outfit and your silver teeth."

"Platinum, shawdy."

Fool, she thought. *I know damn well they are silver, all three of them. Stop fronting.*

They sat at the bar for a while talking, laughing, and joking. After a couple more drinks, Bambi said she was tired. He followed her to her hotel room in his car to make sure she got there safely. She didn't ask him in because she wasn't sure if Cook'em-up was up there. Then again, they hadn't planned for him to be that stupid.

"You know I got drinks tomorrow," she said as she ran her hand along his arm.

"I know. I'm 'pose to be going out with my brother and them tomorrow at the Silk Hat, so make sure you come through. I'll be there about one," he told her.

"Okay, I'll be there."

He smiled his silver smile and drove off in his funky-ass car.

Bambi was nervous about the next night, but Cook'em-up sat her down and had a heart-to-heart talk with her. "Look, you know how much your baby need y'all back together as a family, right? You know Lynx didn't kill Smooth, right?"

"Right." Bambi nodded her head affirmative.

"You know for a fact he was with you."

Again Bambi nodded.

"You done seen firsthand how that pig Columbo is, right? Well, he'll do whatever he has to, to make Lynx take the fall for this. And you know this."

He handed her a small vial and looked in her eyes as he continued. "I need you to slip this into his drink. It's just a mild tranquilizer to put him to sleep. Once he's asleep, call me and I'll take care of the rest from there."

"I hope it don't come down to giving him no ass."

"If you have to, work your magic. Whatever you do, don't let this fool get away. We got to get him, you understand?"

She nodded as tears rolled down her face. She had gotten an old prescription of Valium from her mother. She wasn't sure if they were any good or not, but she dropped one hoping that it would relax her. Even though she was scared, she took a deep breath and got her mind together. She knew what she had to do to ensure immunity for her man. *Girl, it ain't no ifs and ands about it, you gotta hold it down!* she said to herself.

She let the Valium take its course, got dressed in a skimpy little "come and fuck me" Gabon outfit, and went to the club. Cook'em-up wasn't far away, but he played the background, watching her every move. Bambi went over to the bar and walked up behind Ronnie. She covered his eyes from behind and said, "Guess who?"

He removed her hands, and she greeted him with a big hug and his silver teeth. She could smell the liquor all over him. "How long had you been here?" *Damn, I didn't notice this dude had a slightly cock eye last night. Did I have too much to drink last night? That's exactly why I don't drink—I can't be focused.*

"Too long. You trying to go with me?" he asked, looking confused. She wrote it off as the liquor talking.

"Where your brother and your boys at?" Bambi asked.

"They in the back room getting pussy and gambling. I am ready to go get some too. What's up?"

"Let's go get a room, then," Bambi purred seductively.

"Damn, you fast, girl," he said. But he jumped right up and followed her out of the club. They walked past Cook'em-up as they exited.

You are some kind of dog, Bambi thought, pushing his hands off her in the car. He was all touchy-feely, doing everything he could to unbuckle her pants. He had his head halfway down her pants as she drove to the hotel.

Bambi waited by the elevator while Ronnie paid for the room. She didn't want anyone to be able to identify her, and luckily no one else was around as they walked down the hallway and found the room. As soon as they entered it, she pulled the Hennessy and Absolut out of her bag.

"Fix me a drink. Then after I have my drink, I am going to fuck the shit out of you. You heard?" he said. He was a lot more demanding than he had been the night before, but maybe he'd just been playing the gentleman to reel her in then, Bambi thought.

She fixed him a stiff drink while he got undressed and slid under the covers. She dropped the vial of stuff that Cook'em-up had given her into the drink and then walked over and handed it to him. He gulped it all down and then lay back in the bed. His little dick was standing straight up. She reached out to stroke it; she could see he was getting excited.

"You know what time it is?" he said. "Time to take your clothes off. I ain't pay for this room fo two days for you to beat my dick. I can do that shit myself." He reached over and started unbuttoning her blouse. Bambi pulled back.

"Hold on, wait a minute. No, no, no." She waved her hand in his face. "This ain't going to be no hump, jump, and pump a bitch. I'm a woman with needs. There are places I need to be touched. Believe me, I'm going to touch you in all the right places and in ways no bitch is ever going to come close to," Bambi said, kicking her gift of gab to him. Of course, he fell for it.

Bambi had calmed him down. He went from being a pit bull after a steak to a meek little puppy who only wanted some attention. She rubbed baby oil all over him. As she did tears formed in her eyes, but she kept taking deep breaths and thinking of her, Lynx, and the baby being together.

While she massaged his back, Ronnie suddenly jumped up and started acting crazy. He was dancing, shaking his butt to the music, telling her to "cut the music up louder." She didn't know what the hell Cook'em-up had cooked up in this poison, but she knew he had mixed it with some kind of animal tranquilizer.

"Get this fat midget off me," he said, sweat dripping from his forehead. "Come on now. Get it away from round me." He seemed to pleading to someone. Then he started muttering, and she couldn't understand what he was saying. She backed away, terrified of him, but he didn't even seem to know she was still in the room.

Finally the tranquilizer fully kicked in, and he wobbled to the bed. Bambi had never been so scared in her life. He passed out across the bed diagonally. She poked his back, but he wasn't moving. His breathing sounded short and ragged.

Bambi quickly got back into her clothes, gathered up her things, grabbed her cell phone, and called Cook'em-up.

"He's out cold," she said. "I'll leave the door open, and you can do whatever."

"Did he drink all the stuff?"

"Like a fish," she said, glancing once more at the naked man sprawled over the bed.

"Then you can lock the door behind you. You've done all that needed to be done. You can go ahead and leave. He won't be waking up."

As she realized what had just occurred, Bambi became angry. She felt double-crossed by Lynx's right hand, whom he loved like a brother. Lynx had told her that if he ever died or had to go to prison that Cook'em-up would take care of her.

How could this man ever take care of me if he just set me up to commit murder? Damn, I had no idea that I was going to have to do Ronnie in myself. Cook'em-up lied about it being only a mild tranquilizer. I know this wasn't a part of Lynx's plan.

She knew Cook'em-up had never trusted her, and she realized that now that she had murdered someone, Cook'em-up felt like he finally could accept Bambi fully into Lynx's life. With a murder under her belt, there was no way possible if the heat ever came that she'd be able to cross him up with the police. These were hard pills for her to swallow. For a minute she contemplated killing Cook'em-up herself. Now that she had actually killed, it wouldn't take much for her to kill again.

"Why you worrying about me? You better be watching your step, Cook'em-up," she said to herself as she locked the door behind her and hurried down the hallway to the elevator. She pushed the *down* button.

CHAPTER 38

The Truth Shall
Set You Free

As Bambi put the baby down for a nap, she knew it wouldn't be long before they found Ronnie's body in North Carolina. Once they did the charges against Lynx would be dropped since Ronnie was the only witness. Soon Lynx would be able to return home. Having his passport stamped by Canadian officials would give him all the alibi he needed in case they wanted to try to pin Ronnie's murder on him, too.

While she put the cover on the baby, Egypt and Tricia waited for her at the door.

Tricia took her into the living room and sat her down.

"I asked Egypt to be here for support while I tell you what I need to get off of my chest," Tricia said nervously.

"What is it, Mommy? Please, I can't take any more bad news right now."

"Well, let me share with you my news then, first," Egypt cut in. "You know I have been going to the prisons for years to see dudes. Well, I am getting married to my baby, Shawn."

"You mean the dude that was in the fed with Lynx?" Bambi asked in shock.

Egypt nodded. "I know he got life, but he makes me happy. He stimulates my mind, and I love him like I've never loved a man. So please be happy for me."

Bambi looked into Egypt's eyes, which were shining with tears of happiness.

"I am happy for you, if you are happy. I will even be there with you when you get married," Bambi said.

"Thank you so much! You are truly the best friend in the world," Egypt said while she hugged her friend. "Ruby even said she'd come over to go with us."

Bambi was happy for Egypt, but she dreaded hearing bad news from Tricia. She hoped she didn't have some sickness or something from when she was drinking all the time. What if she'd gotten a disease from some man? Whatever it was, she'd better face up to it.

"Now, Mommy, give it to me. Tell me," she demanded to know.

"It's not that bad, actually. It could be good after the initial shock wears off," Egypt assured her friend.

Tricia began to cry, and Bambi went over to the plastic-covered sofa and hugged her mother. Egypt moved over to be closer to Bambi and put her arms around Bambi to comfort her. Bambi told her mother in a soothing tone, "You know whatever it is, I'll understand. We've been through hell and back, so what can be so heavy that I can't handle?"

Tricia wiped her eyes with the tissue that Egypt handed her. "Look, baby, every decision that I have ever made concerning you has always been with your best interest at heart."

"I know that, Mommy."

"Since I've stopped drinking and been going to church, I've

been thinking a lot, wanting to get this off my chest, so I can be free and not have to carry any burdens around."

"Okay, Mommy." Bambi glanced at Egypt, who already seemed to know the big secret.

"Since you were small, you've always asked me why your middle name is Lloyd'dess. I've always told you it was after someone who was dear to me, right?"

"Yes, you said a close friend who lived far away but was always dear to your heart," Bambi said.

"Well, that man's name is Lloyd, and he is your father."

"What?" Bambi said, shocked.

"Listen, let her finish," Egypt interrupted, because she knew questions were being conjured up in Bambi's head.

"His name is Lloyd 'Slot Machine' Pitman. We grew up in the same neighborhood. He was older than me, and I loved him so much. But he had a girlfriend at the time, and he loved her more than he could ever love me. He was known for robbing banks and for his money. I started seeing your father—well, Bob—to make him jealous."

Tricia took a deep breath and continued. "Once Lloyd found out I was pregnant, there was no doubt he knew it was his, but he got locked up two days after I told him. He didn't have any way to get me any money because his girlfriend had all the money, and he couldn't tell her about me because then he'd put himself in the situation of her leaving with all of it. Being the hustler that he was, he didn't want to see you without, so he told me to play on Bob and use Bob as my ticket out of the ghetto. I did that simply to make a better life for you."

Bambi said, "So Bob isn't my father."

Bambi was confused, but happy knowing that she hadn't been written off by her father. Although her mother had no reason to withhold such a heart-wrenching secret from her, she was relieved because she was sure that anything that Lloyd could offer her was better than Bob ever had.

"No, he isn't. I'm sorry, baby. It's killed me over the years to withhold that information from you for so long. I see so much of Lloyd in you. Everyone says you take after me, but when I see your finesse and how you can look into the ugliest situation and find a hustle in it, I could never take the credit for it. That's all Lloyd. Baby, all I can say to you is that I am sorry."

"Ma, there ain't no need to be! I know you did best—and what you did was out of love. I only wish you would have told me earlier while I was dying for Bob to love me. I would have been happier having a father in prison who loved me than a father out here who could give a damn."

"I didn't know how you would react."

"Where is he now? Lloyd, I mean."

"He just came home from jail a couple of months ago. He's asking about you but agreed not to bother you if you are happy."

"I want to see him."

"It's more," Egypt said. Bambi turned to look at her friend. "I know I have always been the closest thing you've had to a sister, but you have a real sister. Her name is Yarni, and I met her. She's just like us."

"For real!" Bambi got excited.

"Yes! I met her for lunch. She's a year older than you. Y'all have the same birthday. Y'all have the same taste. She has one of the same Prada bags you have; she's fly like you. Y'all even walk alike."

"For real! I can't wait to meet her."

"You will soon," Egypt said.

"So, Ma, when did you see Lloyd?"

"Well . . ." Tricia looked like she was at a loss for words.

"Well, he was actually the one who gave me the other half of the money for my plastic surgery."

"For real?" Bambi was shocked, but then a thought ran across her head. "Well, dag where he get money from if he's been locked up all those years?"

"Bambi . . . baby, let me tell you. I told you yo daddy is a stone-cold hustler from the heart. He could take soda cans and turn them into millions. But seriously he's just spending his money from the seventies, that's all."

"Dammmmnnnn . . . tell Daddy Warbucks I said 'Don't hide it, divide it.' No, I'm just playing. I really can't wait to see him," Bambi said. It felt like her life was finally coming together. She had it all—the man, the baby, and now, finally, her daddy. This was her payday, as far as she was concerned.

Bambi turned to her mother and hugged her. As she felt her mother's arms around her, she said, "I'm so happy. Thank you for telling me everything. Thank you so much."

CHAPTER 39

At the End of the Day

After the whole ordeal in North Carolina, Bambi had to rush to New York for a live taping of *Oh Drama!* to discuss party planning. She didn't want to go, but she also didn't want to upset her new publicist, who had been working so hard for her lately. With all Bambi's personal drama, she had missed a couple of things the publicist had set up. No matter how she was feeling, she knew she had to put on her game face and pull it together, and she did.

Never in her wildest dreams did she imagine that far back in the rain forest of Central America, BET would even be an option and Loot'chee would be watching. He damn near shit his pants when he heard her voice and saw her in the flesh still maintaining, looking like a million dollars, hands and ears blinging. And federal prison khaki brown wasn't the color she was wearing, either.

"This bitch played the fuck out of me!" He shook his head and said, "I don't believe this slick-ass, conniving *bitch*!" The more he studied how relaxed and carefree Bambi looked, talking about her life as a party and event planner, the madder he got.

"I am really happy, and I love what I do," she said with a wide smile.

"This no-good beeitch got me sitting down this ma'fucka living like Tarzan, getting ate up by vampire mosquitos and shit. While this bitch is living the damn glamorous life." Loot'chee laughed a little because he couldn't believe how she had played him.

"What would you say to up-and-coming party planners who desire to be at your level in the game?" the host of the show asked.

Bambi looked confidently into the camera and shot straight from the hip. "Never give up; always know that you can do anything you put your mind to. Just stay focused and don't let the haters or any people who mean you no good stand in your way."

At that moment Loot'chee felt like she was talking about him. He screamed at the television as if she could hear him, "*Bitch,* you wanna fuck wit me? You crossed me! Don't nobody cross Loot'chee Meney and get away with it!" He guzzled down his Guinness Stout and slammed the bottle on the table. "You wanna play with me? Try Lotto. You would've had better chances winning! I promise you, you gone be dealt wit. Yo ass ain't untouchable!"

He pulled out his gun and shot the television set, emptying the entire clip into the television.

"Damn that bitch made me waste my new hollow-point bullets on her scandalous ass! Now I gotta kill the bitch twice now. A no-good bitch!"

Once she was done filming, Bambi's cell phone rang. It was Brent Jackson the attorney, calling to confirm that the charges had been dropped against Lynx because the case was flimsy at best and there was no witness. Bambi knew that Lynx would be returning soon. Her life would be normal again.

Meanwhile, Columbo was at the police station canceling all the arrangements he had made for his retirement party. Since Ronnie's death had been ruled a suicide, he had no case against Lynx. So he had to start over from scratch and find a cunning way to build a new case against Lynx, his number-one nemesis. After all his phone calls were made, he went out and got drunk with his police buddies.

Across the North Carolina border, in a small apartment in North Durham, on the television, a news reporter updated: "The body found in the Town Hotel has been identified as Ronald Shaler. The medical examiners have ruled this death a suicide."

Ronnie sat, tears streaming down his face. His identical twin brother, Donnie, was dead and somehow had been identified as him.

He knew that there was only one person who could pull off such a clever plan: Lynx. The beautiful girl the night before . . . Everything was all a set-up, and he'd fallen for it. He hadn't seen it coming because the drugs had his mind. He'd had no idea that his brother would have to pay the price for his mistakes. He had paid dearly by losing his brother, but out of every bad situation comes something good. Well, now all his problems were washed away. Columbo would leave him alone. Lynx would forget about him. Although a part of him had died, he felt that the rest of him could live.

Now he could start a new life somewhere. Maybe he'd get clean and find a new game. But one thing was for sure, Ronnie thought. Lynx was gonna pay someday.

At the end of the day everyone thought that they could start a new life, turn over a new leaf, and toast to new beginnings, but they all seemed to forget that *sometimes you just have to charge it to the game.*

All in all, the saga continues. . . .

I was always told to make my visions so big that the only way they could ever come into existence is if God stepped in! So, first and foremost, I have to give all the glory and praise to God. It is only because of His favor and blessings that I am here today.

I reflect over the period as I breathed life into this book.

I lost tragically and gained tremendously. I lost a couple of friends. Money was stolen from me without a gun. I was backstabbed time and time again, and had a major surgery. But the most detrimental thing, the straw that really broke the camel's back, was when I talked and laughed until 11:30 p.m. with my grandmother, who was so full of life and also the most influential person in my life, only to get a call at 6:00 a.m. that she had went on to glory. Through all that I had experienced in life—the pain, the heartbreaks, the struggles—*nothing* could prepare me for such a life-changing blow. But through it all, I weathered the storms in my life.

For years I never knew who my true warriors were.

Kennisha and Timmond, you two are the joys of my life. Thank you for understanding and being excited about my career. Mommy, as always you stood beside me. You were the general in my army, taking on the nanny role at times when you had your own life going on. My stepfather, Balldey, thanks for loving my mother as you do. Lord knows I know she can be a real boa constrictor (smile). Elouise Perry, for loving me as if you birthed me, you have the power to make me find the best in a bad situation. I am so thankful for our unique relationship!

Dee, I can sometimes drive you crazy with all my drama, but without a reasonable doubt, I know you got me. Niecey Butler, *wow*! You are one of my dearest friends. I thank you for being so loyal to me through it all. To my "twin" Tamia Washington, there is no way I could ever repay you for being my backbone during my surgery and for being my caretaker, surrounding your *own* life around my medicine times and doctor appointments and never complaining about my whining and all my extra theatrics. Katona, I can't thank you enough for always being on standby and available when I need you to meet me at the mall in thirty minutes! Your opinion is greatly appreciated. Sheva, throughout all the years we've fought like strangers and we've had some of the best of times. But all in all I love you, and never forget it. Dedria, I know you got me and I got you. Melissa, I know I am constantly worrying and pressuring you to get a million things done for me. After my lip smackin' and tantrums, you always come through for me. This is to the talks and laughs we have . . . you know which ones I am talking about. Pat MacEnulty, although we are very different, we are so much alike. I love you like my mother pushed you out too. Joi, as always, you continue to hold me down and are always on point early *whenever* I ring your phone, eternal love to you. My sistah Wahida, who would have thought two chicks with so much spunk would turn out to be so close, look at us. Chandra Steward, it amazes me how we both are caught up in our own lives, but it only takes one phone call for you or me to hit 64. It's only a minute before your magazine (damn, damn, damn) is going to be a *major* publication! Diaamah, you are such a sweetie pie.

To my three divalicious friends: Sharissa, keep smashing 'em baby! I know that our daily talks are so routine, but when you call and you ask, "You OK?", it means so much. Thanks for sharing all visions with me for your soon-to-be-multiplatinum-selling album, *I Found Love*. The book diva, Neechie (Chunuchi), girl . . . we have got to keep the clown radar on at all times (smile). Maybe we should write a book on that. You are so talented. My shopping partner, BT (Brenda Thomas), there are so many great things I could say about you. Thanks for being ready to go to combat at the drop of the dime for me, and also for being able to tell me to calm down and cease-fire.

Uncle Sonny, you have been like a father to me, loving me as only a father could love his daughter, always wanting to be my protector, watching out for my best interests at times when I don't know what's best for me. Dad and Joanne, Kim, you will never know how much it meant when you drove eighteen hours to see me on Thanksgiving. Thanks bunches.

Brenda Williams, thanks for stepping in, assisting me in my matters big or small when I felt so overwhelmed. You were right . . . you are the best at what you do. To the best promoter of all times, my Auntie Trena Buck, girl, Don King ain't got a thing on you . . . Oodles and ca-zoodles of thanks to the official Internet Queen, publicist, and travel companion. Cousin Cha, you wear so many hats and you never complain. Much love! The whole Alan Furs family, especially Dena, my personal furrier, you keep me laced in the latest hottest furs. Thanks so much!

To my Wayne, I owe you so much. I thank you for making me your first priority over everything. I know that you wouldn't let me hit the ground if you were falling yourself. My brother Jerron, although at times you are like a wedgie, always on my butt and full of do-do, I love you and I know that you only want the best for me. Craig, for keeping me on my toes and loving me under all conditions. What would I do without you? Knowing I have your boundless love is more than anybody can ask for. David Slatton, I don't have to put it out there, but you know what for, thanks a bunch! Kathy always being so pleasant and working me in.

To the fallen soldiers on lockdown, to the ones I know and the ones I don't. I know your pain, struggle, and the hourly battle you fight within the unjust system. At times you may feel like you are alone, but never are you, for you are in my heart. There is not one night that doesn't go by that you are not in my prayers.

Endless thank-yous to my Johnnie Cochran of the literary world, Pam Crockette. I am so proud to say that you represent me. Thank you for believing so passionately in my career. You have been more than just an attorney. You've been, at times, my inspiration and motivator. After our talks I feel I can conquer the world.

To my Random House family, thank you all for assisting me in making history and for welcoming me into your world with open arms. Extra special thanks to my editor, Melody, for allowing me to keep my voice, making my transition to the majors as painless as possible and for stressing to everybody just how important this project is. Also for seeing my vision for *Street Chronicles,* A Nikki Turner Exclusive. Danielle Durkin, always being so patient no matter how crazy my question is. Carl Weber, thank you bunches for thinking of me when putting out some of the hottest projects! Marc, for getting me such a great deal that put me in a situation that, without a doubt, I could provide for my children. Earl Cox, for consulting me through all the endless drama no matter.

To the people who make all this possible, *my fans.* I could never thank you enough. I thank you and love you not only for